YOU'RE the ONE

Gene Taylor

Dreamspinner Press

Published by
Dreamspinner Press
5032 Capital Circle SW
Ste 2, PMB# 279
Tallahassee, FL 32305-7886
USA
http://www.dreamspinnerpress.com/

Cover Art by Paul Richmond
http://www.paulrichmondstudio.com

Cover content is being used for illustrative purposes only
and any person depicted on the cover is a model.

ISBN: 978-1-62380-852-5
Digital ISBN: 978-1-62380-853-2

Printed in the United States of America
First Edition
July 2013

THIS story is dedicated to the memory of my mother and father, who *really did* give me nickels to play the jukebox like the one mentioned in the prologue. They even bought me boxes of used records from a local jukebox distributor to play at home. There was always music in our house—along with plenty of love. The main character is not really me, but I actually got that jukebox that 'Graham' and I always wanted!

PROLOGUE

Amarillo, Texas 1953

"OH, DADDY, look! They've got a jukebox!" cried the six-year-old little boy.

"I see that, son, but let's sit down over here at this booth and order some lunch before we worry about that jukebox," the father replied.

"Couldn't I please have a nickel so I can play a record? Huh, Daddy?"

"Wouldn't you like a nice cold Orangette or maybe a Dr. Pepper first while we study the menu?"

"Oh, Daddy," the boy groaned in his little voice. "You know I always get the same thing anyway when we eat out at a café—a hot steak sandwich."

"He's right, Conrad," the mother interrupted with a grin. "Let him go watch the records play."

"Do you think I could have a nickel?"

The father sighed, giving in. "Okay, Graham. Let me get out my change and see...." He picked out some coins and studied the excited, expectant look on his little boy's face. "I know you love to play the jukebox, so here are two nickels... but you come right back to the table when you're done watching them play...."

Graham grabbed the coins with a gleeful "Thanks, Daddy." He raced to the big old Rock-Ola jukebox in the corner of the café.

"Conrad, he can't even read the names of the records."

"I don't think it matters much. He just likes to watch the records spin."

"Maybe so, but he really does like the music… and he's got his favorites from the radio. I'll go help him out. You order something for us. We've been married long enough that you can pick something for me…. "

Graham was already nearly glued to the front of the glowing red, orange, and blue colored plastic front of the jukebox. His eyes were like saucers as he stared expectantly at the machine, which at the moment stood silent and still.

"Want some help, Graham?"

Graham looked up and smiled. "Sure, Mommy. Read me some songs."

"Well, there's Hank Williams and Ferlin Husky…," she began. "Oh, here's one by Teresa Brewer. I know you like to sing along with her songs sometimes on the radio at home… and on the car radio, too. And here's one by Patti Page! You like her, too."

"What are the songs?"

"'Ricochet' by Teresa Brewer… and 'Doggie in the Window' by Patti Page…."

"Oh, *yes!*" Graham cried. "Show me the numbers to push," he exclaimed as he put his two nickels in the slot and waited for the "clunk" as each one dropped inside and registered with a little round light that blinked "Thank You."

"Here," she replied, pointing to number 7, "and this one," she said as she indicated number 16.

Graham gleefully pushed the numbers and stared, fascinated, as the big silver rim around the 78rpm record swung out and waited for the turntable to rise from the bottom of the window. It slowly raised the disk to the top where it began to spin very fast. Then the tone arm obediently met the record and the jukebox burst into a perky tune with the big musical voice of Teresa Brewer exploding over the captivated little boy.

"I love records!" Graham exclaimed.

"I know you do, honey."

"I want one," he murmured.

"I'll talk to Daddy, and maybe we can stop at a record store on the way home and buy one of the records."

"No, Mommy. I meant I want a jukebox… just like this one!"

His mother smiled as she watched her happy little boy. "Somehow I think you really mean that," she said softly. "And I wouldn't be a bit surprised if you actually got one someday when you grow up…."

CHAPTER ONE

Chicagoland, August 1968

GRAHAM THOMAS sat at a table in the cafeteria of Maine Central High School in Des Plaines, Illinois. He looked around at the crowd of other teachers also sitting in the stuffy cafeteria. He wondered how much more they all could take of this boring first day of teachers' meetings. The first day of classes for students was the next week, but the district required three days of so-called "in-service days" to prepare for the beginning of school.

At the moment, there was a fifteen-minute break between speakers, but Graham felt too tired to even get up to go get a soda from one of the soft drink vending machines in the room. He looked at his watch and sighed just as a rather handsome, tall, slender young man with curly black hair pulled up a chair and sat down next to him.

"Hi," the man said and smiled at Graham. "I can tell you're as pumped up as I am over these first-day meetings. Are we having fun yet?" He grinned and flashed a smile that made Graham nod at the sarcasm.

Graham studied the man quickly. "Oh, yes. I find these speakers truly inspiring," he said while shaking his head slowly to indicate otherwise. He turned to look at the appealing man next to him and said the first thing that popped into his head. "My name is Graham Thomas, and I'm new in the English department. I know you look familiar, but there are so many new faces that I just don't remember your name."

The man grinned. "I know what you mean. I'm inspired about as much as you are. I'm a new teacher here, too. We met briefly this morning on our way from the parking lot, but as you say, there are just too many of us to remember all the names. I'm Ron McWilliams, a new Spanish teacher."

"Hi, Ron," Graham said. "I'm sorry about not remembering your name."

"Don't worry about it. I just wondered if you'd like to go out for a bite to eat later. I'm from West Virginia so I'm new in town too… and I don't know anyone."

Graham smiled and shook Ron's proffered hand. "Sure. That sounds good to me. I was going to stop someplace on my way home anyway."

"How about that steak house a couple of blocks from here?" Ron asked. "I hear it's pretty good."

"Okay, Ron, I'll meet you there when this terrible torture is finally over." Graham settled back in his seat to endure the rest of the meeting.

Graham wasn't knockdown handsome, but he wasn't ugly, either. He was five foot nine with a medium body build, and he had enough chest hair and hair on his arms and legs to make himself interesting, in his own "almost modest" opinion. His moderately wavy hair, a little long, not quite to the collar, was dark brown, almost black, and his eyes, which someone once flatteringly called bedroom eyes, were chocolate brown. He wore dark-rimmed glasses to read and drive, but vanity made him put them away the rest of the time.

Graham had come to Des Plaines this fall of 1968 from his hometown in Amarillo, Texas. He'd never even been to the Chicago area before arriving in July for an interview for this position. He had thought of it as a chance to see Chicago for the first time and to have a fun little trip. He was surprised that he was so well liked at his interview, and the fact that Mr. Knotts handed him a contract to sign right on the spot had truly been a shock.

"I'll stay at least two years," Graham had said to himself as he gazed at the contract, "just to show I can hold a job. Then if I don't like it up here in the North, I'll quit and go back home. But at least I'll have a couple of years of teaching experience." He had smiled at Mr. Knotts and signed the contract.

Without warning, the microphone at the front of the room squealed, and then, just as it stopped, a voice boomed across the cafeteria. "If I could have your attention, please…. We need to get back to business so we can draw our first day to a close. If you'll just take your seats… I would appreciate it. Now, would all our new teachers please stand?" Marvin Knotts, the principal of Maine Central High School, looked over the faculty seated before him.

"We have seventeen new teachers this fall, most of whom have some previous teaching experience, but there are two or three others who are brand new to our profession. We'd like to give a hearty welcome to all of our newcomers, so please join me with your applause as I introduce each one to you individually."

When the introductions were complete at last and everyone thought they were soon to be dismissed for the day, the principal had one last unhappy surprise. What made it worse was that Mr. Knotts appeared to be so pleased with what he had to say.

"To conclude our first day back on the long path of this school year to educate the fine young people in our community," he went on in his long-winded drone, "it is my pleasure to call upon our illustrious superintendent Dr. Maynard Watts once again. He has some inspirational thoughts to guide us on our way."

Mr. Knotts smiled at his faculty, not at all aware of the inner silent groans from his restless teachers around the room, who tried to hide behind forced enthusiasm and fake smiles at the announcement. "Dr. Watts, we're all on the edge of our seats, I'm sure, to hear your inspiring message this afternoon."

The superintendent grinned and approached the microphone.

Graham looked around at his fellow teachers and hid a little smirk behind his hand. He was pretty sure most of the teachers were wondering how they were going to take naps with their eyes open while giving the impression that they were interested in yet another boring speech. At least Graham felt that way. He found his own solution by burrowing deep into his own thoughts, pondering the state of the Chicago gay bar scene, while pretending to listen with rapt attention.

Graham's reverie came to an abrupt end as applause from his fellow teachers signaled the end of the superintendent's address. Graham hoped there wasn't going to be a test over it later, because he hadn't heard a single word.

The principal took the microphone a final time to say, "It's been a long day, teachers, so I'm not going to prolong it any further. I just wanted to remind you that tomorrow morning we'll meet by departments with your department chairs, and then the afternoon is yours to work in your classrooms to prepare for the first day of classes next week. Thank you for your kind attention. You're dismissed for the day. Everyone have a good evening."

Grateful to be released to go home for the day, Graham turned to Ron and saw that Ron's eyes looked glazed over, too, probably from the superintendent's lengthy speech. "Now, about that steak house?"

"Just follow me in your car," Ron replied. "It's not very far...."

Graham made his way out of the cafeteria, following closely behind his new friend.

"I'm right over there," Ron said as he turned and pointed to a little VW import. "See the green Volkswagen Karmann Ghia in that second row? I'll pull over to the entrance of the parking lot to wait, and then you can follow me...."

By the time Graham reached the restaurant, parked, and entered the place, Ron had a table and was waving to him. When the waitress had left, Graham and Ron sat sipping soft drinks and awaiting their dinner.

"You said you were from West Virginia, Ron. What brings you to Des Plaines?"

Ron laughed. "Same as you, I imagine. I just wanted a job near the big city, and this was as good a place as any, I guess. What about you?"

"You're right. That's pretty much my story, too. I'm from Amarillo, Texas, and I just thought it would be interesting to live in the Chicago area after my first year of teaching near Denver."

Ron gave Graham a mysterious look. "I have a feeling there's a lot more to your story than just that. How long have you been 'out'?"

Graham blinked in surprise. "Out where?" he asked, knowing what Ron really meant... but trying to give himself a moment to think how much, if anything, he wanted to reveal to this stranger.

"You know what I mean. You're gay. I'd bet on it. Don't get all defensive, though. I'm gay, too."

Graham now turned his full attention to Ron McWilliams. He had just been trying to be polite and make a new friend on the faculty when Ron asked him out. Now he analyzed the man a little closer. Ron had a smooth, kind of "college fraternity" look about him that didn't especially appeal to Graham. Graham hadn't particularly thought about Ron being gay, but he was now trying to imagine Ron as a potential playmate. He was having a lot of trouble with that idea.

"I see the wheels spinning in your head," Ron said. "Don't bother giving me a speech about whether you're a top, bottom, or versatile. I was only interested in making a gay friend... I'm not looking for a boyfriend. I've had a few relationships, and that's just not what I want. I like to go to the bars and play around. A gay bar is like taking a trip to a candy store. You can pick out something different to eat each time you put your hand in the box, so to speak."

Ron laughed at the shocked look on Graham's face. "I can see you and I have very different ideas along those lines."

"I have to admit that I'm more on a crusade to find a lover, if that's what you mean," Graham replied. "I enjoy a night out as much as the next guy, but I'm hoping to find someone to keep for longer than just the evening."

Ron chuckled. "That's fine. We can be friends without going to bed together. I had in mind that we could just be bar buddies. You know... drive into Chicago for a night of hunting once in a while. Do you know your way around the gay scene in Chicago yet?"

"Not at all," Graham said. "I haven't even been to a single bar yet."

"Then I have an idea. Let's go to the Annex Saturday night, and I'll show you around."

"I assume that's one of the gay bars...."

"Of course. Interestingly, it's on North Clark Street. Does that ring a bell?"

"Not especially. Should it?"

"It depends on whether you're a history buff," Ron replied. "That's where the infamous St. Valentine's Day Massacre took place in 1929 when Al Capone's men shot all those gangsters to death in a garage. As a matter of fact, the site is only a couple of blocks from where the Annex is now. It's a real part of Chicago history."

Graham considered Ron's offer for a moment. "Okay. Let's go make some history of our own on North Clark Street on Saturday night."

The waitress arrived with their order, but after she left, Ron said, "Great. How about I pick you up at your place around ten Saturday night?"

"Ten? Isn't that kind of late to be driving to Chicago?"

Ron laughed. "Not at all. You really *are* new at this. Nobody goes to the bars before eleven, and it'll take about an hour to get there and park."

"Whatever you say," Graham replied, unfolding his napkin.

RON was prompt when he arrived at Graham's apartment Saturday in his little green convertible, top up for the evening. They headed for the Northwest Tollway, south of Graham's apartment.

"You need to remember how to get to the bar," Ron insisted, "since you'll probably want to go on your own next time. You take this toll until it becomes the Kennedy Expressway. Then a little further along you can exit at Fullerton, and from there you go north or south on the cross streets, depending on which bars you want. I'll tell you about the best ones and how to find them."

As Ron had said, it took nearly an hour before they reached their destination bar.

"I really appreciate your help. Otherwise I'd have to buy a gay bar guide and figure out how to find the bars," Graham said.

"Well, the Annex, where we're going, is a pretty good pickup bar, but there are other good places like the Inner Circle, the Normandy, Sam's, Faces, and the Trip. There are more than that, of course, but those are just the ones I've visited so far."

"Sounds exciting. We only had one bar in Amarillo—the Back Door. I can't wait to see all the choices in Chicago."

"We're almost there. See? The parking lot is full already. I'll have to drive along this next block to see if I can park on the street." Ron slowed down until he found an empty space not far ahead. Then he parallel parked his car, and they started walking back to the bar.

"I'm excited already," Graham said.

"Where are your glasses?"

"Oh, I left them on the dash of your car. I really won't need them in there."

"Now, there's something we didn't talk about, Graham," Ron said and stopped on the sidewalk. "When we get in there, let's split up. Okay? Neither one of us will get lucky if we hang around together. We'd look like a couple. Can you handle walking around on your own?"

"Sure. I'm a big boy now," Graham replied with a frown.

"Now, don't get your feelings hurt. You know what I mean. We'll check on each other about every half hour or so. That way we'll know if the other one scores."

"What if one of us *does* score… and finds someone to go with?" Graham asked.

"We'll figure that out if it happens. Come on. Let's go inside and see tonight's pickings."

Music from the jukebox was overpoweringly loud when they arrived. The Doors' "Hello, I Love You" blared throughout the bar. The irony of the bone-shattering music was Mayor Richard Daley's edict that there was to be no dancing between members of the same sex in any gay bar. That made the jukebox and sound system seem sort of sad, but that was the way it was, Ron explained to Graham.

That didn't stop many of the boys and a few girls from enthusiastically gyrating with each other as they stood in place around the bar, just short of dancing together. Some of the bartenders and bouncers occasionally roamed through the crowded bar patrons to make sure it didn't go too far. Often they threatened to throw the near-dancers out on the street if they didn't cut it out.

The Annex was fairly dark, lighted mostly by various neon beer signs along the walls on the left and in the back. The right side had a mirror that stretched along the entire wall from about halfway up to the ceiling. A few dimly lighted pool tables were at the back just past the bar, right on the way to the restrooms in the rear of the building. The line to the men's room testified that action was to be found there if one had the courage to participate in stroking at the urinals or sucking and fucking in the stalls. Graham didn't think he had that much nerve.

The main room was narrow and very long. A two-sided bar ran the length of the room with space on both sides for standing and cruising, which was the reason that most of the hot young men were there.

As they walked along the length of the bar after buying beers, Ron pointed to a section of the mirrored wall toward the back. "See over there? That's the notorious 'grope corner.' Notice how few overhead lights it has and that it's partially blocked from view by huge clouds of cigarette smoke? That's because so many guys are hanging out over there… and lots of them are smoking. It really is just what they call it—a haven for groping. Let's go take a look. You need to experience this. I'll go first, and then you follow a few steps behind me."

Graham did as Ron directed, slowly making his way along the wall. When Ron stopped, Graham stopped, too. Ron lit a cigarette, and Graham lit one, too, deciding to follow the example of his teacher.

Sure enough, as soon as he stopped, he was slightly shocked at having his crotch felt and rubbed, causing it to tingle. But it *was* kind of thrilling. Ron then walked back to him.

"Okay, time to split up. Let's just wander around on our own and see what happens."

Graham nodded and began to circle around to the other side of the room, away from Ron, who stayed in the grope zone. He finished his cigarette, drank his beer, and watched as guys cruised each other around the room. Since no one spoke to him, Graham was feeling a little shy and out of his element. He merely moved slowly from place to place, mostly watching others.

He went up to the bar, ordered another beer, and found a place to stand along the left side of the room. He gazed lustfully at all the handsome men who filled the place, but no one returned his stare. A few minutes later, he tried another spot farther down the wall. Nothing. He smoked another cigarette, giving himself something to do with his hands. His throat was beginning to feel dry and raspy so he stared at the almost burned-out cigarette in his hand with distaste. *I think I'm quitting these things,* he thought. *I'm glad I haven't been smoking for very long....*

He continued his routine, which by now was becoming really boring. Another beer. Another spot along the wall. Another beer. Still nothing. Damn it. He knew that a lot of his problem was his being too shy to speak first. But he wasn't sure how to strike up a conversation with these handsome big city boys.

He decided to try the grope corner again. He didn't see Ron there this time so he just waited at a vacant spot he found along the wall. Again nothing much happened. Suddenly he felt the warmth of a body standing rather close to him. He turned to look.

"Is that your calling card?" a guy asked as he reached inside the top button of Graham's shirt, fingering the modest hair on his chest.

"Yeah. So who's calling?"

The guy chuckled and held out his hand, "I'm Robin. Rob for short. And you are?"

"Graham. Nice to meet you."

"Hmmm. Graham? Sounds like a sweet cracker," Rob replied and smiled.

"Want a bite?" Graham immediately blushed. He couldn't believe he actually said something so forward to a stranger.

Choking his laughter back a bit, Rob said, "Maybe... but let me suck on it first!"

Graham blushed even more, but he decided to continue playing the game. "We'll see. Rob for short, huh? Is it? Short, I mean?"

"That's for you to find out, honey. Let's go to my place and play Seek and Hide."

"I thought it was called *Hide and Seek*," Graham said.

"In this version, I get to *seek* what you've got to *hide* in those tight pants of yours."

Rob reached into his own pants pocket and retrieved his car keys with one hand while he placed his other hand right on Graham's cock and rubbed gently, causing it to stiffen somewhat inside his pants. "What do you say?"

Graham was flattered by the attention and kind of taken in by Rob's quirky sense of humor. *I wonder if I dare to go home with this guy?* He replied aloud, "Uh, I'm here with a friend in his car. We live kind of far from here, and we drove to the bar together...."

"That's okay, you *delicious thing*," Rob said. "I promise to bring you back here... later, that is.... "

"Well, let me look for my friend and tell him I'll be gone for a while," Graham said.

"I'll meet you at the front door in about ten minutes," Rob said. "I need to go piss anyway. Don't be too long."

Graham methodically searched the bar, but he couldn't find Ron anywhere. *What now?* He went to the front of the bar where Rob was waiting.

"Ready to go?" Rob asked.

"I can't find my friend," Graham said. "I'm afraid to leave without talking to him…."

"Hey, he's either found someone and gone home with the guy… or maybe he's just sitting outside in a car making out with someone. Either way, let's go. We'll be back before he even notices you're gone."

"I still feel funny about just leaving this way. Would you mind driving by his car as we go? I want to make sure it's still there."

"Okay, show me where it is."

The car was just where he and Ron had left it… so Rob headed for his place, which was in a quiet neighborhood still on the near north side of the city. Rob's apartment was on the second floor, so they walked up the stairs, not saying anything. Even though Graham was excited about his first Chicago "date," he was still a little apprehensive about going home with a stranger like this in the big city. His small-town background hadn't prepared him much for Chicago. But it was a little too late to worry about it.

Graham could tell that despite being relatively handsome and well-built, the guy was several years older than he was. It worried him just a little to be with someone who was so much more experienced at picking up bar tricks. He felt a lot like a student on the first day of class.

Rob unlocked his apartment door and let Graham in. Then he locked and bolted the door, sliding the chain lock securely in place. Somehow the sound of that sliding lock made Graham gulp and grow a bit more nervous. Instead of leading Graham on a tour of the place or taking him to the bedroom, Rob pulled several oversized throw pillows from the sofa and tossed them onto the floor, making a sort of bed in the middle of the room. He went to his console stereo, selected two or three record albums, and started the music.

"Come and join me, Graham," Rob said, taking off his shoes and socks. He unbuttoned and discarded first his shirt and then his pants and underwear, and lay down on the rug-covered floor completely naked with his head on a pillow.

The only light in the room came from the lights of Chicago that glittered through the large, undraped bay window next to the sofa. Still, it was bright enough for Graham to see the hardened cock gently bouncing on the flat belly of the nude man waiting for him on the floor. Graham was intrigued, and he quickly undressed, throwing his clothes onto the sofa.

Graham lay down next to Rob, who wrapped his arms around him. Cuddling as close as he could, Rob began kissing Graham lightly all over his face. Startled at first, it took Graham a moment to relax and enjoy the moment.

Rob rolled over on top of Graham and began rubbing their swollen cocks together, gently at first and then urgently. He kissed Graham deeply, invading and possessing his mouth. He placed his hands on either side of Graham's face and whispered, "You smell so good, and I love the feel of your hair in my hands."

Although Rob was certainly doing the right things to stimulate him, Graham somehow felt there was something not quite right about Rob. As he lay there, Graham puzzled over his obvious hesitant response to Rob's fervent efforts.

Then Rob rolled onto his side, reached down to grab hold of their two cocks, and began to stroke them. "You're really cute," he told Graham. "I've never seen you in the bars before. Are you new to Chicago?"

By now Graham was having a difficult time concentrating on what Rob was saying because the stroking on his dick was finally arousing him so much, but he didn't want to come too fast. He tried to focus on what Rob had said.

"Uh, yeah. I just moved here from Texas last month. I live in the western suburbs. Des Plaines, actually."

"How old are you, my little Texas friend?" Rob asked.

"Twenty-three," Graham replied. "How old are you?"

Rob stalled for a moment, apparently trying to decide on his response to the question. "I'm thirty-two," he said at last.

Wow. That's old! He's nearly ten years older than I am. But out loud he merely replied, "Really? I couldn't tell.... "

"You're lying," Rob said with a grin, "but that's okay. I know that I don't look all that old. After all, I got *you* here tonight, didn't I?" He chuckled.

Graham thought, *Yeah, but that's because I didn't know your age. Nine years! Maybe that's what I was sensing. I've never been to bed with such an old man before. Still, he's nice looking.* Aloud, he said, "Let's skip all this talk and get to the good part."

"That works for me." Rob proceeded to kiss Graham again while fondling Graham's cock and balls. Then Rob moistened two of his fingers in his mouth, slid them below Graham's balls, and began to try to insert them into Graham's ass. Startled at Rob's attempt, Graham pushed Rob's hand back to the two pulsing cocks. Rob responded by rolling back over on top of Graham and pushing his dick up under Graham's balls, aiming for an entry into Graham's ass. Rob's dick was pretty thick and rather long.

This scared Graham, who had never been fucked by anything that big. And Rob hadn't even produced a tube of lubricant. Graham pushed Rob's hips away and said, "No, I don't want to get fucked."

"Come on... I promise not to hurt you." Rob urged his dick back toward Graham's ass.

"No, I said. Stop. You don't even have any lubricant handy anyway. I'm not about to help you jam that big dick up my ass!"

Rob shrugged and said nothing, but he pushed himself into a simulated fucking position. He pulled Graham's thighs tightly together and stuck his cock between them, right up against Graham's balls. He began pumping his cock in and out until finally the friction caused him to come, squirting juice all over Graham's ass and onto the rug beneath them.

Then Rob just rolled over onto his back and lay there, catching his breath. After a moment, he fumbled for his cigarettes, a lighter, and an ashtray from the coffee table next to him.

Graham reached between his legs, scooped Rob's come into his hand, and spread it over his own cock, lubricating himself. Then he stroked until he came a few minutes later.

"You really are new at this stuff, aren't you? When I saw you at the bar, I thought you'd be a lot more fun... than this turned out to be."

"Sorry to disappoint you. Uh, I guess I've always been kind of shy in bars. It's hard for me to strike up a conversation."

"You mean it's hard for you to pick up tricks."

"I guess you could put it that way. But a lot of that is because I really want a lover, not just a trick."

Rob snickered. "You must have been watching Doris Day movies with a happy ending."

"So what? I know there must be somebody out there for me."

"I hate to rain on your parade, but life isn't like that. I know from my own experience."

"Just because you've had bad luck doesn't mean that I will. I'll get a lover one of these days."

Rob stubbed out his cigarette. "Have it your own way. Why don't you go clean up a little in the bathroom and get dressed. I'll drive you back to the bar."

"Okay. Be right back."

When he was done, he came back to the living room where Rob was waiting for him by the door, already dressed.

"Okay... let's get going," Rob said with a frown as he put out another cigarette in an ashtray on a little table next to the front door.

Within just a few minutes, Graham found himself being dropped off in front of the Annex... feeling rather disappointed with this first Chicago trick.

Rob-for-short had barely said a word on the way back to the bar, and that was fine with Graham. They both just mumbled "Bye" at each other as Graham got out of the car, which then sped rapidly away into the darkness.

Well, that was kind of a bust. And he doesn't know what he's talking about anyway. He's just a bitter old man scrounging around for sex.

Since he was already outside, Graham walked a block and found Ron's green Karmann Ghia still parked in the same place. *Good. Now to go find him so we can get out of here.*

Graham looked at this watch and saw it was already nearly three. He couldn't believe it was so late. And he was amazed that the bar was still open at this hour. At home a bar had to close by two.

The bar was not nearly so crowded this time when Graham entered, and that made it easier to search for Ron. To Graham's dismay, Ron was nowhere to be found. Graham circled the bar three or four times and even checked the men's room despite his trepidation. There was no Ron in the Annex anywhere. He practically ran out the door and down the street to check on the car again. But there it was, still parked in the same spot. It dawned on Graham that Ron had left with someone, just as he himself had done. Graham had no choice but to go back inside and wait. Instead of drinking beer now, Graham ordered Coke after Coke as he waited. He was tempted to smoke cigarette after cigarette as the hours dragged by, but he decided to stick to his vow to quit.

Finally, Graham found himself being ushered out the front door as the bar closed. It was five in the morning, and Graham was out on the sidewalk in a strange city on the same street where the infamous gangster murders had happened nearly forty years ago. Graham's imagination began to run away with him, and he felt real fear. He didn't know anyone in the city, except for the lackluster Rob-for-short who naturally hadn't given either a last name or a phone number.

Finally, anger at being deserted in the city by his "friend" began to overcome the fear. He decided on a plan. He was fortunate because at that moment a yellow cab began slowly cruising down the street. Graham hailed the cab and directed the driver to the downtown bus station. Graham figured that if he went there, he might be able to get a bus to Des Plaines so he could at least get back closer to home. He'd worry about the rest of the details if he could get that far.

The cabbie let him off as he requested, but Graham was disappointed to learn there wasn't a bus to Des Plaines until much later in the day, about mid-afternoon. He was not about to sit around a bus station all day, so Graham sat down by the window and looked across the street. The answer to his problem suddenly appeared. There was a car rental business there, and amazingly it was still open.

Graham walked across the street, pulled out a credit card from his wallet, and went inside to rent a car to drive home. He was slightly dismayed when he remembered that his glasses still rested on the dash of Ron's car, but he figured he'd have to risk it and drive without them. Fortunately he could see well enough to read street and road signs, and it wasn't too long before he found himself back in Des Plaines, angry enough at Ron to do him some real damage if he ran into him at the moment. He parked the rental car and went inside his apartment to get some sleep.

The sound of his telephone ringing a few hours later awoke Graham. It was a little after noon. Sure enough, it was Ron McWilliams.

"Hi, there," Ron greeted him cheerily. "I see you got home okay."

"I got home all right, but no thanks to you! That's the last time I ride anywhere with you. If we ever go out together again—and that's a *big if*—it'll be in my car or in separate cars," Graham grumbled.

"Hey, I'm sorry it worked out this way. I met this guy and—"

"You don't have to give me the details. I get the idea," Graham said, wondering if he should mention that he had done practically the same thing. *But I didn't leave Ron stranded in Chicago,* Graham reminded himself and kept his aloof tone.

"How did you get home anyway?" Ron asked.

"I took a cab downtown and then rented a car."

"Oh. Well, I'll tell you what. I'll split the cost of the cab and the rental car with you to make it up to you. How does that sound?"

"Okay. I'll just let you do that. And there's another thing you can do. Drive over to the local Avis agency when I return this rental car. Then you can give me a ride back to my apartment."

"Sure thing, Graham. When do you want to return the car?"

"Meet me there in about twenty minutes. I'll throw on some clothes and look the place up in the yellow pages."

"Okay, I'll see you there—" Ron began, but Graham had already slammed the phone down and was muttering to himself as he went to dress.

CHAPTER TWO

Their friendship had gotten off to a rocky start at best, but it grew to somewhat friendlier levels as the next three years passed. However, Graham never quite forgot the feeling of being stranded on a cold street at five in the morning in a city that he didn't know. He was not particularly sad when Ron McWilliams found a new job in Ohio and left at the end of those three years. But at least Ron had introduced Graham to gay life in the city of Chicago, albeit in a very unforgettable way.

August 1971

GRAHAM sat in a student desk near the center of a classroom teeming with other English teachers in his department. Large travel posters of England and movie posters from film adaptations of Shakespeare's plays around the walls indicated that this room was like a United Kingdom outpost in the middle of America. In other words, senior English—British literature—was taught here. It made Graham a little envious because he would like to have had the resources to create an environment as elaborate as this in his own senior English classroom. The English Department chairman had traveled a great deal, which permitted him to collect all these items, and he had also been teaching a lot longer and amassing an impressive collection along the way. Even the two other senior English teachers in the department had grand and colorful rooms. His own classroom was neatly adorned with some posters and pictures but not as fully decorated as he hoped to make it in years to come. He sighed and resigned himself to being the new kid on the block among senior teachers.

Other English teachers around him chatted softly about their summer vacations and various trips, but Graham didn't think anyone would be too interested in hearing about another hot summer in dry West Texas. A few of his casual friends who taught in the same hallway nodded and smiled at Graham because he was fairly well liked on the staff. They were all waiting for their chairman to arrive for this first departmental meeting of the new school year.

"This is so tedious," Graham muttered to himself. "I hate just waiting around to hear the same old pep talk we hear about this time every year. I could be working in my classroom and getting things ready for the first day of classes...." He stopped complaining to himself abruptly. A tall, handsome blond man walked into the room and looked around for a place to sit.

"Is this desk taken?" he asked Graham as he approached. The newcomer pointed to the desk next to Graham.

"Uh... no... not at all... have a seat." Graham fumbled in his excitement at seeing the good-looking man, who promptly sat down next to him. "You're new in the department? I guess that's a stupid question since you're here with the rest of us."

"Hi. I'm Mark Matthews," the man said as he offered his hand to Graham. "I'll be teaching freshman and sophomore English." He smiled and his eyes seemed to twinkle.

Graham almost stared too long because the man was so attractive. He appeared to be a little taller than Graham, probably about six feet tall, and he had a terrific body that showed through, even in his school dress clothes. His glacier-blue eyes practically pierced Graham's heart on the spot, but he reined himself in with great difficulty and smiled as innocently as he could manage at Mark.

Graham said the second thing that came to his mind. "Hi back. My name is Graham Thomas, and I teach freshman and senior English. It's nice to meet you."

The first thing that had come to Graham's mind had been, *Damn, you're hot! Can we go someplace after this meeting so I can suck your cock?* But Graham had decided it wouldn't be prudent to say that to a new teacher. He might scare Mark off... and it would certainly give away his orientation to the whole department sitting around him.

"So is this your first year to teach?" Graham asked, hoping to move the conversation forward.

Mark grinned. "Yes. I just graduated from the U of I in May."

"Really? How did you like Champaign-Urbana? I've been there a few times and really liked it."

"Cham-bana," Mark said with a chuckle. "I liked it fine, but I'm anxious to actually get started teaching. I was so bored with all those education classes."

"I know what you mean. Are you from around here?"

"DeKalb," Mark replied. "But I didn't want to go to Northern Illinois U. I wanted to get away from home, and it's quite a ways to Champaign. Are you from here in Des Plaines?"

Graham chuckled softly. "Not quite. I'm from Texas."

Mark tilted his head quizzically. "I'm surprised. You don't have a Texas accent."

"That's because I watched so much TV when I was a kid that I picked up more of a Midwestern sound instead. When strangers meet me for the first time back home they think I'm a Yankee."

Mark laughed. "Is this your first year, too?"

"No. It's my fourth year here… my fifth year altogether. I taught for a year near Denver."

"Wow. You've been around…. "

"In some ways, I guess…. "

Their conversation was interrupted by the arrival of their chairman, Jack Richards, who put his briefcase down on his desk and walked to the podium. "I'd like to welcome everyone back to a brand-new school year." He beamed.

Graham glanced around and saw that many of the eyes in the room had begun to glaze over already in anticipation of a dull hour to follow.

WHEN the meeting was concluded at last and they were all dismissed, Graham turned to Mark. "Want to go have a Coke or maybe a cup of coffee in the teachers' lounge?"

"Sure. Lead on… I still don't know my way around here very well."

"Oh, just a moment, Mr. Matthews," Mr. Richards interrupted as they were about to leave his classroom. "May I speak with you about a few things relating to the required evaluations of new teachers? I'm sure you remember the process, Mr. Thomas," he said with a kind smile. "You just sailed through with flying colors when it was your turn… before you got on tenure."

"Thanks, Mr. Richards… I'll catch you later, Mark," Graham replied as he reluctantly left his new acquaintance.

As it turned out, that was about as close as Graham got to befriending the new teacher… except for occasional chance meetings from time to time. He had been excited about the new guy, and he had intended to see if he could discover if Mark might possibly be gay. But it was a large department in a large school, and so much had to be done at the beginning of the school year. Graham grudgingly gave up on his quest and fell into his usual routine as the first weeks of fall slipped by.

Part of that routine included frequent weekend trips to the gay bars in Chicago. Graham was only twenty-six, and he had no intention of sitting home watching television… except on Saturday nights at 8:30

when *The Mary Tyler Moore Show* came on. It was almost required viewing among the gay crowd to watch the adventures of Mary and Rhoda just before getting dressed and heading out for the big city.

On this particular late September Saturday evening as Graham's yellow Impala sped along going east from Des Plaines to the city, he was especially eager to put the school week out of his mind. School was always really stressful this time of year, and Graham was ready to leave it all behind. He turned up the car radio as the jingle "WLS Chicaaago!" sang out over the airwaves, followed quickly by a new up-and-comer on the charts, the DJ happily informed his listeners. The Chi-Lites began to warble "Have You Seen Her?" Graham happily sang along.

As he pulled up on North Clark Street just past the Annex, he couldn't help but remember that night long ago when his so-called friend Ron had stranded him in the dead of night at this same location. "So long, Ron!" Graham said softly with a grin as he parked on the street and headed for the bar.

Graham walked inside and took a few steps toward the bar. Without warning, a hand grabbed his shoulder and spun him around. Then a voice cried out, "*Whorella*! Where the hell have you been?"

As he was turning, he grinned and then embraced his old friend Adrian Sellers. "*Bitchie Sue*! You old queen! How are you?"

They both laughed and quickly kissed each other on the cheek.

"Really, Graham... where've you been?" Adrian asked.

"I've been here and at the Inner Circle mostly. I guess I've just missed you in the crowd."

"Well, anyway, it's great to see you. I suppose you spent the summer back in dry old Texas?"

Graham sighed. "You got that right. One of these days I'm going to bite the bullet and actually enroll in some graduate classes to begin work on a master's degree. I'm considering Arizona State...."

Adrian giggled. "My, but aren't we *academic* these days? But ASU? Phoenix is really hot in the summer. Didn't anyone ever tell you that?" He laughed.

"That's true... but I'm used to hot summers. I graduated from Texas Tech, after all... and the weather there is hot, too. But enough about school stuff. How have you been? Any new romances I should know about?"

"Well, I did have a little summer fling with this really cute guy from Wisconsin...."

Graham grinned. "And? What happened?"

Adrian sighed. "He went back to Wisconsin! That's the end of the story."

"Damn. Sorry to hear it...."

"Don't shed too many tears over me... I'll find somebody one of these days. By the way, are you still doing that little *thing* you used to do with the guys that you see in the bars?"

Graham stared at him. "What little thing do you mean?"

Adrian chuckled. "You know very well what I mean. You already told me about it, so you don't have to pretend you don't know what I'm talking about. You look at a cute guy, close your eyes, and imagine him in bed with you... as your lifetime lover. You *know* you do that...."

"Well, it's just that I'd really like to have someone in my life... someone who would be there longer than a week or two... or a month or two...."

"Or an hour or two?" Adrian chuckled. "Yes, I know. So you're mentally trying guys out by pretending in your head that you're living together, taking vacations together, and doing the things that ordinary couples do together...."

Graham nodded. "That's it exactly."

"Has it helped you?"

"Look around! Do you see me here tonight with a lover?" Graham asked sarcastically.

"Sorry, sugar. Maybe one of these days you'll find... well, anyway... speaking of all this, I guess we should split up for a while and see if either one of us has any luck tonight."

"Okay," Graham agreed. "I'll see you around the bar... and maybe we can visit some more later."

Adrian nodded and headed off while Graham wandered over to the bar to order a beer. As always, the loud booming of the jukebox hit Graham in the face. He placed and received his order, and then he strolled over to the bar's long wall, beer bottle in hand, to find a spot where he could nest for a while and scope out the pickings this evening. He grinned and looked around.... The cruising never stopped. *This joint hasn't changed even a little bit since I first came here with Ron a few years ago.*

Unfortunately, Graham was still a little shy about making the first move when it came to cruising or even making friends in a bar, so nothing much happened for a while. From time to time Adrian came waltzing by and spoke, but Graham's rather quiet nature was keeping him pretty much all alone.

When he finished his beer, he realized he needed to go to the men's room. He remembered what a friend had once told him: "You don't buy a beer; you just rent it." Sure enough, it was time to return the rental. As notorious as the men's room was, Graham had no choice but to go inside. It was that or go take a leak on the parking lot. But that would mean a risk of getting ticketed or even arrested for indecent exposure. He decided to brave a trip to the men's room.

Surprisingly, there was no line at the moment, so he walked on in. Four of the five urinals were occupied, leaving the one against the back wall open. As he entered, he thought he saw some kind of quick movement all along the row of urinals, but it happened so fast as he opened the door that he wasn't completely sure he saw anything at all. All four guys at the urinals were staring straight ahead at the wall.

As Graham walked up to the empty urinal to do his business, the guy next to him turned and smiled. Then the guy winked. While his own golden showers flowed, Graham stole a glance sideways and saw that his neighbor was watching Graham's dick as he peed. But then the guy quickly looked in the other direction toward the guy on his right side. Then Graham noticed movement again, this time out of the corner of his eye.

He turned to look and saw that the two cute guys next to him had both backed up to expose rock-hard dicks. Graham couldn't take his eyes off the two guys, who were now playing with each other's cocks. Graham looked farther to his right and saw that a similar thing was happening at the other two urinals along the way... except that now one of the guys knelt to the floor and began to suck the other guy's cock.

Graham could clearly see the two cocks next to him and the fourth one down the line, bobbing in and out of a mouth.

His own dick grew hard as he continued to watch all this action despite having finished urinating. He was mesmerized and couldn't take his eyes away. Suddenly the cute guy on his right gasped and squirted his load into the urinal. Then he leaned over and quickly kissed the guy who had stroked him to climax. Finally, he stuffed his cock back into his pants, zipped up, and left the room. Not too surprisingly, he didn't bother to wash his hands. The remaining stroker on his right now moved over next to Graham and smiled. This guy was not just a little cute... he was really handsome.

Graham looked down and saw the guy's huge cock sticking out over the urinal directly in his line of sight. The guy nodded at Graham as though to say, "Have a feel of it if you want to." While Graham was thinking about it, the handsome guy reached out, hesitantly at first, and then gently took hold of Graham's dick, which immediately got even harder. The guy grinned and began stroking Graham. Graham's reflexes took over, and he started playing with the stranger's huge cock. Sex games in the men's room were new to Graham, and he found it rather thrilling to have a stranger manipulating his cock, obviously trying to get him to come.

Graham could feel his climax fast approaching, so he braced himself while continuing to stroke the stranger. He couldn't suppress a moan as he came hard into the urinal. *Wow, that really felt good. Maybe it was just what I needed.*

Trying to be helpful, Graham started stroking the stranger even harder, but the guy shook his head, put out a hand to stop the stroking, and muttered, "Huh-uh. No." Evidently he intended to play with even more dicks as the evening went along and didn't want to come yet.

Graham gave the guy's cock a last squeeze, and then he put his own dick back into his pants, zipped up, and washed his hands. As he left, a new guy entered the men's room and took his place, evidently ready for a little tearoom entertainment.

Just before the door closed, Graham heard someone moan and yell, "Oh, God, *yes!*" from inside one of the stalls, and he had a pretty good idea of what was going on in there. Graham just smiled and shook his head as he threaded through the crowded bar to find a spot where he could lean against the wall again.

This new experience left Graham needing to recuperate a bit, so he decided to have another drink before hitting the road back to Des Plaines. He figured the one beer he'd already downed was really enough since he had to drive quite a way to get home. So he ordered just a plain Coke from the bar. He looked around for Adrian, but he wasn't immediately in sight.

He decided to try the grope corner to see what action was going on there. When he did, all those memories of Rob-for-short and his first Chicago trick on his first night in the bar came flooding back. It still made him cringe to remember that night. He knew how lucky he'd been to get away relatively untouched. Rob had been very disappointed when Graham refused to be fucked, and if Rob had been the violent type, Graham could easily have been overpowered and raped in the stranger's apartment. He didn't intend to be so naïve again.

"What's with that really odd look on your face?" someone asked.

Graham snapped back to the present. "Oh, hello again, Adrian. It's nothing…. I was just thinking about the first time I was in here and nearly got… more than I could handle." He smiled.

"You're not ever going to snare a trick if you just stand there and won't talk to anybody."

"I get lucky once in a while," Graham replied defensively. He thought about relating his recent experience in the men's room, but he decided against it. "I guess the real problem is that I'm not looking for just a one-night stand."

Adrian shook his head. "You already told me. You keep telling me… you're looking for a full-time boyfriend."

"That's right. So we don't need to go over it all again. I don't want just a little sliver of the pie… I want the whole thing."

Adrian laughed. "Did you just say that you wanted the whole thing and not just an itty bitty sliver? I feel the same way… I want a big one, too! Size really does matter." He grabbed his crotch and playfully fondled it.

"Ha. Ha. Very funny, Adrian. You heard what I really said… and *stop doing that*."

"You're not going to satisfy your... uh... sweet tooth if you don't try some samples once in a while, though."

Graham smiled ruefully, shook his head, and said nothing. Then he heard the strains of one of his favorite songs from the sixties, "Dream a Little Dream of Me," as it began booming from the jukebox.

He was about to ask Adrian who sang it, but then he remembered. *Oh, sure... Mama Cass from the Mamas and the Papas. It was from 1968.* But then the song was gone abruptly, replaced on the jukebox by "Mr. Big Stuff" by Jean Knight.

That's funny. Why would the jukebox start a song and stop it in the middle like that?

"Did you say something?" Adrian asked.

Graham shook his head, but that was when Graham noticed that someone slightly to the side was listening intently to his conversation with Adrian. It was kind of dark in the grope corner, so he couldn't see the guy very well. He turned to his right very slightly so that he could see the snooping stranger. He was shocked when he got a better look because he could swear that he looked like the movie star Robert Redford.

"Adrian! Look at the guy behind me and slightly toward the wall," he whispered. "Doesn't he look familiar?"

Adrian glanced at the guy Graham had indicated. "No. Do you know him?"

"Of course not! I think it's Robert Redford."

"What?" Adrian laughed loudly. "Are you kidding me? He doesn't look a thing like Redford. How many of those drinks have you had anyway?"

Graham turned and looked again at the stranger by the wall. The man was studying Graham intently, but then he smiled suggestively. "But look at his blond hair and blue eyes... that face... the way he's grinning at me. It looks exactly like Robert Redford."

"Honey, I think you'd better give me that glass and let me call a cab to take you home. That guy doesn't look anything like... well, never mind. He just doesn't."

Graham realized Adrian was either being stubborn or was looking at the wrong person. But he decided to quit arguing so Adrian wouldn't try to take his expensive Coke away. "Okay. I was just teasing you. Can't you take a joke? Besides... this is just a plain old Coke."

Adrian frowned. "I guess I can take a joke all right. Only it might have been funnier if the guy had even remotely resembled—oh, forget it. But I'm going to keep an eye on you, so maybe you'd better keep to drinking the soft carbonated stuff."

"Yeah. I'll do that...."

"All right then... I'll come back and check on you in a little while...."

After Adrian walked away out of sight, the stranger edged closer and finally stood so close that he was actually touching Graham and leaning up against him.

"Hey! What's the idea?" Graham exclaimed as he turned around and stared at the guy.

The guy who looked so much like Robert Redford winked at Graham. "Hi, there... you sexy guy." Robert grinned, showing white teeth that sparkled even in the dim bar light. "I was just trying to get your attention... that's all. I hope I didn't scare you."

Graham's mind was racing, and he could hear echoes of *Butch Cassidy and the Sundance Kid* ringing in his ears. This voice really sounded exactly like Robert Redford. Then he closely examined the guy again, and Graham couldn't get over it. The man touching him really did look like an exact double for the actor.

"Uh... that is... I mean... hello," Graham stammered. "You kind of scared me, sneaking up like that... I mean, standing so close to me and all...."

Robert now smiled softly and put his arm around Graham. "I'm sorry about that. Are you okay now?" His arm gently caressed Graham's back.

"Uhhhhh... I'm fine." His heart had been pounding, but at last Graham began to regain his composure a little bit. "I guess it serves me right for not paying attention to who's around me. I know you've probably heard this before, but did anyone ever tell you that you look exactly like Robert Redford?"

The guy chuckled cheerfully. "Only all the time," he replied. He lowered his arm and now gripped Graham around the waist. "But never mind any of that right now... I'd like to talk to you, *in private*," he said, caressing the last word with his sexy inflection.

"What do you mean? Outside?"

Again the stranger gave Graham a quick little wink. "Well, sure. Where else? Why don't we just step outside and have ourselves a little chat out on the street by the curb?"

"I don't mean to be rude or anything, but couldn't we just talk in here?" Graham asked. This guy was beginning to make him more than a little nervous. "By the way, my name's Graham."

"I know it is, handsome. I know it is."

"What's yours?"

"You can just call me... uh, Robert.... That will be fine."

"You say that like it isn't really your name," Graham replied.

"Well, it *has been* my name. Among other names, of course."

"That's a very strange thing to say."

"Well, there are different *roles* people play in life all the time. Wouldn't you agree?"

Graham nodded. "Oh, you mean like actors in a movie or in a play...."

"Yes. Sort of like that. But never mind all that right now. Let's go outside for a few minutes so we can *really* chat."

With that, Robert took a firmer grasp of Graham's waist and steered him toward the front door of the bar... none too gently, either.

Graham found himself powerless to keep from being swept outside the door. "I really don't like this very much," he protested as they reached the steps outside the front door.

"I tell you what, Sport," Robert said. "We'll go sit in *your car*. Would you feel safer there?"

"A little more, I guess. It's that yellow 1970 Impala over there."

"I know... uh, I mean... what a nice car," Robert said. "Just unlock the doors, and we'll sit and have our little visit."

Graham did as he was told and nervously sat behind the wheel, ready at a second's notice to start the engine to drive away. He hoped he could find a cop to get this crazy guy out of his car.

"Who *are* you exactly, anyway?"

"Don't you recognize me?"

"Well, you look and sound like the actor Robert Redford from the movies, but I know that you just couldn't be. Where is the *real* Robert Redford? In Hollywood?"

"I guess you don't keep up much with the news from out there in Hollywood. He's busy shooting a movie called *Jeremiah Johnson*, due out sometime next year I believe."

"You're just not going to tell me who you really are, are you?" Graham asked.

Robert just smiled and slowly shook his head. "It's not important. Now first of all, Graham, I made a special trip here tonight just to see you. I know this is going to sound very strange and unbelievable to you, but trust me. I'm going to be perfectly honest with you."

"Honest about what?" Graham asked, beginning to panic a little.

"About what I'm going to do for you, naturally."

"*Do* for me? What does that mean?"

"Why, Sport, I'm going to give you a great *power*. Such a great power that you're going to have to be careful with it!"

"Oh, you are, huh?" Graham replied. "Look. If this is about drugs, you might as well know right now that I'm not a bit interested. I don't do drugs of any kind. Unless you count liquor… and I don't."

Robert laughed. "That's pretty funny. Drugs. Well, this *is* the day of the hippies all right. And I guess all that flower power stuff and whatever else is still going around… but I'm not here about any drugs. What I'm going to do for you is a *lot* more powerful than any drugs. You might even call it a gift."

"A gift? What kind of a gift?"

"The gift of love, Sport. The gift of love. I'm going to give you the power to make anyone fall instantly in love with you. All you have to do is pick out the person."

"That reminds me of that old song 'Love Potion No. 9'," Graham replied. He began to hum it for Robert.

"You really like old Top 40 music, don't you?" Robert said, looking a little bored. "I've noticed you have a thing for old songs.

That's going to be ironic later, but I'm getting ahead of myself. Anyway, the old songs are not it at all. I'm really going to give you a wonderful power."

"Oh, come on!" Graham protested. "This has gone just about far enough. Get out of my car and go away!"

"But I'm being perfectly serious, so don't be so ungrateful. You're going to have a wonderful time with my little gift."

Graham decided that the only way to get rid of Robert was to humor him. Then he was going to get out of here fast and drive home. Never mind saying goodbye to Adrian tonight. He'd explain his sudden departure when he saw his old friend the next time.

"Okay. Give me the gift, and then I gotta go home. I live out of town...."

"Yes, I know. Des Plaines, isn't it?" Robert asked.

"How did you know that?"

"Why, uh... you have a Des Plaines city sticker here on the windshield of your car. That's how I knew... of course," Robert stammered.

"Oh. Yeah, I forgot. Well, anyway... just give me the gift so I can go home."

"Fine, Sport. Hold out your right index finger."

Graham had visions of the guy flashing a knife and cutting his finger off, so he hesitated. But then he figured he could just jerk away before that happened and jump out of the car, so he held up his finger. Robert touched it with his own index finger, and that was it. There was no lightning, no tingling, and no sensation of any kind... and there was certainly no scary knife appearing out of nowhere.

"There you go," Robert said, happily grinning at Graham. "It's all yours, Sport."

"Okay. Thanks a lot. You'll have to get out of the car now. I'm going."

"Don't you want to know how to use the power?"

"Then tell me... but be quick about it because I've got to go."

Robert shook his head slowly. "Such a lack of gratitude...." he muttered." All right, then. Whenever you want someone to fall in love with you, point to the person with that finger and say the words, 'You're the one.' That's all there is to it."

"You're the one," Graham repeated. "That sounds so *familiar*.... Oh yeah. That's an old song by The Vogues.... I've got the 45 at home. Okay, I've got it. Thanks. And bye!"

"Not so fast," Robert said. "I don't think that you're taking this seriously at all. You really *do* have the power. And you have to be very careful, because the person *will* fall in love with you... and I mean *right then*! So if you point to anyone with that finger and say those words, it *will happen*. Incidentally, it will work on girls as well as the boys so you better be aware of that."

"Uh-huh. I see," Graham said, still trying to humor Robert and get him out of his car.

"And one other thing," Robert added. "Your ability to use the power will need to be replenished from time to time. That means I'll have to visit you once in a while and charge up your finger. Is that okay with you?"

"Yeah, sure. You do that."

"Would you rather that I meet you in a bar... like here, for example... or at your apartment in Des Plaines?" Robert asked. "It doesn't really matter to me where we do it."

"How about you just meet me here at the Annex some Saturday night when I need recharging. That would be better for me. Then I wouldn't have to explain you to anyone who might see you come to my apartment building."

"Okay, Sport. That's a deal. And you'll know to expect me when you hear that song again. Remember?"

"What song?"

"'Dream a Little Dream of Me.' And by the way, sometimes I may come in a disguise... dressed as someone else. Don't be surprised."

"This is beginning to sound like *Name That Tune* for the 1960s," Graham said.

"Ha, ha," Robert chuckled. "That's very cute. I'll have to remember that. Do you have any more questions, Sport?"

"No. Now I have to go—"

"Oh, you will have questions, Sport… by the next time I see you," Robert said. "Okay. I'll let you go. But do be cautious with this power… okay, Sport?"

"Sure, I'll be careful," Graham promised.

And then without warning, Robert was gone. Just vanished. Graham hadn't even heard the passenger door open or close.

"I don't care…." Graham muttered softly out loud. "At least he's gone, and I can finally get outta here!"

Wait till I see Adrian next time! But of course he won't believe a word of this. Maybe I'd better just forget the whole stupid thing.

CHAPTER THREE

GRAHAM started the car and drove down Clark Street to make the connection to the freeway that would lead him back to Des Plaines.

"Dream a Little Dream of Me"? That's pretty ironic! This whole dumb thing is like a bad dream. I don't want to think about any of this anymore. I just need to get away from these crazy people in Chicago.

Graham Thomas had a dream that night, really more like a nightmare. And it had to do with good-looking but weird Robert from the Annex. Graham was at a fancy dress ball—like the one the prince gave in the story of Cinderella. As a matter of fact, it seemed to be the same ball that was in the Disney movie. He could see the prince dancing with a girl wearing glass slippers, and the scene was in a stylized medieval castle. The music was the most beautiful waltz Graham had ever heard. Then it dawned on him that he was dancing alongside the famous couple, too. He just hadn't noticed who his partner was. Now he looked to see with whom he was dancing, and it was *Robert Redford*. And Robert was wearing that famous Robert Redford smile as he whirled away on the dance floor in his cowboy boots and western wear from that Sundance movie.

"Are you having a good time, Sport?" Robert asked.

Graham awoke with a jolt. It was then that he decided not to return to the Annex for a while. For the next two weeks Graham decided to go instead to the Normandy on Saturday nights. *Besides, the Normandy is much bigger and lots more guys go there.*

But he knew that he was just rationalizing. The real reason was that he didn't care to run across Robert again. And he wanted to forget all that nonsense about the power and pointing with his index finger. So he stayed away from the Clark Street bar.

In the meantime another, different kind of problem began to plague Graham. He was having trouble with his television set at home. He'd splurged a little bit when he bought a seventeen-inch color set a couple of years ago, primarily so he could watch football games in color on Saturday afternoons. There was only a one-year warranty, of course, and Graham was afraid now it would be costly to fix the tuner. It seemed to be the tuner because the set wouldn't hold a picture for more than a half hour or so without losing the channel. It had to be constantly adjusted.

One morning on his way to his classroom, he stopped in the principal's office to talk to the secretary, Olive Morgan, who he'd learned was a real authority on most things. He told her about his television troubles and asked for a TV-repair recommendation.

"Oh, Mr. Thomas!" Olive exclaimed. "That's not a problem. All you have to do is talk to Kent Cassidy over in the technical arts building. He teaches electronics, including TV repair. He and his students are always looking for items to repair. They do it as a service for the faculty as well as for other students and their friends. The students get good practical experience, too. They only charge for parts since it's part of the classroom curriculum. It's very inexpensive. I'm surprised you didn't know about it."

"Gee, thanks, Olive. I don't think I've ever even talked to Mr. Cassidy in the four years I've been here. He's in a completely different building, of course, and another department, you know. I'd recognize him from faculty meetings, I guess, but I don't know him at all. What's his room number?"

"Hang on just a minute." She reached for a little pad and wrote down some numbers. "I put his phone number, too, in case you need it. Good luck."

Later in the day during his conference period, Graham made a quick call to Mr. Cassidy, who assured Graham that the problem was minor.

"Mr. Thomas, we can take care of your little problem pretty quickly. Why don't you just bring the set with you to school tomorrow, and I'll have one of the students carry it into the technical arts building for you."

"Just call me Graham. And thanks. I'll bring my car keys to you in the morning. I'd rather not carry a TV from my car all the way to your building, Mr. Cassidy."

"You can call me Kent. See you in the morning, Graham."

The next morning Graham found himself in the technical arts building for the first time, reading room numbers as he searched for Kent's room. At last he found it.

"Hi, Kent," Graham called as walked in.

Kent Cassidy held out his hand to shake with Graham. "Hello, Graham. I don't think I've ever really met you before." He smiled as his eyes roamed over Graham as if for the first time.

Graham tried not to stare as he gave handsome, dark-headed Kent a similar visual inspection. He liked what he saw and wondered how he had missed out on getting to meet Kent sooner. But there wasn't time to mull it over now, because it would soon be time for first period class.

"I'll let you know when your TV is ready," Kent promised as Graham waved and began to make a hurried exit. "And I'll send a student in a little while to return your car keys."

Graham suffered through that evening without a TV, but he turned it to his advantage since he made himself get a lot of schoolwork done instead. The next afternoon as Graham sat at his kitchen table grading papers from the day's assignments in class, he was surprised to hear a knock at his apartment door. He looked through the peephole in the door and was stunned to see Kent's smiling face. He threw open the door and saw that Kent was standing at the door, with Graham's television sitting on the floor of the apartment hallway.

"Your television's ready," Kent announced with a huge smile. "I knew you were probably missing it last night, and I didn't want you to have to spend a second evening without it. I just looked you up in the faculty directory, and I brought it to you myself. Where do you want me to put it?"

Graham stood there for a moment, still a little shocked that Kent was making a home delivery. "Uh, it goes over here on this TV stand. I'll give you a hand with it."

"Oh, no. I've got it!" Kent exclaimed, sweeping the television up into his arms and bringing it into the apartment as though it were a lightweight toy. Kent's muscles, which Graham had not noticed before, rippled with the effort.

"I really expected you to just send a student to put it into my car at school when it was ready," Graham protested. "I hate that you went to so much trouble to actually bring it to me at home."

"Oh, it's nothing. Our supplier had the parts we needed right at his shop… so all I had to do was call over there yesterday and get what I needed this afternoon to fix the TV. And as I said, I didn't want you to be without it any longer than necessary."

"How much do I owe you?" Graham asked.

"Oh, don't worry about that. I'll put an invoice in your mailbox at school. I think it only came to three or four dollars for the parts."

"This is just so nice of you, Kent. And please forgive my poor manners. Won't you sit down? Can I get you a drink or something?"

"I'll take a beer, if you have one."

"Sure. Just take a seat over there on the sofa, and I'll get it for you."

When Graham returned from the kitchen with two beers, he noticed that Kent had taken out a cigarette and was just about to light it as Graham set the beers down on the coffee table. Oddly enough, Kent's hands were slightly trembling. *How curious,* Graham thought as he sat down beside Kent and took a drink from his beer bottle.

"Want a cigarette?" Kent offered.

"No thanks. I quit a couple of years ago."

"Would you rather I didn't smoke?"

"No. It's fine. It doesn't bother me at all."

Kent looked at the ashtray at the end of the coffee table and then back up at Graham.

Graham smiled at the question in Kent's eyes. "I kept the ashtray for guests," he explained.

As Kent started to light his cigarette, he fumbled and dropped the lighter, which bounced on the floor and landed at Graham's feet.

"Let me get that for you." Graham retrieved the lighter. Then he turned to Kent. "Here, I'll light it for you...."

Graham couldn't help but notice that as he lit Kent's cigarette, Kent made contact with his fingers to seemingly touch as much of Graham's hand as possible.

This is getting stranger by the minute.

They sat in silence for a little while. Kent was smoking somewhat nervously and drinking beer, but he was saying almost nothing. Graham tried looking into Kent's eyes in an effort to figure out what was going on, but Kent pointedly avoided looking back.

Just as it was really becoming uncomfortable for Graham, Kent said, "You really look sharp in those shorts. That's how I like to dress around the house, too."

Graham glanced down and realized that he was wearing really brief and nearly worn out old gym shorts from back when he was in college, and his T-shirt was nearly in rags. He was also barefooted. His appearance was about as casual as was possible, but he hadn't given it a second thought since he'd been working alone and hadn't expected any company.

"Yeah. I figured I might as well be comfortable while grading papers."

"Are those gym shorts?" Kent asked.

"They are," Graham replied, wondering why Kent was so interested in his appearance. This was sounding very awkward and seemed to be going in a very odd direction since Graham had never considered that Kent might be gay. And he had certainly not even had a private conversation with the man except at school the day before.

"The ladies would say you look very *sexy* dressed like that," Kent said, trying awkwardly to grin. "I wonder if those shorts would fit *me*?"

"Uh... I wouldn't know," Graham said, as a sense of reality began to dawn on him now. His gay intuition was clanging loudly inside his head. "I don't remember what size they are. Probably just large. I'm not sure. I wore these in college, and that was a few years ago."

"You've kept yourself in pretty good shape since college," Kent remarked, once again eying Graham closely.

"Uh... thanks." Graham didn't know what else to say. Despite his scanty clothing, he was beginning to feel overly warm sitting here like this next to Kent Cassidy.

"I know this will sound a little bit unusual, but would you mind if I tried on your shorts?" Kent asked. "I'm just curious to see if I could wear them."

At last it became crystal clear to Graham what was probably going on and where all of this was headed. He looked closely at Kent and made a decision. Kent was good looking, and he was a teacher. Ideally Graham had wanted a relationship with another gay teacher, and this just might be his chance. Maybe Kent and Graham had more in common than he had thought... since Kent was so obviously coming on to him. This whole encounter with Kent over the television repair was turning out to be something completely unexpected in more ways than one. He felt a little thrill of excitement surge through his body.

"Sure, you can try them on." Graham quickly slipped them off and sat there in just his underwear and the T-shirt as he held out his shorts to Kent. Before taking the shorts, Kent moved so fast that he looked like a blur as he took off his shoes, socks, and dress pants, tossing them all on the floor.

By now, Graham was not at all surprised when Kent looked over at Graham's underwear and said, "Do you suppose that I could try on your underwear, too?" He grinned shyly at Graham, who understood perfectly what that meant.

"Okay," Graham replied, "but only if you'll let me try on *yours*, too." He was enjoying this rather unique way that Kent had maneuvered them both out of their clothes. It was kind of like a gay game of show and tell.

Kent wasted no time as he unbuttoned and tossed his shirt aside and practically ripped off his jockey shorts. This revealed a big, rock-hard cock that bounced up and hit Kent's belly as he stood to hand the white jockey shorts to Graham.

Kent's totally naked body made Graham's cock blow up like a balloon inside his own underwear, which he now took off and handed to Kent. Then he quickly stripped off his T-shirt as well. The two naked men stood looking at each other.

Graham almost laughed when Kent really *did* take Graham's jockey shorts and put them on. So Graham did the same, feeling more than a little *queer* wearing Kent's white underwear.

It was a relief when Kent finally brought the "exchanging clothes" pretense to an end and stepped over to put his arms tightly around Graham, rubbing their hard cocks together in their embrace.

Without further hesitation, Graham took Kent's hand and led the man to the bedroom, where they both stripped off their borrowed underwear and lay down together on Graham's bed, exploring each other's bodies with their hands and then with their tongues.

Kent eagerly reached over and took Graham's dick into his mouth first, slowly licking the head and then inching down the shaft ever so carefully until he had taken it all. Kent's fingers gently massaged Graham's balls, causing Graham to groan softly.

Graham carefully shifted 180 degrees on the bed so he could move his head down toward Kent's cock while being careful not to interrupt Kent's sucking. Graham licked the slit on Kent's hard cock and then licked around the head before taking it into his mouth as Kent was doing with his own dick. Graham stuck a moistened finger into Kent's ass, searching for the prostate as he continued to suck Kent.

"Don't make me come yet," Kent pleaded. "When I come, I'm all finished! You'd better come first if you want to come at all."

Graham took Kent at his word and slowed down while Kent picked up speed sucking Graham's dick. Moments later as Kent continued to suck faster and faster, Graham cried, "I'm going to *come*. Take it out if you don't want a mouthful!"

Kent ignored the warning and took all of Graham's come down his throat and sucked until Graham was dry of sperm.

That was Graham's clue to suck harder so Kent could come, too. Amazingly, Kent came even faster than Graham had.

Graham had hoped that now with the urgency of their orgasms over, they might lie in bed and cuddle. But Kent was true to his word about being all done after his climax. He immediately pulled away from Graham and put on his own underwear, leaving Graham to do the same.

Without even waiting for Graham, Kent headed back to the living room and began to dress. Graham followed and put on his own skimpy clothing again.

"What's your hurry, Kent?" Graham asked. "Don't you want to finish your beer and talk about this a little? What just happened is kind of a big deal."

"No. I've got to get home. My wife will be wondering why I'm taking so long to get home from school. She's very suspicious when I'm late. And she gets sort of cranky being there with just our baby daughter all day...."

Graham's hopes were dashed at once when he heard this. "You're *married*? And you have a baby, too? I had no idea. I thought you were just single... and probably a closeted gay man."

"*Gay?*" Kent laughed bitterly. "I'm not gay. And I'm not bisexual, either. This was just two guys having a little fun together. There was nothing serious about this."

"I don't know, Kent," Graham replied. "Sucking cock and coming in another guy's mouth sounds kind of *gay* to me."

"Don't make so much out of this, because it was really nothing at all. And don't look so disappointed." Now Kent gave Graham another huge smile. "But any time you're up for some more *fun*, just leave me a note in my mailbox at school, and I'll try to come over here after school. I'm sure we can find some very inventive ways to get ourselves naked together again. We could have a lot of fun if you just won't take it so seriously."

Graham was still dumbfounded. "Sorry, Kent, but sex with another guy is pretty serious to me. I've been looking for a serious relationship… and with our *fun* this afternoon… you made me think I might have found it!"

"See? You're making this afternoon into a big deal already," Kent insisted.

"The worst part about this is that you're married. It makes me feel like I helped you cheat on your wife."

Kent was making his way to the door now, extremely anxious to leave. "I didn't cheat on my wife. It doesn't count if it's with another guy. It's just *fooling around*. Look, I've gotta go. As I said, if you want to play with me again, just leave a note in my box at school. See you." He closed the door firmly behind him, leaving Graham more than a little shattered.

Kent was gone, taking with him any hopes Graham had for something serious to develop with the sexy vocational teacher. In a way, he felt sorry for Kent, because Kent was in such obvious denial about his sexual identity. Oddly enough, it had not even occurred to him that he could have tested Robert's power trick on Kent. But that was all silliness, wasn't it? Nevertheless, after the disappointing ending to the afternoon with Kent, it was time for some out-of-town diversion for Graham Thomas.

The next time Graham was in Chicago on a Saturday night, he went to one of his old favorite bars, the Inner Circle. It was larger than the Annex, but it wasn't as noisy or quite so much a pickup bar as the Normandy. The more spacious of the two rooms had an impressive bar with plenty of standing room on either side for the cruisers in the crowd. But there was also a slightly raised platform section by the wide bay windows that looked out onto the street. In this area there were small wooden tables with bentwood chairs, almost like an old-fashioned ice cream parlor. This was a social area where friends met for drinks and gossip, rather than for cruising. Although the jukebox was loud, it wasn't so overpowering that you couldn't be heard above the music.

As Graham walked into the bar, the jukebox was blaring out Mary Hopkins' song, "Those Were the Days."

Oh, brother. Graham looked at the table section on his way to order a beer. *Just look at all those queens singing along with that old record! I guess they identify with that one. And that will be me singing along with them in just a few years, too.* He sighed and shook his head.

Graham secured his beer and wandered around the club for a while, slowly sipping his bottled beer to make it last longer. As he rounded the end of the bar, he glanced along the wall for any interesting prospects. To his great surprise he saw a familiar face, one that he had not seen for quite a long while.

"Oh, my God," he said slightly under his breath. "It's Rob-for-short! My first Chicago trick." There he was with a guy who looked a lot like Graham in his general appearance but a little younger. *I guess he cruises for a certain look or type. I must have fit the pattern.*

He walked up to Rob and grinned. "Hi there, Rob. How are you doing?"

Rob stared at him. "Do I know you?" he asked coldly.

Graham thought about just letting it pass and walking away, but he couldn't resist. He unbuttoned the top button of his shirt, exposing his chest hair. "Don't you remember my calling card?"

Rob turned a little pale, and the guy with him started laughing. "So that's his pickup line?" he asked Graham. "He just used it on me a minute ago." He chuckled and turned to Rob. "Look me up when you get a new line." And then he walked off.

Sensing that his interruption had not been appreciated, Graham said, "Uh, well… it was nice seeing you again, Rob."

"Hang on just a second. You do look familiar after all. What's your name?"

"Uh, it's Graham."

"Oh yes. That's an unusual name so maybe that's why I remember you. You're the little Texas guy who was afraid of losing his friend in the bar that night when we met. And you were so intent on finding a lover, weren't you?"

"That's right. You tried to fuck me, and I wouldn't—"

Rob chuckled. "I remember it. Well, did you find what you were looking for in the big city bars?"

"I guess you mean did I find a lover. No. Not yet."

Rob leaned in a little closer. "It might be that you're looking in the wrong places. Haven't you noticed after all this time that most of the guys in these bars are just out for an evening's fuck and not great romance?"

"You could be right, but the odds are better of finding a guy in a crowd of gay ones. I'm not giving up. At least not yet. Besides, don't relationships start in the bedroom?"

Rob laughed this time. "Yeah, and they end there, too, usually an hour or so later. Maybe you're just as shallow as I am. But at least I admit it to myself."

Graham blushed. "I'm not shallow! I'm just sampling—"

"I'm not going to argue with you about it." Rob stuck out his hand to shake Graham's. "Good luck, kid. See you around." Graham was left alone before he had a chance to say anything more so he angled back around to the other side of the bar to have a look around. He ambled through the crowd for a while and then checked the time on his watch. He noted that it was nearing midnight, and the crowd of bar patrons grew noisier as more and more guys came straggling into the bar. It was getting hard to find a place to stand.

Maybe it's time for me to go home.

He happened to be close to the front door when three very noisy guys came in and pushed by him, brushing against him as they passed. Graham might not have paid any further attention to them except that the three guys kept leaning in together, whispering, laughing, and behaving very oddly… even for guys in a gay bar.

Something's up with those guys. Maybe it's just drugs…

He watched the three newcomers. They marched up to the bar and ordered beers, and then they worked their way into the middle of the crowded room closest to Graham. Nothing else happened for a few minutes so Graham just stood and watched curiously. Without warning someone let loose a high-pitched, blood-curdling scream.

"Oh, my God!" someone else screamed from the same general direction.

Then a chorus of screams, even louder than the jukebox, pierced the loud music. Next, a few rather effeminate guys rapidly struggled through the crowd as if in a panic, and continued to scream as they rushed for the entrance. They scurried past Graham in obvious great fear, trying to escape the bar. In their haste, they dropped beer bottles and lit cigarettes all along the floor, marking their path. Graham reached with his shoe to stomp out two burning cigarettes, but he didn't have time to even look up as a stream of screaming guys suddenly ran past him. Soon it was a flood of guys running by as he stood jammed against the wall.

What the hell is going on? Is there a fire? Maybe I'd better get out of here!

Above all the screaming, someone yelled, "It's alive!"

It crossed Graham's mind then that those three suspicious guys that he had observed just might have something to do with this hysteria. That was the only thing that kept Graham from joining in the mass exodus from the bar. He didn't smell or see any smoke, other than cigarette smoke, so he didn't feel in any immediate danger. He watched as bartenders, bouncers, and waiters scurried all around, trying to determine what the trouble was.

At last the standing room area was clear enough for Graham to see the three mysterious guys standing there together, still drinking, smoking their cigarettes, and laughing as if over some huge joke. Graham, puzzled by their actions, moved closer now that the place had emptied out.

Then Graham finally saw what had happened. The guy in the center had opened up his shirt almost to the waist, and a boa constrictor wrapped around his chest was winding around so that its head was playfully sniffing the air, just next to the guy's neck! The snake squirmed and squeezed slightly as it slowly wound upward so it could see the bar better, its tongue flicking in and out.

CHAPTER FOUR

In the background, softly at first and then louder and louder, sirens screamed in the dark Chicago night. *Someone must have called the police or fire department.*

Rather than being called as a witness to this little drama, he decided it was time to venture back to Des Plaines while the getting was still good. The three mysterious strangers must have figured that they'd better leave, too, because they suddenly pushed past him and beat him out the door, with a cursing bartender right on their heels.

Graham shook his head. *Only in Chicago. Maybe Rob-for-short was right. This is a crazy place to look for a lover.*

He hurriedly found his way out of the bar and sped around the corner to his car, just as he heard the police arrive. He saw their blue lights flashing and reflecting from the wet street, and he didn't know whether to laugh or be angry at the sudden end to his night's excursion to the big city.

He thought, *At least the snake's appearance was more exciting than Robert Redford's had been over at the Annex! I wonder if that snake's name could be Kent?*

BY MID-OCTOBER, Maine Central's football team was having a remarkable season. This year the Vikings were winning every game, which was a little bit of a surprise. But it also began to cause a problem for Graham in one of his senior English classes. The team's quarterback was in his eighth period class. That wouldn't have mattered, but the quarterback, Trevor Randich, was getting cockier and more conceited as the season wore on. He had started the semester as a fairly nice and well-mannered young man, but the string of football victories was definitely going to his head. He became more difficult to manage with each passing week. He seemed compelled to show off in class with wisecracks and often with disruptive behavior.

In Graham's opinion, it didn't help that he was also an extraordinarily good-looking boy. He was six feet two inches tall, trim and muscled, and he had a clear, tanned complexion that fairly glowed. He had fashionably long, dark brown hair and thick, almost black eyebrows that topped the most startlingly beautiful green eyes Graham had ever seen. He was a true beauty, but his fortunate good looks seemed to fuel his arrogance almost as much as the team's success, which Graham thought took away from his good looks. It made Graham shake his head and yearn for the kid to graduate.

One Thursday afternoon, which happened to be a unit test day, as Graham arrived at his classroom door after a trip to the faculty men's room during passing period, he saw someone had written the word "fag" in neat block letters with a permanent marker on the right-hand side of the wall next to the doorframe. It wasn't all that prominent at first glance, but it certainly made a statement to anyone who looked very closely at the door or to those who entered the classroom. It didn't take Graham but an instant to figure out who he thought had done the deed, but of course he had no proof. He sighed to himself. *How am I going to get rid of this? I'm going to have to deal with this quickly.*

He went into the room and found a small chess club poster that was tacked onto his front bulletin board. He taped the little poster next to his door in the hall, masking the offensive word from view.

Next, he walked into the room just as the bell rang and proceeded to take roll and fill out absence slips as usual. He noticed immediately that there were a few giggles coming from the back corner of the room where Trevor sat. The student wore a self-satisfied smirk on his face. That made Graham feel almost certain he knew who was guilty.

"I'll give you a few minutes to go over your notes before the test," Graham announced, "but let's please review silently and individually." He stared directly at Trevor, who obediently took out his spiral notebook and began to read through his notes. Then Graham went to the door to post the absence slips.

At that moment, one of the other students, Anita Latham, slipped out of her desk and approached Graham by the classroom door.

"Mr. Thomas," she whispered, "I know who wrote that ugly word on the wall—it was Trevor Randich. He was doing it when I came to class. I just thought you'd like to know." She smiled and headed back to her desk.

"Thank you, Anita," Graham said loudly enough for everyone to hear. "I appreciate your help." He looked at Trevor and saw that he was frowning now, knowing that the teacher's pet had once again told on the guilty party.

As the students studied quietly, Graham walked up and down the aisles between their desks, pretending to check on their study progress and also answering any questions they might have. When he reached Trevor's desk, he stopped and looked at him. Trevor defiantly returned his stare.

Without thinking about what he was doing and saying, Graham pointed to Trevor with his finger and said in a low voice, "So you're the one who defaced the wall."

Instantly Graham heard a tiny jingle, like a small bell. He looked around quickly for the source, but he couldn't find it. No one else seemed to have heard the sound. However, the look on Trevor's face changed immediately. His eyes grew large, and his lips began to tremble. Graham thought he saw large tears start to form in Trevor's eyes.

"Oh, Mr. Thomas," he said softly, "I'm *so* sorry! I did it as a joke, and I know now that it was a cruel thing to do. Please forgive me."

At first Graham thought it was an act so Trevor could show off a little more in front of his buddies. But he wasn't going to give the boy an audience of his classmates.

Graham decided it would be wise to take Trevor out into the hallway where the rest of the class wouldn't hear what was becoming an embarrassing scene. Once they were out of the classroom, Graham closed the door and turned to Trevor.

"What do you intend to do about this?" Graham calmly asked. "It looks like you used permanent ink. Perhaps your mother and father could help you figure out a way to fix it."

"Oh, *please*, sir," Trevor pleaded, "don't tell my parents. I'm so ashamed!"

"Maybe Coach Patterson would be interested in this little problem," Graham suggested. "Especially how those letters got on the wall. I bet he'd have some good ideas for you."

"You wouldn't tell the coach, would you?" Trevor exclaimed, clearly close to breaking down in tears. "I promise you I'll fix it—today." He reached out, took Graham's hand, and held it for a second, rubbing Graham's fingers. "Won't you please give me a chance to make it up to you?" He smiled at Graham. "I'll do anything you want."

Graham was more than a little startled at this sudden turn of events. He snatched his hand away from Trevor and stared curiously at him. On the one hand, he was almost sure Trevor was playing games with him, but on the other, Trevor seemed terribly sincere. He quickly looked through the window in the classroom door to see if the other students had observed or heard any of this little scene with Trevor. No one appeared to have noticed anything—they all seemed to be still preparing for the unit test, figuring the teacher was right outside the room.

This is crazy! How could the other students have not noticed something of what was going on? I take it back... this is beyond crazy... it's utterly weird! He shrugged and turned back to Trevor.

"Come in after school before football practice, and we'll discuss it then," Graham said sternly, turning to open the door and then taking Trevor back to his desk.

The rest of the class period went smoothly without further incident, although Graham noticed that Trevor looked up and stared at him intently from time to time, even while taking the test. At the end of the class, Graham gave a reading assignment for the next day and quickly dismissed the students at the bell. He left without giving Trevor a further chance to talk to him and made his way down the hall to the teacher's lounge for a Coke. He sat at a table in the corner, sipping his drink and grading his test papers while wondering what to do about Trevor.

After he finished the papers, he gathered them and his unfinished drink so he could join another English teacher, his acquaintance from earlier in the fall who was reading a magazine at another table. Mark Matthews had been of great interest to Graham since that first meeting, but he and Graham still only knew each other very casually. They saw one another occasionally since they were in the same department, but they had not really become friends. Graham regretted not knowing Mark better, because he was still very attracted to him. He was glad they had the same conference period since it gave him a chance once in a while to gaze at good-looking Mark.

Graham assumed Mark was straight, and he had no reason to suspect otherwise. They had never really talked on a very personal level. Mostly they had just chatted about school or sometimes about movies. Besides, the odds were pretty good that Mark was just another straight hunk.

"How's it going?" Graham asked.

"Good, I guess. Those sophomores are a real challenge. I think they're even worse than the freshmen."

"Oh, I'll take freshmen any day over sophomores," Graham said. "At least the freshmen are still a little scared and don't think they know it all… like the sophomores do."

Mark laughed. "That's true. You have freshmen, too?"

"Yeah, I've got seniors *and* freshmen. My classes are pretty good." Graham toyed with the idea of telling Mark about what had happened with Trevor and his calligraphy talents, but he decided against it. He didn't want Mark to know that even *one* of his students had thought of him as a fag, especially enough to write it on the wall by his classroom.

Mark looked at the clock on the wall. "Wow. Ninth period is almost over—it's nearly time for the bell. I've got to get over to my classroom, grab my things, and leave early today to run a few errands. I'll see you tomorrow, Mr. Thomas."

"Call me *Graham*. I'm not the department chair, and you're only a few years younger than I am."

"Okay, *Graham*," Mark replied. "I'll see you later."

The final dismissal bell rang, and Graham headed for the English office to see if the secretary had mimeographed the papers he needed for the next day. The papers were indeed ready, but he stopped for a few minutes to visit with Gertrude, their department secretary who had worked for the school for many years. She had become friendly with Graham and didn't mind doing little favors for him once in a while, like putting his papers ahead of someone else's if he had an emergency and really needed them in a hurry. By the time Graham got back to his classroom, it was about twenty minutes after school had ended. He wondered if Trevor would show up for their conference about the door.

He was amazed to see that Trevor was busily trying to remove the letters on the wall with a bottle of rubbing alcohol, an old rag, and even a small bottle of mayonnaise. Almost as amazing was the fact that Trevor was already partially dressed for football practice—he wore a skimpy gold T-shirt and purple, very brief shorts. The school colors looked a little risqué on Trevor today as he stood there in the hallway like this.

"Well, Trevor," Graham said, "I see you've already started trying to repair the damage you did to the wall."

"Oh, yes sir!" Trevor exclaimed. "I figure this alcohol will take most of it off pretty well. The mayonnaise was just in case the alcohol didn't get it all. As you can see, I've got it mostly cleaned up!" His face beamed as though he were quite proud of his ingenuity. "Just a little more rubbing ought to do it...."

"Mayonnaise?"

Trevor giggled. "My mother taught me that... it takes out all kinds of stains."

Graham shook his head. "That's a new one on me...."

Trevor looked up and grinned. "It works best on wood surfaces, though."

"You sound like a TV commercial! Where did you get the rubbing alcohol and the mayonnaise?"

"Oh, I dashed over to the A&P on the corner a block down from school right after classes, before I changed into these practice clothes. I told the coach I would be late for practice because I had to do something for *you*. He didn't seem to mind...."

"Well, that's very thoughtful of you, I'm sure," Graham said. "I think you're right that the letters are just about gone. You might try just a little more of the alcohol, and I bet you'll get it. It's a good thing you didn't write really large letters on the wall. It might have taken you quite a while to get rid of them. You might have even had to paint over part of it." He watched as Trevor applied more pressure to the fast-fading letters. "You know, what truly bothers me the most, though, is why you did this in the first place." Graham pointed to the place where the letters had been. "Do you really dislike me all that much?"

Trevor looked straight into Graham's eyes. "No, sir. Not at all. As a matter of fact, you're my favorite teacher."

"That's rather hard for me to believe."

"I was just being a smartass. Pardon my French! I just wanted everyone to think I was *cool* enough to write on the wall. But I'm really sorry! You won't have any more trouble out of me. I promise."

Graham looked at him doubtfully. "I hope you mean that...."

"Mr. Thomas, could you unlock the door? I'd like to talk to you privately inside for just a minute," Trevor asked.

Graham hesitated, saying nothing and then starting to shake his head.

"The letters are gone now, Mr. Thomas, and I wanted just a little of your time! Okay?"

"I suppose so," Graham said. He unlocked the door and switched on the lights. He was surprised when Trevor stepped inside the room, closed the door behind them forcefully, and snapped the lights off again. He was even more shocked when Trevor threw his arms around Graham in a big bear hug!

Graham spun away from Trevor and fended him off at arm's length, glaring at the boy. Graham sensed something else was about to happen, and he was right. Just as Trevor strained to lean over toward Graham, puckering up his lips as though to kiss him, Graham shoved his hand up—palm against Trevor's chest—and blocked him for no gain, like a thwarted running play on the football field. Trevor had been quick, but Graham had been even faster.

"I love you, Mr. Thomas," Trevor murmured.

Graham felt like an electric bolt had charged through his body, giving him quite an unpleasant shock. As Trevor leaned forward once again to try again to kiss him, Graham broke away completely.

"Trevor, what are you doing?"

"I told you, Mr. Thomas, I love you." Trevor reached toward Graham yet again, but Graham backed away.

"Can't you tell how much I want you?"

That made Graham retreat even farther, determined to keep away from the boy. "Trevor, what's the matter with you? You can't be serious!"

"Oh, but I am. I really want you—right now. I never knew it before today. Something just happened and I knew. I know how crazy this sounds, but I suddenly realized that I needed to let you know that I'm gay—and I just don't care who knows it. I want you to hold me and love me. You're all I care about."

Graham scurried away from the boy and made it to the door. He flipped the switch to turn the lights back on. "Trevor, have you had a head injury in football practice lately, or in a game?"

"Well, yesterday afternoon I did get tackled pretty hard and bumped my head on the turf. What has that got to do with anything?"

"I, uh… I think maybe you're just suffering some aftereffects of it, that's all. Why don't you go back to practice and tell the coach you're not feeling very well. Maybe he'll let you go home early, and you can get some rest." Graham put his hands on the boy's shoulders, a gesture he hoped Trevor would find friendly and reassuring—and not at all simply a way to hold him at bay. "I think you just need to recuperate a little bit. We'll forget all about what happened here today and start all over again in class tomorrow. How would that be?"

At first Trevor dropped his gaze and opened his mouth as if he wanted to speak but couldn't find any words, and again Graham thought it looked like the boy would cry. But then he seemed to have an idea. His jaw tightened and he looked square into Graham's eyes. In a solemn voice, he said, "I'll do anything you say." Graham cringed at the way he drew out the word *anything*. But he quickly recovered.

"Good. Now you just run along. I'll make sure that the wall looks like it did before, and we'll forget all about that, too."

"Okay, Mr. Thomas. I'll see you tomorrow in class. Can I call you Graham when we're alone?"

Graham spun around and yelled, "No!" but Trevor was already part of the way down the hall and Graham was alone.

When Graham got home to his apartment, he was still quite a bit in shock over all that had happened at school.

Why would a smartass kid decide to come on to me like that? It just doesn't make any sense. Surely it's not the stupid power that idiot Robert was talking to me about at the bar. That's just too fantastic to believe. Still, I did use the phrase "you're the one" when I accused him of defacing the door. Nah. It's just a coincidence.

The next day, Graham was a little nervous about his afternoon eighth period class. When he came to the door, Trevor was waiting for him. He had a small plastic bag of apples in his hand.

"These are for you," Trevor said. "You know… an apple for the teacher and all that." He grinned. "But I wanted you to have a whole bag of them."

"Uh… thanks, Trevor, but you really didn't have to do this.… "

"Oh, I *wanted* to." Then he winked at Graham and walked into the classroom to take his seat.

Graham did his best to avoid getting anywhere near Trevor during the period, and he did not call on him during the literature discussion. He was relieved that Trevor left with the rest of the students at the end of class.

But after school, when Graham returned from the teacher's lounge after his conference period, Trevor was waiting for him again at the classroom door.

"Why, Trevor, what are you doing here? Don't you have football practice? This week's game is tomorrow afternoon, remember."

"Oh, I know," Trevor replied, "but I just wanted to spend a little time with *you* before practice."

"Uh, that's very nice, but won't Coach Patterson be upset at your missing so much practice?"

"Aw, he won't care. Besides, I'm thinking of quitting football anyway. It takes up too much of my time after school. I'd rather come in and be with you every afternoon." He winked at Graham again. "Maybe I could even come up to your apartment every day. I could wash your car, help you keep your place straightened up, cook dinner for you...."

Graham would have laughed out loud if the kid hadn't sounded so earnest.

"Trevor, this is getting ridiculous. Surely you can see that. You're a student, and I'm your teacher. We can't have any kind of social relationship together. You know that. And you can't quit football. You're too good at it. Besides, you might get a scholarship for college out of it."

"What do you want me to do?" Trevor asked.

"I want you to forget this nonsense about spending time with me and quitting football. I want you to go on to practice as usual."

"Okay, I'll go to practice because I want to do what you want me to do. But I'm not going to forget about how I feel about you and about being with you someday. If it takes all the rest of the school year, I'm going to prove to you that we belong together." With that, he walked off toward the gym.

Graham rolled his eyes and shook his head. "That kid is either a really great actor, or that head injury earlier this week has messed him up pretty badly. There can't be anything to that dumb power stuff from the other night!"

CHAPTER FIVE

WHAT started out as a bad dream in the parking lot of a gay bar in Chicago had now turned into a sort of living daily nightmare for Graham. Each time he went to his eighth period class, Trevor was waiting for him outside the door. Sometimes Trevor gave him some little present or another. Occasionally it was candy, and once or twice it was more apples or perhaps just a little note that said something like "Just thinking of you!" and it would be signed "T" or it might say "From T to G." It was all very silly romantic nonsense. No matter how many times Graham told Trevor not to do it, the boy too often brought something. By this time, Graham had already decided that the cause of all this nonsense might actually be the ridiculous-sounding power curse Robert had supposedly given him… but he didn't know how to stop it.

When Trevor started copying Shakespeare's love sonnets onto parchment paper written in fancy calligraphy, Graham really started getting worried. The other students were beginning to notice Trevor's attention to Graham and were starting to make fun of Trevor—and probably Graham, too—behind his back. But Trevor didn't seem to care.

The only good thing that had happened was that Trevor was studying harder than ever and trying to prove his worth to Graham in class. His grades were now practically straight A's. *At least maybe he'll earn a scholarship,* Graham thought, not having a clue what to do about Trevor's schoolboy crush.

One afternoon, a week or so after Trevor developed this curious attachment to his teacher, Graham had a visitor during his conference period. It was definitely not one of Graham's favorite people—it was Clayton Weinert, senior class dean of students.

Dean Weinert was in his early sixties and had a military bearing about him. His only concession to modern fashion was oddly incongruous longish gray hair, which Graham thought looked totally ridiculous on him. But he brooked no nonsense from his seniors… and not even among the faculty, whom he liked to dominate if he could get away with it. As a matter of fact, he was Graham's least favorite administrator at the school.

Usually Graham and the dean got along on the surface, at least in a coldly formal and polite way. Today, however, he could tell from the way the dean requested a conference with him that something unpleasant was up. But Graham had no choice except to invite the elder administrator into his classroom.

"Good afternoon, Dean Weinert. Won't you sit down?"

"Good afternoon, Mr. Thomas." Dean Weinert took a seat in one of the student desks. "I just want to talk to you for a few minutes about one of your students. I'm a little worried about him, and I think you can be of some help."

Graham sat in a desk next to the dean. "And which student would that be?" Graham asked, already knowing the answer.

"Trevor Randich. Coach Patterson has told me that the young man has said he wants to quit football. I called Trevor into my office because we all know he has the potential for a good athletic scholarship when he graduates next spring. We've even heard rumors that the University of Illinois is interested in him. We can't have him ruin his chances for college, can we?" Dean Weinert smiled coldly.

"And what did Trevor say?"

"He claimed that he has lost interest in football, but I think I managed to talk him into staying with it to complete this season."

"But why are you discussing all this with me?" Graham asked. "He's doing very well in my class—almost straight A's."

"Trevor told me that he considers you his role model." The dean shuddered slightly as though this were inconceivable. "He says he wants to be an English teacher like you and someday teach here at Maine Central in your department."

"That is certainly a legitimate goal, isn't it?"

"Of course, Mr. Thomas. Of course it is. But Trevor's family cannot afford to send him to school without a scholarship. And Trevor's grades so far in high school do not merit consideration for an academic scholarship. No, sir. Trevor is going to have to do it on his athletic ability in football. That's why I've come to you. I want you to help influence his decision to stay with football. May I count on you to help in this endeavor?"

"Naturally I will, Dean Weinert. I'll certainly do what I can."

"Good. Good. And there's just one other thing. I understand that he spends a lot of time with you."

"Time with me?" Graham asked. "Well, he drops by after school on his way to practice sometimes."

"That's what I'm referring to, Mr. Thomas. Do you think that's wise?"

"What do you mean?"

"I mean he's late to practice every day. I should think that you would not keep him from valuable practice time," Dean Weinert said frostily. "You seem to be the one who makes him late."

Graham was beginning to fume over this last accusation. "I don't make him late on purpose. I've encouraged him day after day to go on to practice."

"Don't you find it a little *queer* that he stops by to see you every day?"

"Just what are you implying, Dean Weinert?" Graham asked, his voice rising in volume.

"Only that it seems awfully strange to me that a once-normal young man can't seem to stay away from his young male English teacher."

"I've had just about enough of this conversation, Dean Weinert," Graham replied and stood up. "It sounds to me as though you are accusing me of fostering some kind of unnatural relationship with the boy. And that is simply not true. I've said I would help in any way that I can. And I will. But just remember, Dean Weinert," Graham added, "you're the one who came to me for help with Trevor! Don't forget that." Again a tiny bell sounded in Graham's ear. Too late Graham realized that he had pointed his right index finger at the dean as he spoke. *Oh, no!*

Instantly the frosty look on Dean Weinert's face disappeared. He smiled warmly at Graham. "Oh, Mr. Thomas, may I call you *Graham?* I certainly apologize for giving you the wrong impression. I know you'll do your best to help us with Trevor. I'm dreadfully sorry for offending you. It's just my clumsy way of handling things sometimes. I hope you can forgive me."

"Of course, Dean Weinert," Graham replied, nervous at what he knew was happening but powerless to stop it. "No offense taken."

"I feel so bad that I said those things," the dean said, wringing his hands. "I don't know how I'll ever forgive myself. You know, you're one of my favorite teachers here at Maine Central High, and I just can't stand it that I have given offense. Surely there is some way I can make it up to you. I know. Let me take you out for a drink after school. I know a nice, quiet little bar downtown where we can have a friendly chat together." His eyes glittered with pleasure at his own suggestion. "That's just the thing."

"That's really very kind of you, Dean Weinert, but it's totally unnecessary. Besides, I'm really very busy this afternoon, and I have plans for this evening anyway."

"Well, perhaps another time," Dean Weinert murmured. "But you simply must let me take you out some evening. I really want to make amends. But for now I'll just get out of your way and I'll certainly be in touch." Unsurprisingly, he winked at Graham as he walked out the door.

"Oh, no!" Graham exclaimed softly. "Now I've got two of them after me. What have I done?"

Graham was right, too. Beginning the next morning, and every morning after that, Dean Weinert stopped by to wish him a cheery good morning. Graham was shocked that the man started to bring little presents too—usually small boxes of candy. He also pestered Graham each day with invitations for drinks after school, and frequently he suggested that they have dinner together.

Trevor hadn't let up, either. He still brought a gift to Graham most days and stopped by after school to visit on his way to the gym for football practice. The drawers of Graham's desk were beginning to fill up with little presents from the two admirers, much to Graham's dismay.

I can't believe this is happening to me. It was bad enough with Trevor, but it's even worse with Dean Weinert. There's got to be something I can do about the two of them. Thank goodness the day after tomorrow is Saturday, and I can get away to the city.

But the surprises weren't quite over for Graham for the week. That very afternoon he had another visitor—Trevor's mother. The office sent a note during the school day that Mrs. Randich was requesting to visit with him during his conference period. Graham didn't know what to think when the lady arrived at his classroom.

She was a handsome, dark-haired woman. Her complexion and eyes reminded Graham of Trevor. Graham thought it was obvious where Trevor got his good looks. Mrs. Randich offered her hand and smiled as she walked into Graham's classroom.

"Good afternoon, Mrs. Randich. I'm Graham Thomas, Trevor's English teacher."

"Good afternoon, Mr. Thomas."

"You must call me Graham."

"Then you must call me Olivia. I am so pleased to finally meet you," she said. "Trevor has talked about you so much that I feel that I already know you. As a matter of fact, you're almost all he does talk about where school is concerned. And that includes that precious football of his. You know, I'm sure Trevor now intends to be a teacher someday, and that is entirely your influence. We're so grateful to you for being such a positive role model for him."

"How kind of you," Graham said. "I assure you that Trevor is doing very well in my class. May I show you some examples of his very excellent work?"

"Oh, no. That won't be necessary. That's not the reason I've come. It's something else entirely."

"Oh?" Graham replied, puzzled.

"Mr. Thomas, uh, I mean Graham... you're from Texas. Is that right?"

"Yes, ma'am, I am. From Amarillo, Texas, to be specific. It's in the Texas part of the old Route 66 highway."

"Oh, how interesting," she said. "I don't know much about Texas, since I've never been there. But I was wondering... are you going home for the Thanksgiving holidays next month? That's an awfully long way."

"Well, no, I'm not. That's a little too far to go just for a four-day holiday. But of course I'm flying home for Christmas."

"Naturally," she replied. "Well, I was wondering if you would like to spend Thanksgiving Day with our family? Trevor suggested it... well, *insisted* on it, actually. He practically demanded that I come down here to meet you and invite you personally. We would consider it quite an honor if you would accept."

"That is so very kind of you and your family, Olivia. I don't know what to say."

"Just say yes, Graham. Trevor would be so pleased. He's just so eager to have you over for the holidays. I was really surprised at how much it seemed to mean to him. He'd be so disappointed if you didn't come."

Graham did some fast thinking. How was he going to get out of this? He really didn't want to encourage Trevor any further, but his mother had actually come all the way down to school to issue this personal invitation. It might look funny if he refused... and it would be rude as well. With great misgivings he said, "Of course, Olivia. I'd be very happy to come. Thank you for thinking of me."

"Oh, I'm so glad you'll come. And Trevor will just be jumping for joy when he finds out," Mrs. Randich replied. "Well, I know you must be very busy so I won't keep you any longer.... I'll just run along. It was such a pleasure to meet you. I'll be in touch with you later about the details. Good-bye, Graham."

"Good-bye, Olivia."

And after she left, he said softly to himself, "This is beyond belief. I don't know what I'm going to do about all this. I may have to marry Trevor when he turns eighteen and graduates, and then we'll spend our vacations with Dean Weinert and his wife!"

As the jingle on WLS radio kept insisting between Top 40 records, "The hits just keep on happening!" It was continuing to be true for Graham. When he got home to his apartment after school, the phone was ringing. It turned out to be an unpleasant surprise.

"Hello, Dean Weinert. How may I help you?"

"Oh, Graham! Please just call me Clayton. We don't need to be so formal."

"Uh, okay... Clayton. What can I do for you?"

"Well, it's Thursday night, and you might not know that it's barbecue night at the American Legion. I thought it might be fun if we went out for a pleasant little meal tonight," Clayton said hopefully.

CHAPTER SIX

"Gosh, Clayton, that *does* sound like fun, but I've got so many papers that I just have to grade tonight before tomorrow's classes. I'm sure you know what a heavy grading load we English teachers have." Graham tried to chuckle conspiratorially. "These are essays, and I just have to get them done."

Dean Weinert sounded deeply disappointed. "Are you sure you couldn't put them off, perhaps until sometime next week? I was really counting on a little dinner for us."

"I wish I could, Clayton, but you know what happens when you put off work and let it pile up on you. I don't dare get behind. But thanks for thinking of me. Goodbye." He hung up before Dean Weinert could get in another word.

I don't know how much longer I can keep putting him off. I think I'd better go back to the Annex tomorrow night. I've got to find Robert and ask him how to turn off this power that's getting me into so much trouble. The worst of it all is that I haven't even had a chance to try it... on the man who's really the one for me... whoever that is. It's all been accidents so far.

EVEN though Graham was already planning to go to the city on Saturday night, he decided he needed a night out on Friday, as well. But he figured he would make this a local night out... and not at a gay bar. The stress of his two unwelcome suitors was wearing thin on his nerves so he thought the distraction of visiting a local pizza hangout for an hour or two would be helpful. He drove to one of the more popular ones, a place called The Captain's Keg. Not only did they serve excellent pizza, but they had a wonderful variety of domestic and imported beers, many of them on tap.

As he had expected on a Friday night, the place was fairly crammed with patrons, a great many of whom were college students and others in their twenties or so. Despite the crowd, Graham spotted two or three empty tables scattered around, all but one of which had not yet been cleared by a bus boy. He selected the only table that *was* ready and waiting for him. Graham barely had enough time to sit down and examine the menu already on the table before he was interrupted—by a visitor, not a waiter.

"Graham?" a voice cried happily. "How wonderful to see you."

A little startled, he looked up to see Dean Weinert standing next to him.

Damn! Aloud, he replied, "Why, Clayton... this is a surprise. I didn't know you ever came to the Keg." *I wouldn't have set foot in here if I thought you'd be here.*

He feigned a smile as pleasantly as he could.

"I'm here with my wife, Margaret. She's over there." He pointed to a somewhat frumpy and frazzled-looking woman about halfway across the room. "We like to keep up with the young folks, you know."

Graham knew that Dean Weinert probably expected to be asked to sit down at his table, but he just couldn't quite make himself do it. He needn't have worried. Clayton Weinert pulled out a chair and sat down right next to him, obviously beaming with joy at their accidental meeting.

"What can I get you gentlemen to drink?" a waiter asked.

Graham hadn't even noticed the guy approaching the table so he was again a little startled. "Uh... do you have dark beer on tap?"

"We sure do," the waiter replied. "We've got Löwenbräu dark, and—"

"You can stop right there," Graham said. "I'll have a half yard of Löwenbräu dark, please."

"And you, sir?" the waiter asked Clayton.

Clayton chuckled. "Well, I was sitting over there at another table, but I guess I have time for another beer with my *good friend* here." He reached down and tweaked Graham's knee playfully. "I'll have the same thing he's having." Clayton smiled so brightly that his eyes sparkled. Then he reached over and patted Graham's hand.

Graham inwardly groaned and reached for the menu again, as much to get his hand away from Clayton as to really see the pizza offerings.

"Here," Clayton said. "Let me make a suggestion to you." He reached over, practically fondling Graham's hand as he grabbed the side of the menu where Graham gripped it. He pretended to look over the menu while casting admiring glances at Graham. "The house specialty pizza is excellent." He grinned, still holding on to Graham's hand.

This is eerie. Kent Cassidy did practically the same thing when I lit his cigarette. But Kent wasn't under the spell of the so-called power. On the other hand, he was *obviously trying to seduce me... but Dean Weinert is almost panting as he tries to get his hands on me!*

Graham hastily dropped the menu onto the table, thus breaking contact with Clayton's hand. His mind was racing. *How am I going to get rid of this guy? Surely he'll take his beer and go back to his wife in a minute or two.*

He looked over at Mrs. Weinert. Her face was set in stone, and it wasn't a pretty picture either. She was obviously annoyed and impatient with her wayward husband.

"Don't you think Mrs. Weinert might be missing you, uh, Clayton?" Graham asked.

"Who? Oh, you mean Margaret. She'll be fine. Don't worry about her," Clayton replied, not even glancing over to check on his wife.

Graham looked around, praying for the waiter to come back. *I think I'm stuck.*

At that moment the waiter finally arrived with their drinks. "Here you go, gentlemen," he said, sliding two tall and frothy tankards across the table. "Have you had time to decide on your order?"

Not even having actually thought about pizza since Clayton had joined him at his table, Graham was silent for a moment. "Hmm. I guess I'll have a small Italian sausage and mushroom pizza."

"Original crust, thin crust, or pan pizza?"

"Thin crust, I guess," Graham replied.

"I'll have that right out for you, sir. Anything for you?" he asked Clayton.

"No, thanks. I already ate. I'll just have the beer. And put everything on my tab. I was at that table right over there," he said, again pointing to his previous table where Mrs. Weinert still sat, apparently growing angrier by the minute.

"You know, Graham," Clayton began, "this place is terribly busy tonight. I'm afraid you might have to wait for a really long time to get your order."

"That's okay," Graham said. "I don't mind having to wait."

"Nonsense. Let me see if I can help you out...."

"What do you mean?" Graham objected, staring at the odd look on Clayton's face.

Clayton surveyed the room and spotted three tables now empty but still not yet cleared. "It's a shame how people waste food, and they have such good pizza in here, too."

A warning light came on in Graham's head, but he didn't quite know what it might mean.

Clayton suddenly rose from his chair. "Just a minute, Graham, and I'll fetch something tasty for you."

Before Graham could stop him or protest, Clayton scurried off to the first of the empty tables. There he picked up a pizza pan, which still held three or four slices of whatever kind of pizza the previous patrons had ordered. Then Clayton was off to the next table, where he scooped up three slices of uneaten pizza. He made it to the third table and finished filling the pan with the leftover pizza that he found there. Beaming with pride, Clayton returned to Graham's table with his prizes.

"Here you go, my boy. I don't think these slices are even completely cold yet. And even so, pizza is really better at room temperature or maybe cold anyway."

Graham was mortified. Just about everyone in the room had watched Clayton by the time he reached the second table, and the chuckles and laughter were in full chorus by the time he came back to Graham.

Clayton chose a slice of pizza and held it up. "I don't know if you like the different kinds of pizza that those people ordered, but they look pretty good to me!" He stuffed the first bite of his selected pizza into his mouth.

This time Graham groaned aloud.

"Come on, Graham, eat up."

"Uh… I'm still drinking my beer." Graham desperately offered an excuse not to eat from the pan of other people's leavings. He gulped some beer.

Mrs. Weinert had finally reached the full limit of her patience… and perhaps beyond. She had watched as her husband snatched the pizza from the three tables, and her face was an angry purple as she rose and stormed over to Graham's table.

"All right, Clayton Weinert!" she yelled, not bothering to keep her voice down. "I've had enough of this foolishness. How dare you keep me waiting like a second-hand hooker over at that table while you first of all fawn all over this young man… and then make a spectacle of yourself by stealing used pizza from empty tables. You're a disgrace! Get up from there and take me home this minute!"

Cheers and applause greeted her outburst as her audience goaded her on. "You tell him, Granny," someone hollered.

"Let him have it," another voice yelled. "Give it to him *good*."

"We've got some leftover pizza over here that we're not going to eat… if you want it," another voice called out, laughing.

"See what you've done?" Mrs. Weinert exploded again. "Everybody in here sees what a clown I married! My mother was right about you all the time. I insist that you take me home right now."

It finally became clear to Clayton that perhaps he had gone too far. He blushed a deep red and stood up. "I apologize to you, Graham. I didn't mean to embarrass you like this."

"What do you mean you didn't mean to embarrass *him*? What about *me*, you old goat? Don't I get an apology, too?"

"Of course, my dear," Clayton mumbled. "Now lower your voice and let's go home."

"It's about time, Clayton Weinert… that you came to your senses and got yourself…."

The rest was lost as the unhappy couple left their raucous spectators behind. Thunderous cheers and applause broke out.

The waiter arrived with Graham's pizza. "Would you box that up please and make it a carryout order?" Graham asked. "I think I've lost my appetite for pizza for tonight."

"Sure thing, mister," the waiter replied. "And hey, your mother and father really put on quite a show tonight," he grinned broadly. "We should pay them. By the way, do you want a box for the other pizza, too?" He smirked as he pointed to the pizza scraps Dean Weinert had gathered.

Graham gave the waiter such a thundercloud of a look that the waiter scurried away without waiting for an answer.

A few minutes later as Graham left the restaurant with his pizza box balanced carefully in one hand, another round of applause and cheers accompanied his exit. Graham decided he probably wouldn't be visiting The Captain's Keg again anytime soon.

One more result of his accidental use of Robert's untimely *gift* happened even before Graham had a chance to look for Robert. The very next morning he was awakened at nine o'clock by a loud banging at his apartment door.

"Who the hell is here this early on a Saturday morning?" Graham muttered angrily as he stumbled to his living room. He looked through the tiny peephole in the door and saw Trevor Randich.

"Shit!" he exclaimed angrily. "What is it, Trevor?" he called through the door.

"Come on, Mr. Thomas, please let me in. I want to talk to you."

Without thinking, Graham unlocked the dead bolt and opened the door. "Oooooh, Mr. Thomas," Trevor gushed. "You're just as beautiful as I thought you would be!"

Too late Graham realized he was standing there still dressed only in his white jockey briefs. His face turned red and his heart sank.

But before Graham could retreat to throw on some clothes, Trevor rushed through the door and closed it firmly behind him. "I just *love* your body!" To Graham's astonishment, the boy stripped off his T-shirt and tossed it to the floor. The flimsy cotton shorts nearly bursting with a raging-hard cock that pointed invitingly towards Graham were about to follow.

Graham blushed even harder and cried, "Stop! Leave those on!" But as he stared at the boy's beautiful body, he couldn't help but notice his own cock was starting to respond. *Damn! I've got to stop this before it's too late!* He rushed to Trevor just as the boy got his thumbs under his gym shorts' waistband and was about to pull them down. Graham panicked and grabbed Trevor's wrists to stop him from pushing them both over the edge.

Suddenly Trevor's eyes rolled upward, he quivered and jerked and whimpered, and a dark stain spread in his shorts. "Damn it! I came already!"

Graham's eyes stared in fascination at the creeping stain on the shorts. *Thank God he came so fast, or this could have gotten a lot worse!*

"Gosh I'm sorry, Mr. T! I just couldn't help it. I never came so fast before in my life. Please forgive me. I promise to do better in the future—"

"Now listen to me, Trevor. There's nothing to worry about... because there isn't going to be a next time. What happened was just a natural reaction, but you and I are not meant to be together like this ever again. Now why don't you trot around the corner there and clean up in the bathroom while I get dressed. Okay?"

Trevor nodded and headed where Graham had directed, still looking a little sheepish. "But we still need to talk," he announced as he entered the bathroom and closed the door. Graham hurried to his bedroom and threw on a shirt and some pants. Then he rushed back to the living room where Trevor already waited, pacing slowly up and down.

"Trevor, you've got to stop all of this. I really mean it. You're not even legally old enough to… uh… do anything with an adult!"

"Oh, yes I am! My birthday is today, and I'm eighteen. I can do what I want to, and seeing you, uh, undressed that way, was like a birthday present for me."

Graham shook his head slowly and pointed to a side chair. "Have a seat for a minute, Trevor. You're right—we need to talk. Please think hard about what I'm going to say. Promise me?"

Trevor sat down and nodded. "Okay."

"Look, Trevor, I'm still your teacher even if you *are* eighteen. You know very well how much trouble there would be… for both of us… if you and I got involved in a relationship. You're a really smart guy so you know this already."

Trevor looked down at the floor. "Okay. I realize you're right. I don't want to cause you any trouble—"

Trevor looked up straight into Graham's brown eyes with those startlingly green eyes of his. There appeared to be a tiny touch of acceptance in the midst of the yearning still there.

Graham thought, *If I were eighteen years old and a student, I'd say why the hell not? This guy really is beautiful and he wants me. But I'm* not *eighteen, and he's still more like a kid, despite his birthday. Maybe he's got the good sense to understand this must stop. I've got to reason with him.*

So Graham looked solemnly at Trevor and slowly shook his head. "I can tell you know I'm right."

Trevor suddenly changed tactics and smiled sweetly. "I told you that I love you, Mr. Thomas," Trevor said softly and looked down at the floor again as if he were a little embarrassed. "That's a very difficult thing for a gay guy to admit to his teacher. I know you see that. Surely you can tell I mean it, or I wouldn't be here. Please let me prove it to you… someday. And even though you haven't told me, *Graham*, I just know that you love me, too."

"Back up a minute. Let's look at this realistically, Trevor. Are you sure you really want a gay life? It wasn't that long ago that you were writing ugly letters on the wall next to my classroom door at school and giving me a hard time in class. Now you think you *love* me? Think about it, Trevor. There's something wrong with that picture."

"Oh, I know it all happened very suddenly, and I really can't explain it," Trevor insisted. "But I'm feeling things about myself that I've hidden away for years. Now I know why I never tried very hard to find a girlfriend. Actually, I used to worry because I just wasn't interested in girls. Now that I've been in your class and have gotten to know you a little, I can see what I was waiting for."

"But you really *haven't* gotten to know me, Trevor. Not more than anyone else in the class has. Don't you see how unrealistic this all is? And be honest about this, Trevor. Have I ever given you any reason to believe I was gay, or have I offered you any encouragement that I desired a romantic relationship with you? Wasn't it all just in your imagination?"

Trevor thought about that for a moment, and then he hung his head as he looked down at the floor again. "You're right about that part. But the rest of it is true. I've been gay all along, and I just hadn't let myself consciously acknowledge it. And it doesn't change the fact that I'm attracted to you, Mr. Thomas. That I care for you. That I love you!"

Graham passed over that last part. "You mean to say you think that you were gay all along?" Graham asked, somewhat surprised.

"Yes. I know I'm gay and always have been, but I would never have told anyone that," Trevor replied. "Not while I was still in high school anyway. This sudden feeling for you has just made me realize it and finally admit it to myself."

"All right, Trevor. Since you've been honest about this, I guess I will be, too. I *am* gay, but nothing can happen between us because you're my student. I already told you that. Now, I feel bad about talking to you this way, because I don't want to cause you any pain. But it's very difficult in this world to be gay. I'm sure I don't even have to tell you that."

"Don't worry for a minute about telling me you're gay," Trevor reassured him. "We'll keep it as our secret. If you want me to, I'll stop bringing you presents and coming to your room after school. I know people are beginning to suspect something, so I'll be more careful in

the future. As long as I know we have a connection in spirit, at least...
it'll be enough for me. As an English teacher, you'll appreciate this...
we'll be like *kindred spirits*."

Graham chuckled. "I don't know where you heard that
expression, but I suppose it does apply. And that's very wise of you,
Trevor, to slow down the obvious show of affection. You do need to be
more careful. And I want you to think this over very carefully... since
I'm about eight years older than you are. That's a lot at your age. Even
if it were a year from now and you were out of school, it would still
feel very inappropriate to me for us to become a couple."

"It doesn't bother me a bit. I don't care about the age difference."

"Maybe you don't right now, but you might in the future. Let's
just see what happens when you go away to college next fall. Will you
agree to that? No more open displays of affection at school, and just as
importantly, no more visits to my apartment. After all, please remember
we are still teacher and student."

"Okay, Mr. Thomas," Trevor agreed. "Whatever you say. As I
said before, I don't want to cause any trouble for either one of us. But
when I've graduated next spring, I'll be all *yours*!"

Graham groaned inside. *I've just got to find Robert and get both
of us out of this.* He said aloud, "We'll see how we both feel in a year
or so from now... and by the way, happy birthday, Trevor."

"Thanks." Trevor stood up to leave, but he looked at Graham for
a moment and happily smiled. There was a tiny gleam of what looked
like hope in his pretty green eyes.

CHAPTER SEVEN

DESPITE what Trevor had promised him, Graham still felt uneasy about the impossible situation that seemed to be simmering between them. It wasn't so much a matter of Trevor's age exactly, since Trevor was now legal, but Graham certainly didn't love Trevor and wasn't likely to ever feel that way about him.

It was simply a fact that Trevor would always seem to be one of his students in his eyes, and that feeling would never go away. He did admire how attractive Trevor was... and he liked the kid... but he wasn't interested in a relationship with *any* eighteen-year-old man. It was fortunate that Trevor would most likely be going away to college next fall. But just in case Trevor hadn't taken seriously their recent conversation at his apartment, Graham had to find a way to completely end Trevor's interest in him before it got even more out of hand.

Then a terrible realization came to Graham. If Trevor wanted him so much, what would it be like when Dean Weinert finally found a way to get Graham all alone? He shuddered as he imagined the elderly administrator chasing him around some bedroom somewhere, cock bobbing and long gray hair flying cheerfully behind him in the air. That was a disaster in the making!

As Graham drove to Chicago that Saturday night, he earnestly hoped he would be able to find Robert and get some answers to help him out of these two dilemmas. *Oh, please be at the Annex tonight, Robert.*

Just as he was about to pull into the bar's parking lot, a flashing blue light appeared behind him. Graham knew instantly it was one of Chicago's finest—a cop who was evidently prowling around the gay bars. Everyone knew the Chicago police sometimes did that, often just to harass the gays.

Graham obediently pulled over to the curb and waited for the inevitable ticket on some trivial or trumped-up charge. He looked into the rearview mirror and then the side mirror to get an idea of what would be facing him. The cop was out of the squad car, checking the license plate of Graham's car. He had a little traffic citation book in his hand, but only when the cop approached the car could Graham get a good view of the guy. This cop looked young and cocky... the worst kind, Graham figured. He had heard these guys could be real smartasses and abusive with gays. *This guy is kind of cute, in a military sort of way*, Graham thought. *Just my luck.*

"Good evening, *ma'am*... uh, I mean, sir," the cop said, smirking at Graham. "In a hurry to meet the rest of the girls?"

"No, Officer," Graham said. "But I thought I was driving the speed limit."

"I just bet you did, honey," the cop answered. "But you didn't come to a full stop at that last stop sign. What you did... we call it a 'rolling stop.' You must have a hot date tonight at this fag bar."

Graham was afraid to be too defensive with a Chicago cop. He had too much at stake to be arrested near a gay bar, and he knew the cop would certainly include the specific location somewhere in his report. So he said nothing.

"May I see your driver's license, please?" the cop asked sarcastically. "Just take it out of your wallet so I can check it, and keep your hands where I can see them."

It dawned on Graham that there might be a way to avoid an expensive ticket and an ugly scene with this cop. So far this was just a minor annoyance, but it *could* get worse. And it did.

The cop looked up from Graham's driver's license and noticed the sticker on the windshield for the faculty parking lot at Maine Central. "Say, are you a teacher?" The cop grinned crookedly.

Graham gulped. "Yes, I am."

"And someone like you is actually teaching our innocent young children?"

"What's that supposed to mean?"

"It means the kids need protection from perverts like you." He smiled viciously. "You know, I ought to just make a little radio call to headquarters so they could relay a little information about you to the police in Des Plaines. Yes, I saw your city sticker on the window. I bet the good folks there would thank me."

"You wouldn't do a mean thing like that, would you? I don't fool around with the students."

"How do I know that? You might be fucking little boys all the time! I think I'll just—"

Keeping his hands up where the cop could see them, Graham pointed to the cop with his right index finger and said, "You're the one I saw around the corner, aren't you?"

A bell sounded. It was working again! The cop stopped in his tracks and looked searchingly at Graham. Then he smiled gently. "Your name is Graham?"

"Yes, sir," Graham replied.

"That's such a pretty name. I really like it. Mine's Carlton. Carlton Safranski. My friends call me Carl so of course you can call me Carl, too." He held out his hand to shake with Graham after putting the citation book away in his back pocket.

"Uh, hello, Carl," Graham replied, smiling and accepting his hand.

"Oh, what a nice class ring you're wearing," Carl said, examining Graham's hand. "May I look at it?"

"Sure," Graham said. "Want me to take it off?"

"Heh, heh," Carl chuckled. "No. Just let me hold your hand a minute. You're from Texas, are you?" he looked at the ring, observing the insignia, and playing gently with Graham's fingers.

"That's right," Graham replied. "I moved here about three years ago last August."

"Isn't that something," Carl remarked. "Did anyone ever tell you what lovely eyes you have? A fellow could just drown in 'em." He winked and smiled at Graham again.

"Uh, thanks, Carl. You're real sweet to say so."

"Say… are you in a hurry? I know a real nice coffee shop right near here, and they've got real good doughnuts."

"Well, to tell you the truth, Carl," Graham replied, "I sort of had my heart set on a drink. A beer, at least."

"Oh, that's too bad, Graham. I'm on duty for a couple of hours more, and of course I can't drink while I'm on duty." He looked terribly disappointed. Then his face brightened. "I know. You go on in and have a drink or two, and I'll wait around in my squad car, circling through the general neighborhood until I get off duty. Then we can go somewhere *together*. How would that be?"

"Oh, that's just fine, Carl!" Graham said, hoping he would be able to get out of this little cop date later. "Let's do that...."

"Okay, Graham... but don't you go picking up someone else in there—I'm mighty jealous!" He handed the license back to Graham.

"Oh, I won't," Graham quickly promised. "I'll just have a couple of drinks and meet you later."

"Now don't you have *too* many drinks." Carl chuckled. "It wouldn't do for you to get too drunk to drive. Then I'd have to put you under house arrest for your own protection. My house, that is." He laughed softly. "But now that I think about it, maybe that's a good idea after all."

"Oh, I'll be careful and not drink too much," Graham answered with a big cheery smile. "See you later, Carl. Don't give out too many tickets to the other boys."

"I won't," Carl promised. "I'll be *waiting* for you...."

Graham started his car, drove into the parking lot, and walked toward the bar. He glanced at the street and noticed that Carl was still watching him closely. As Graham turned to go in, he saw Carl wave playfully at him, so he returned the wave.

"Oh, *brother*," Graham said softly to the nearest parked car. "What have I done this time? Now I've got a cop crazy about me. Robert just better be here to get me out of all this!"

Graham hurried up to the bar and ordered a beer. Then he proceeded to search the bar for Robert. But he wasn't there. "Damn!" Graham muttered out loud. "Just when I need that nut, he isn't here."

But Graham kept slowly circling the bar, waiting and hoping Robert would show up sooner or later. Not even his friend Adrian popped up this evening, so he had no one to talk to.

By the time Graham was sipping his second beer, he had just about decided to give up. He wandered back to the grope corner again and was checking his watch.

I've got to try to get out of here before Carl's shift is over! Maybe I could leave unnoticed while Carl's in another part of the neighborhood, and I can get away. Surely Carl wouldn't drive all the way to Des Plaines looking for me if he's on assignment here in the

North Clark Street area. My place isn't in Carl's jurisdiction. He's a Chicago *cop after all.*

Since Robert had not shown up, Graham figured that he had waited as long as he dared. He checked his watch once again and saw that it was about half an hour before Carl's shift would be over. Hopefully the cop wasn't out front right now, and Graham could make his getaway. There was nothing to do anyway but drive back to Des Plaines, since he hadn't found Robert.

Graham headed back toward the parking lot, carefully watching for Carl's squad car. Just as he reached his Impala and thought he had it made, a blue light flashed again. "Oh, no!" Graham groaned.

"Hi, there!" Carl called cheerfully. He pulled up next to Graham just as Graham was about to open the door and drive away. The blue lights went off, and Carl rolled down his passenger window so Graham could hear him. "C'mon, Graham. Get in…. I've got a great idea. I'll call on my radio to clock out, and then I'll take you to my place for a drink. Later… much later, I hope… I'll bring you back to your car. I'm pretty sure it will be safe while we're gone."

Graham's heart sank. He could not think of a good excuse not to join Carl in the police car… and the guy was pretty sexy… so he reluctantly climbed into the passenger seat. "Are you sure about this, Carl? We just met, you know."

Carl grinned broadly at Graham. "Hey, I know a nice guy when I meet one, and you're awfully cute, Graham."

"Uh, thanks, Carl," Graham replied. "You look nice, too."

Now that he was sitting inside the squad car with Carlton, he had a better chance to really study this young cop. As they drove along after Carl completed his call to a police dispatcher, Graham examined the man's square jaw, straight nose, bright and cheery eyes, and other handsome features. Since the guy was a cop, Graham figured there was a very fit body inside that uniform. It seemed that he was about to find out.

Carl's long legs indicated that the guy might be a few inches taller than Graham, and those legs really were shapely in those uniform pants. Now that he could see him up this close, Graham decided the cop was actually very desirable. He would have preferred that Carl have longer hair, but you can't have everything. *Maybe this could be a thrilling little adventure after all. I guess I'll just relax and see what happens.*

In a remarkably short time, Carl pulled into the parking lot of an attractive apartment building on Chicago's west side. He turned to Graham and said, "Let's go inside. Just follow me... and I'm sure we're going to have a really good time. My place is on the third floor, so we'll take the elevator."

Graham did as he was told, since he really had very little choice. He decided he might as well make the best of the situation. *How bad could this be?* he asked himself as he gazed at the tall, good-looking cop beside him.

When they got to Carl's apartment, Graham wasn't surprised that it wasn't completely tidy and neat. It wasn't dirty by any means, but it was as casual as Carl himself appeared to be.

Once they were safely locked inside the apartment, Carl grinned shyly and said, "I have to tell you, Graham... I've never done this before. It's my first time with another guy! I think I've always wanted to try it, but I never had the nerve until I saw you tonight. You'll have to guide me along."

"Well," Graham replied, "I guess we should start by going to your bedroom and getting undressed. You lead the way."

"Okay." Carl took Graham's hand and led him into a short hallway. They turned to the left, entered a bedroom, and Carl took Graham to the room's unmade bed. Carl flipped on a nightlight and smiled ruefully. "Sorry about the wrinkled-up sheets.... I was in a hurry this morning."

"Don't worry about it."

Carl stood by the rumpled bed with a confused look on his face, as if he were wondering how to go about an encounter with another man. He turned to look at Graham with questioning eyes.

Poor guy. He doesn't know what to do. I'm going to have to get the ball... or balls... rolling and help him out. Graham decided.

"Okay, Carl. Let's get you more comfortable." Graham reached to unbutton Carl's shirt most of the way to the belt.

Then he put his hand inside to gently massage each of Carl's nipples, one after the other. They immediately hardened as Graham's fingers lingered on each one. Carl moaned a little when Graham ran his fingers lightly through the chest hair and worked their way to the navel.

Graham looked down at the bulge that had exploded in Carl's pants. "Officer, it looks like you've got quite a weapon there… inside your pants, I mean. But I think you need to put the other one away someplace before one of us gets hurt."

Carl's hand went instantly to his firearm, in an automatic reflex. "Oh yeah. You're right. I better get this out of the way."

While Carl was busy storing his gun in the closet, Graham quickly stripped off his clothes, dropping them to the side of the bed. He watched as Carl finished removing his clothing, throwing it on the closet floor, except for his underwear.

"Come here, Carl. Let's get better acquainted." Graham met him at the end of the bed and put his arms around the man's waist, drawing him close and rubbing his stiffened cock against Carl's low-hanging balls and hardened dick which now protruded upward through the waistband of his white jockey briefs. "I can feel that you're holding something against me… and it isn't a grudge."

Carl grinned. "You're funny, Graham. I like that." He leaned to give Graham a tentative kiss.

"I'm not your sister, Carl. You can do better than that." Graham kissed him back, using his tongue to tease Carl's lips open so he could fully insert it. He could tell when Carl barely shuddered that he was a little shocked at first at the invasion of his mouth. But Carl quickly responded with his own tongue.

During the kiss that followed, Graham slowly traced his hands from Carl's waist along to the cop's buttocks, cupping and exploring each firm bubble. While Carl groaned with pleasure, Graham quickly reached up and slid the briefs downward, leaving Carl's throbbing cock jammed against his own stiff dick. That was when he noticed a slight wetness against his cock.

"Is that your precome or mine?" Graham asked.

"I think I'm leaking, and there's more to come," Carl said.

Graham chuckled softly. "That's a good one, Carl. And you feel so good against me."

"I think I've been missing out on the real bedroom fun—" Carl murmured, reaching to explore Graham's dick.

"I've always thought that cops had balls... and I bet yours are exceptional," Graham teased. "Mind if I check them out?"

"Help yourself. It'll be my pleasure—"

Graham nearly chuckled. "You're pretty funny, too, Carl." He reached down and fondled Carl's dangling balls inside a soft and pliable sac that filled Graham's hand to overflowing.

Carl gasped. "You can play with me anytime, Graham."

"Let's continue this by lying down," Graham suggested. He released Carl, climbed onto the bed, and scooted over to allow Carl to lie down. "Now, how about you let me taste a little bit more of you, Carl? How would that be?"

Carl responded by planting another enthusiastic French kiss on Graham, which took Graham a little bit by surprise. Carl was getting good at this quickly. As they lay back on the bed on their sides, their cocks rubbed together, so again Graham took the initiative and put his hand on both cocks at once and began gently stroking. Carl moaned through their kissing, so Graham picked up the pace.

"Not too fast," Carl said breathlessly. "I don't want to come just yet. I want to enjoy you next to me and feel your dick against mine." Carl hesitated, and then he said, "Maybe you'd like to fuck me... I don't have any lube though."

"I don't know about that, Carl," Graham replied. "You've never done it before, and it might hurt you since there's no lube. We can suck or stroke each other off in ways you'll enjoy without you taking it up your ass."

"Whatever you think best, but I'm willing to try. I bet I'd just love your dick in my ass."

"Maybe another time... if we've got some lube. For now, let's just have a good time without any fucking. I'll make sure you enjoy it, Carl."

Graham cupped Carl's balls in his hand again, carefully kneading each one with his fingers. It was turning him on even more how low the cop's balls hung down and how soft the skin around them felt in his hand. Carl moaned even louder. Deciding to take the game a little further, Graham moistened two fingers in his mouth and began to rub the pucker ring of Carl's ass, pushing and rubbing gently until he had inserted them both inside the tight ring that led to the inner Carl. He searched for Carl's prostate, and he knew he found it from Carl's gasping response.

"Oh, Graham. Don't stop! Please don't stop. I'm gonna come...."

Graham stroked Carl to his explosive climax while continuing to massage the sweet spot inside his ass. Carl squirted all over Graham's belly. Graham didn't expect so much sperm, but he liked the rain of it that flowed onto them both.

As Graham scooped up some of Carl's come and began to spread it onto his own cock to stroke, Carl called out, "Wait! Why don't you let me do that?" He coated Graham's dick with a thick layer of come and then gingerly grasped Graham's cock and began stroking. It wasn't long until he brought Graham to his own hot, spewing orgasm.

As soon as the warm liquid stopped hitting his stomach, Carl pulled Graham into another deep kiss. At last Carl broke from their kiss and pulled Graham over on top of him, sealing their bodies together with their man-made glue. He stroked the back of Graham's head softly with his clean hand, running his fingers through Graham's hair.

"That was incredible," Carl murmured. "I knew it would be... as soon as I saw you tonight." He sighed as he held Graham tightly against himself.

"Uh... it's getting kind of late, Carl," Graham said. "I really need to head back home."

"Aren't you going to spend the night?"

"Maybe some other time...."

"Okay." Carl replied. "I'll get us some towels to clean ourselves up. I would offer you a drink before you go, but that wouldn't exactly be the thing to do since you're driving several miles tonight. Well, I guess it's more like early morning by now."

While Carl was in the bathroom, Graham looked around the bedroom. Big posters lined the walls, mostly of famous sports figures. Scattered here and there around the room were various trophies Carl must have won—golf, tennis, bowling, and some that Graham didn't even recognize what the sport was. Carl returned and began wiping

Graham with first a warm damp towel and then with a dry one until he had him all ready to get dressed.

"Carl, you really like sports, don't you?"

"Da Bears!" he grunted. Then he grinned and said, "And the Bulls… the Black Hawks… the Cubs…."

"The White Sox?" Graham asked.

"That's going *too* far," Carl chuckled. "But yeah. I *love* sports. Don't you?"

"Well, I like college football. And even college basketball," Graham replied. "But I think sports mean a lot more to you than they do to me. Do you like to read?"

"Sure. I read the sports section in the *Tribune* every day. And I subscribe to *Sports Illustrated*…. When I was in school, I even read some baseball players' biographies for book reports."

It began to dawn on Graham that he and police officer Carlton didn't have very much in common except sex. And although it was pleasant sex, it wasn't *exceptional* sex. Also, it began to weigh on Graham's conscience that this whole infatuation of Carl's was caused by Robert's strange gift of the power… and now Graham was feeling a little guilty.

Even though Carl had undoubtedly enjoyed himself tonight, it really wasn't Carl's game, so to speak. Graham knew very well that without the magic words he had uttered to avoid a traffic ticket and possibly to keep his teaching career from crumbling into ruins, Carl would never have bedded down like he did with Graham. Graham was feeling more ashamed of this magic trick by the minute and wanted to get out of Carl's place as quickly as possible.

With vague promises of future meetings, Graham managed to get Carl to drive him back to his Impala in the Annex parking lot. Carl thrust a tiny slip of paper into Graham's hand which, not surprisingly, had Carl's phone number scrawled on it. Graham stuffed it into his shirt pocket and waved goodbye to his new admirer. Then he steered back to the expressway and made his escape, driving home as fast as he dared. He glanced at the lighted clock on the dash of his car and noted that it was nearly one thirty in the morning. He was exhausted.

He opened the door of his apartment with a sense of relief. At least Trevor Randich and Dean Weinert had not been out on the parking lot fighting over him. That was a blessing. If they had been, he could always have taken out the telephone number in his shirt pocket and called old Carlton in Chicago to come out to Des Plaines and referee. He smiled at these outrageous thoughts and went to bed, falling asleep in only a few minutes.

A loud knocking at his front door abruptly awakened Graham. "Not again," he muttered sleepily. He looked at the digital clock next to his bed and saw that it was just after three in the morning. *Who in the world? I hope it's not Trevor again,* he thought, *or Dean Weinert visiting in the middle of the night!*

He flipped on a table lamp in the living room and looked through the peephole. His heart dropped in his chest. It was none other than his new conquest, Carl the cop from Chicago. "Oh, no!" he exclaimed softly as he opened the door.

"Graham!" Carl cried. "I missed you so much that I just couldn't sleep after you left."

"Come right on in, Carl." Graham said resignedly as he closed the door behind him.

Now what am I going to do? I've created three monsters, and here's the newest one.

"You sure do look sexy in your underwear!" Carl said. "Do you mind if I get comfortable, too?"

"Help yourself, Carl," Graham said, already reconciling himself to whatever was to come next. "How did you find me?" he asked, knowing already what the answer would be.

"Oh, I wrote down your address from your driver's license. You didn't think I was going to let a good-looking guy like you get away, did you?" He chuckled softly. "I missed you from the minute I let you off at that parking lot."

This time Carl wasn't wearing his uniform, so it was easy for him to strip. He stood there nearly naked, rummaging through the pockets of his jacket. "Look what I bought on my way here!" he announced with a grin, holding up a tube of lubricant. "In case you didn't have any, I stopped and got some of this stuff so you can fuck me this time!"

Carl stood there in just his skimpy briefs. He had changed into a fresh pair, and Graham nearly chuckled out loud because there were little blue sheriff's badge stars all over the shorts. Just like a little kid's shorts with Old West cowboy trim.

Graham studied him and was reminded again that he really *was* a cute young cop. He was probably in his mid-twenties, just like Graham. His body was nicely muscled but not bulging like a weight lifter. There was only a little thin patch of black hair on his chest. His arms and legs were lightly covered with black hair, too, which Graham had admired earlier in the evening. He smiled at Graham and showed even, white teeth. Without his clothes once more, he was certainly quite appealing.

"I can't believe you're up for another round in the sack so soon," Graham said. "It hasn't been very long since the last time, you know."

"I've been saving up, I guess. I just didn't know what I was saving it for. Can't you tell I'm up for another spin?"

"You have a knack for stating the obvious, Carl." Graham saw a bulge growing steadily in Carl's underwear and felt his own briefs beginning to fill up with excitement, too.

Maybe another round of sex won't be too bad after all, Graham told himself, trying to hide from his conscience. *There certainly doesn't seem to be any way out of this anyway. Since I can't find Robert to learn how to turn off the spell, I might as well relax and enjoy it... again.*

"You know what, Graham?" Carl asked slyly. "I'd really like to try on your underwear." He began running his fingers over the front of Graham's briefs, lingering on Graham's ballooning crotch.

"Really?" Graham replied, staring with fascination at the little blue badges on Carl's briefs.

What's with all this trading underpants stuff? This guy must be Kent Cassidy's first cousin, Graham thought. *They seem to use the same gimmicks to get tricks.*

Aloud, he replied, "I guess I'd like to try *yours* on, too. I really like those cute little stars all over them...."

Carl slipped his briefs off and handed them to Graham, revealing his fully hard dick, just as exciting to look at as it had been the first time earlier tonight. "Your turn," Carl insisted, wearing a goofy grin on his handsome face.

Graham stripped off his own briefs, causing his hard-on to spring up and bounce against his belly as he stood back up. He took Carl's offered briefs and pulled them on, smiling at the little badges. He handed Carl his own briefs, and Carl put them on, filling out the crotch more than Graham had. Then Carl pulled Graham into a hug, rubbing their swollen cocks inside the underwear together.

"Umm," Graham murmured. "You feel good. Maybe even better than last time."

"You do, too. But I wonder if my briefs are really a good fit. Mind if I check it out?"

"Feel free, Carl."

Graham watched as Carl knelt down and put his face just a few inches from Graham's cock. Carl reached up and ran his hands over Graham's ass and then moved to the front where he fingered Graham's crotch and gently rubbed his fingers from Graham's balls to the hard cock that struggled to get loose.

"You carry a dangerous weapon, too," Carl remarked with a smile. He put his mouth onto the head of Graham's cock and gently blew his hot breath through the briefs.

"Damn! You're catching on to this stuff really fast," Graham said. "Can I try that on you?"

Carl slowly stood back up. "Sure. Blow away—"

"I think you don't mean to do it, Carl, but you say the funniest things sometimes. But I think I can get my concentration back." He got down on his knees and blew hot air on Carl's dick. "Is that okay?"

Carl moaned. "Perfect. You can blow me anytime."

Suppressing a chuckle, Graham slipped the briefs from Carl's trim body and was about to take the swollen cock into his mouth when he noticed that the head was all gooey again. "You seem to have some ammunition inside that weapon of yours. Is it fully loaded?"

"That's for you to find out," Carl replied.

"My pleasure," Graham said as he eased the throbbing dick into his mouth.

"I think you got that backward. It's my pleasure as much as yours," Carl murmured.

"You've got a really pretty one," Graham said as he took Carl's dick out and examined it.

"I like yours, too," Carl said, pulling Graham to his feet and up against him again. He began to stroke Graham's cock. "I like 'em not too big," he said, "especially since I want you to put that dick right up my ass this time." He put his arms around Graham and kissed him, gently at first, then urgently.

"Let's go into the bedroom," Graham said, already enjoying his cop lover once more. "It'll be better in bed than just fooling around out here."

"Oh, yes. Let's go—I'm ready for you to ride me the rest of the night this time!"

"Don't you want to, uh, play around a little bit more before we try that?"

"What did you have in mind?"

"I thought a little sucking might be in order. Sixty-nine style sucking—"

"Oh yeah! That does sound good," Carl agreed as they reached Graham's bed and lay down, adjusting in a cock-to-mouth position for each one.

A few moments of faint sucking and slurping sounds followed, with a few moans and groans of pleasure thrown in.

Then Carl removed Graham's dick from his mouth long enough to say, "This is a lot more fun than I ever knew it could be."

Graham stopped sucking and said, "Really, Carl? Didn't a girl ever suck you like this?"

"Ha. That's very funny. I could never get a girl to suck my dick. If I'd known how great this was, I'd have tried it a lot sooner. I like this being gay stuff. It's fun! But cut out the talk about girls, Graham. You're spoiling the mood."

Nobody who knows old Carlton here would believe what's happening tonight. I just hope he'll be all right after he goes home. I didn't mean to mess up his life!

"Graham, as much fun as this is… I want you to fuck me now! I can't wait to find out what it feels like with your cock up inside me…."

Graham sighed. "All right, Carl. We'll give it a try, but if it begins to hurt you too much, you let me know right away… and we'll stop and do something else. Promise you'll tell me if you want to stop?"

Carl grinned. "I'm not a baby. I can take it… and I bet I'll just love it." At the frown on Graham's face, he added, "Okay. If it hurts a lot… I promise that I'll tell you."

Graham put his arm around Carl's waist and turned him onto his back. They faced each other, Graham on top, and kissed. Then Graham sucked Carl's nipples, one at a time, and worked his way down Carl's chest with his tongue to the tip of Carl's cock. He sucked it easily at first, then harder as Carl moaned with pleasure. At the same time Graham spread Carl's legs apart again and put two fingers into Carl's ass, feeling for his prostate. But this time he used the slippery lube Carl had brought. Carl gasped with pleasure and came in Graham's mouth quickly.

Then Carl rolled over onto his stomach. "Now spread the lube on your dick, and fill me up!"

"If you're sure you want to try this," Graham said, "we will."

"Grease yourself up good, and put plenty more up my ass, too. Since I've never done this before, I'm kind of excited."

"Just as you say," Graham replied.

"That's good," Carl said. "Now put it in gently at first. Then when I get used to it, I want you to really fuck me hard."

"Okay, Carl." And Graham did as Carl had asked. It felt wonderful, he thought, as he pumped in and out of Carl's tight ass.

"That feels so good," Carl cried out. "Don't stop!"

Graham came quicker than he had expected to, so he lay down on Carl's back, his cock still deep inside Carl's tight ass. "Sorry I came so fast," he said.

"Don't you worry about it. Just rest a few minutes, and then I want you to try it again. I want you to come at least twice." So after a brief rest period with Graham running his hands along Carl's sides and enjoying the masculine feel of him, Graham fucked Carl again. After

Graham once more exploded his load into Carl's ass, he carefully pulled his dick out.

Carl turned over onto his back and pulled Graham close to his chest so they could cuddle for a while. He sighed. "Graham, I thought about staying here with you all night… but the more I think about it, I'd probably better get on home since I'm on duty again kind of early in the morning."

"In that case, I'm sure you'd be better off driving to work from your place than from mine… since it's so much farther away."

A little while later, after they cleaned up in Graham's bathroom, Carl got dressed and kissed Graham a few more times, saying, "I'll try to meet you at the Annex next Saturday night. Maybe we can go to my place again from there. Or if you'd rather go to dinner first, we can do that."

"Okay, Carl, see you next week." He closed and bolted the door after Carl left. "Whew! What a night!" he said softly to himself.

He walked toward the bedroom. *Wow. Carl in bed with me twice in one evening. He's turning out to be a lot more interesting than I thought at first. Even though we don't have a lot in common, he really seems like a nice guy. And he's certainly fun in bed, too. If only I hadn't had to use magic on him. Under ordinary circumstances, I might really think about pursuing this relationship.*

Then something else dawned on Graham. *Now there are three of them after me, and I don't know what to do about any of them. I need another drink.*

He put on a terry cloth robe and walked into the kitchen to get a beer from the refrigerator. Then he sat down at the kitchen table to think about all that had happened to him lately. It was at that moment Graham discovered he wasn't alone!

CHAPTER EIGHT

GRAHAM looked up and saw the refrigerator door open again in the near darkness of the kitchen. It scared him so much he almost dropped his beer. He *did* knock a large wooden pepper mill onto the floor, narrowly missing his foot. "What the hell?" he shouted. "Who's there?"

"Now don't get your panties in a bundle," a voice from behind the refrigerator door said. "I'm just looking for a beer so I can join you."

Graham's eyes grew wide with amazement when he saw who was in the kitchen with him. Of all the people in the world, it was Margaret Hamilton, the woman who had played the Wicked Witch of the West in the movie *The Wizard of Oz*! And she was wearing her witch costume from the movie. Her green face glowed in the light from the refrigerator.

"I can't believe this," he wailed, rubbing his eyes. "I simply can't! I must be still asleep in my bed."

Cackling laughter greeted him. "No you're not, honey! It's just *little old me*."

At last Graham recognized the voice. It was "Robert Redford" in a bizarre disguise.

"Where's the *real* Margaret Hamilton? Doesn't she mind that you're using her identity?"

The voice changed and became the Wicked Witch from the movie. "Oh, grow up, Graham," she said, and then popped the cap off the beer bottle with her crooked teeth. "I thought you liked old movies, so I gave you a treat. Nobody cares if I use a borrowed identity. Besides, the real identities don't even know it."

"Who *are* you, I mean really?" Graham asked, still a little stunned.

"You can call me Margaret, I guess," she said. "I like that better than Robert when I look like this. It just doesn't seem to fit if you still call me Robert."

"I don't understand any of this," Graham protested.

"Of course you do, honey. Of course you do. I told you last time that I might see you next in a different disguise. Remember?"

"Yes, you did, but I also remember I was supposed to hear that Mama Cass song just before you appeared."

"I didn't want to scare you in the dark with sudden music from nowhere. Of course, wouldn't 'Ding-Dong! The Witch Is Dead' have been more appropriate, and more fun?" she asked, grinning broadly.

"I suppose so," Graham agreed. "Did anyone ever tell you that you have a really twisted sense of humor?"

"*All* the time, honey. Simply *all* the time." She cackled again.

"Well, thanks for sparing me the shock of a blast of music. You're so thoughtful. It was *so much better* for you to pop out from the refrigerator light looking like a grotesque witch."

Margaret snickered. "Yes, I thought so, too."

"But you know I didn't believe you about the music or the disguise… just like I didn't believe you about the gift of the power either."

"I know that, sugar," she said. "But I knew you would believe me, once you tried out the power. And you have, too. Haven't you? My goodness me!" She clucked her tongue against her teeth. "A kid, a kook, and a cop." She laughed out loud. "I just love alliteration—you probably appreciate that, being an English teacher." She chuckled some more and sat down at the table with him. "And double your pleasure, double your fun… with that Chicago cop tonight!" She exclaimed delightedly.

"I don't find it particularly funny," Graham retorted. "Did you know you sound like a Wrigley's Doublemint gum commercial? Anyway, the first two were accidents, and the last one was only to keep out of trouble."

"And *did* you keep out of trouble?" she asked smugly, taking a swig out of her beer bottle.

"Not exactly," Graham sighed. "I just ended up with another boyfriend. A *boy in blue,* so to speak. But I only did it to keep the cop from costing me my job at school. He was going to ruin me."

Margaret smiled ruefully. "How true. Well, I hate to say I told you so, but if you had listened more carefully when I told you about the power, you wouldn't have gotten stuck with that teenage Romeo, that aging Don Juan—who even now is plotting to seduce you by the way—and Little Boy Blue who just left. When you think about it, Kid Cop's got pretty good stamina… bedding down with you twice in one night in the space of a couple of hours." She grinned some more.

"When you told me about this power, it was all just too fantastic. You knew very well I couldn't take that seriously… so be fair. Would you have believed such a story from a stranger in a bar—especially a stranger who looked like Robert Redford?"

"I guess not," Margaret agreed. "But now you know better."

"By the way, why are you here in my apartment anyway? You weren't supposed to come here. And why weren't you at the Annex tonight? I came looking for you. That's how I got my latest conquest—he was gonna give me a ticket outside the bar and then report me to my school."

"I know. I'm real sorry about that, honey." Margaret sipped her beer. "I was tied up at the studio in Hollywood because it took me a while to find this old witch costume. MGM had this thing really packed away. It hasn't been used since 1939, you know. Anyway, I wanted to surprise you."

"You did that, all right. You almost scared me to death over there by the refrigerator. And by the way, couldn't you just create a duplicate costume out of thin air?"

"Magic doesn't always work that way, honey. There are rules to follow…."

Graham shrugged. "I just bet there are…. Anyway, you can guess what question I need to ask you at this point."

"You want to know how to break the spell once someone has fallen in love with you, right?"

"Absolutely. I've got to get these three guys off my back."

"It's very simple really," she said. "Just point with your index finger again and say—"

"Let me guess," Graham interrupted. "'Stop! In the Name of Love'!"

Margaret burst out laughing. "That's very good, my dear. I can almost hear the Supremes singing that right now." She started to sing the title, but Graham held up his hand, palm up, to stop her.

"Well, I know how much you like 1960s songs," Graham said.

"That's right… but you've got the wrong song. No, you need to say, 'It Ain't Me, Babe'!"

"Ohhhh," Graham groaned. "That song by the Turtles. You really *do* enjoy those old songs, don't you?" He laughed and then smirked at her. "But that's even worse than—"

"I kind of like the song, myself," she snapped and started to sing it, too.

"Please," Graham interrupted again. "Enough! I'll just do it. What will happen to them? Will they remember everything?"

"You expect them to *forget* it all like magic? Do you think this is some fairy tale or something?"

"I won't answer that," Graham said. "But you're sure they'll remember everything?"

"I know they will," Margaret replied. "And they'll be pretty embarrassed about it, too. Especially the cop."

"Do you think he'll arrest me?" Graham asked worriedly. "Or turn me in at school like he threatened to do before I zapped him?"

"Nah. He'll be too ashamed of what he did… and what you did *to him*! As a matter of fact, he'll feel real bad for taking you to his own apartment… and then driving all the way from Chicago to Des Plaines and barging in here in the middle of the night like he did. He will be afraid you'll press charges. He'll think he seduced you."

"Well, in a way, he did. Twice. At his apartment and after tracking me down at my own place."

"Trying to avoid feeling guilty and ease your conscience, are you? You did use the power on him."

"That's true. It really is my fault for wanting to avoid a ticket. But I told you how he was thinking about getting me into big trouble at school—"

"I guess you didn't have much of a choice. Well, he'll feel guilty, too. That's why he'll leave you alone. And there is one other thing that will come out of this…."

"What's that?" Graham asked.

"He and the other cops have been having a lot of fun using their own power over the gays at the bars. Now he has a whole new insight into what it's like being gay...."

"That's an interesting point. Maybe he won't be quite so quick to harass gays around the bars from now on. He might even turn out to be a nicer person after all."

Margaret smiled. "He will. So don't feel *too* bad about what happened with him. Besides, let's not forget that he *did* enjoy himself both times...."

"What about Trevor? It worries me a lot that he's been getting altogether too friendly with me. On the other hand, I hate to hurt his feelings or embarrass him. He thinks he was gay already. Is that true?"

"He'll take it more easily than the other two," Margaret said. "He's going to thank you because he *was* already gay. He just didn't know how to come out. So you helped him find himself for the first time. See? There's a really positive side to that little romance, too."

"You think so? And he won't feel bad about chasing after me?"

"Oh, I'm sure of it. I even guarantee it. Don't worry about him. He's already got an idea in the back of his mind for a boyfriend his own age. He'll be okay."

"What about Dean Weinert?"

Margaret laughed. "You'll enjoy that one the most. He'll feel so guilty at plotting a sexual rendezvous with you that he's going to leave you alone in the future. Believe me, he'll stay far away from you at school whenever he can. You won't have him as a thorn in your side anymore...."

"So some really good things will come from all of this after all."

"Oh, honey, that's putting it mildly. Just look at all the good that's going to happen."

"All that's going to happen?" Graham asked.

"Well, the dean will leave you alone, Trevor has recognized his sexual identity, and the cop will be a better person while he's doing his job. See what I mean?"

"I guess so. But it sure has been a lot of stress for *me*," Graham said. "I haven't even gotten to enjoy the power, yet."

Margaret grinned wickedly at him. "Are you trying to fool old Auntie Margaret? You had a good time playing with that sexy cop. You certainly enjoyed getting into his pants!"

Graham blushed. "I forgot about that...."

"Sure you did, sweetie. Sure you did. And which time did you forget?"

Graham ignored the question. "So now maybe I can try the power out on someone for real this time. No mistakes."

She looked at him thoughtfully for a moment as though she wanted to say more, but instead of whatever it was, she advised, "Just be careful whom you pick in the future."

"Are there any more little secrets I should know about the power that you haven't told me this time?" Graham asked.

"Nothing that matters just yet. Go out and have a good time with it, like I meant for you to do from the beginning."

"I guess I'd better cancel my Thanksgiving plans for dinner with Trevor and his family."

"Oh, I wouldn't be in such a hurry to do that, my dear," Margaret replied. "Trevor is still going to be your friend and like you a lot for what you did for him. He'll still want you to come to his house for the holiday."

"I guess that makes sense. Okay, I will."

"Well, I noticed when I got here that I took your last beer so I guess I'll be on my way," Margaret announced after chugging down the last of the beer. She tossed the bottle into a trash can in the kitchen corner. "But there *is* one more little thing."

"What's that?" Graham asked suspiciously.

"Hold out your index finger again," she said. "You need recharging after every three times you use the power. Not counting when you take it back, of course. I told you that last time...."

Graham held out his finger, she touched it lightly, and then she disappeared in a puff of green smoke that quickly vanished... as if by magic. No, it *was* magic.

CHAPTER NINE

GRAHAM eagerly drove to school on Monday morning because he couldn't wait to break the first of the two ill-conceived and accidental spells. He didn't have to wait long. As he unlocked the door to his classroom about twenty minutes before the first bell, Dean Weinert came bustling down the hall wearing a huge smile. Graham was pleased that the man wasn't carrying a bouquet of flowers, at least… and he was happy also for the chance to get the man off his back as quickly as possible.

"Good morning, Graham," Dean Weinert greeted him cheerfully. "Did you have a nice weekend?"

"Yes, thanks," Graham replied. "And a very good morning to you, too. I was hoping we'd have a chance to have a little chat this morning before classes."

Dean Weinert looked pitifully pleased that Graham wanted to visit with him. "We have a few minutes before first period," he said, glancing up at the hallway clock.

Graham unlocked and opened the door to his classroom and waved the dean inside. "I just wanted to tell you—"

"Oh, Graham, I'm so excited! I read in the *Chicago Tribune* over the weekend about a concert of classical music coming to the Chicago Civic Opera House in about two weeks. I thought perhaps I would get us tickets, if you'd care to go. I don't really know your taste in music… but I figured that you might enjoy this particular program…."

Graham decided to play the game just a little bit longer, so he smiled and asked, "Do you think Mrs. Weinert would enjoy coming with us to the concert?"

Dean Weinert looked stunned. "Oh. My wife? I hadn't even thought about asking her. My goodness… I'll have to think of something to make sure she doesn't want to go. Uh, I mean, uh, she doesn't really like classical music anyway, so it didn't occur to me to mention it to her. I had in mind some dinner… perhaps at George Diamond's… before the concert. Have you ever been there? It's an elegant steak house not far from the theatre district, rather near the Schubert, actually, and it's very moderately priced. And then after the concert, we could go to a little bar over on—"

"Dean Weinert," Graham interrupted, "I'm flattered you asked me, and it sounds like a truly wonderful evening." He pointed directly at the dean and said, "It ain't me, babe!"

The color drained out of the dean's face, and he stared blankly at Graham for a moment. "What did you say?"

"I believe we were discussing going to a concert in Chicago together in a couple of weeks. What was the exact date on that?" Graham tried hard not to laugh at the look of consternation on the man's face.

"Concert? Oh, yes. Well, uh, it's, uh, a classical music program," the man stammered, "and now that I think about it… I'm sure you wouldn't be interested in longhair music like that. Let's just forget the whole silly idea, Mr. Thomas."

He glanced up at the clock on the classroom wall. "I really should get back to my office," he added, "since there are bound to be students late to first period class… and I'll have to hand out late passes and assign detentions. I'll just be on my way, Mr. Thomas. Good morning." Dean Weinert practically ran out of the classroom in his haste to get away.

I have a feeling I won't be hearing from dear old Dean Weinert very much for the rest of the school year… except for strictly school business. Graham laughed softly to himself. *And I'm so relieved that the spell is finally broken. One down and two to go….*

Graham managed to get through his classes during the day and was glad when the bell rang to end seventh period. He knew it wouldn't be but a few minutes before Trevor would be there for the next class.

When Trevor did come to class shortly afterward, Graham was waiting in the hall outside the classroom door. Trevor smiled pleasantly to see his favorite teacher.

"Hi, Mr. Thomas," he said. "Have a nice weekend?"

"Hello, Trevor. Yes, it was very rewarding. But I wanted to ask you a favor, if I might. Could you stop by after school today for just a few minutes? I'd like to visit with you… if you have time."

"Aw, Mr. Thomas, you know I always have time for you. I'll stop by after my last class, and we can have a nice talk."

"Thanks, Trevor. Go on inside, and I'll see you after school."

Rather than just saying the phrase to break the spell on Trevor out in the hallway between classes, Graham had decided that he owed it to Trevor to carefully handle the situation by giving the two of them a chance to talk it out a little bit. Recognizing one's sexual identity, which is what Trevor had done, was too important to just say some magic words in the hall, break a spell, and go on to class to discuss stories from Geoffrey Chaucer's *Canterbury Tales*. This wasn't just a trivial issue.

With the lesson on "The Pardoner's Tale" completed and the class over, Graham relaxed at the sound of the bell ending eighth period. He stood in the hall as his students filed out, returning the little wave Trevor gave him as Trevor silently left with the others. Graham decided he needed a break, so he went to the teachers' lounge where he found his handsome colleague Mark Matthews already sitting at a table drinking a soda.

"Mind if I join you?" Graham asked.

"Not at all. Have a seat." Mark smiled warmly at Graham. "Did you have a good Monday? Sometimes I have a rough time coming back from the weekend."

"It was fine. It started off with a great beginning and was pretty ordinary the rest of the way," Graham replied.

Mark eyed Graham questioningly, but he let his curiosity about Graham's remark pass. "Do you go out much on the weekends?"

"Some. Not too much around here. Des Plaines is pretty small, and who can pass up a big city like Chicago so close by?" Graham said.

He considered the idea of mentioning some of the Chicago gay bars he frequented, in order to find out if Mark showed any signs of recognizing the names, but he didn't feel quite brave enough for that yet. It was entirely possible that a straight man might have heard the names and would recognize them as gay places. Graham wasn't quite prepared to tip his hand just yet to this young teacher he didn't really know very well.

He decided to steer away from talk about social life in Chicago, so he changed the subject. "Are you a fan of Geoffrey Chaucer?" he asked.

The conference period fairly flew by after that, and soon Graham was walking back to his classroom for his talk with Trevor. Moments later Trevor arrived, loaded down with textbooks for the night's homework in all his classes.

"These are kind of heavy," he said as he put them down on a desk in Graham's classroom. "I can remember when I didn't always bother to even do homework," he admitted with a grin.

"I'm glad you've changed your attitude about that," Graham said as he closed the classroom door. "Your grades in all your subjects are so much better... and when you get to college, you'll be glad you studied harder than you used to. You'll do well, I'm sure, when you get to whatever university you pick."

"Is this going to be a pep talk about college?" Trevor asked, grinning again and looking a little apprehensive.

"Not at all," Graham replied. "I just wanted us to have a little talk about something important."

"I've been good, Graham. Uh, I mean Mr. Thomas. I've stopped pestering you so much, and I've been trying to show you that when I graduate... I'll be a good partner for you. I'm studying hard and doing the best I can in literature. I want you to be proud of me, and I want to join you on the faculty here someday." Then he hesitated and blushed. "And I can't wait for us to get together in your bed for the first time."

"I'm glad you brought that up. I'm impressed with your progress in your studies in school, and I'm equally pleased you want to be an English teacher someday. I only hope it's not just because of me. I hope that deep down you want to be a teacher because you love the subject matter, and you want to share that love with young people who need guidance in their studies. As for the two of us being together as partners, Trevor"—he paused and pointed with his index finger—"it ain't me, babe."

Trevor stared at Graham for a moment... then he blinked and shook his head. "What happened?" he asked.

"I think that maybe you've come to your senses a little." Graham chuckled. "Take a minute to compose yourself."

"Oh, I'm fine," Trevor replied. "I just feel like you do when you first wake up in the morning from a really nice dream!" He looked at

Graham. "I guess I've been dreaming about you! I was imagining that you and I were lovers, Mr. Thomas. I'm embarrassed to say that now. I remember I told you I'm gay… and I also remember you told me you were gay, too. But I really thought I was falling in love with you. I can't believe I'm telling you this. I'm so sorry."

"Don't be sorry, Trevor," Graham replied, smiling. "And you're right. We shared our secret about being gay. It's just that we're friends… not lovers."

"That's right. We're good buddies, Mr. Thomas," he said, winking at Graham.

"And if you can, try to think of me as sort of like an older brother. You can come to me with any problems or questions you have about being gay… or about anything else for that matter. We'll just not let anyone else know exactly how we're such 'good buddies'," Graham said. "I don't want to be accused of too much favoritism, and I don't want you to be teased about being a teacher's pet."

"You're right, Mr. Thomas. We don't want anyone to get the wrong idea about us. We can be close friends without advertising it…."

"Yes. Exactly."

"You haven't forgotten about coming to our house for Thanksgiving dinner, have you, Mr. Thomas?"

Graham smiled. "Of course not. I wouldn't let my good friend down. I've been looking forward to it. My own family is so far away, and I'm really pleased to be spending the holiday with you and your family."

"It's getting late," Trevor said. "I guess I'd better be going." He stood up, gathered his books together, and held out his free hand to shake with Graham. "I'm so glad to have you for my friend, Mr. Thomas. You mean an awful lot to me."

"You're very special to me, too, Trevor." Graham patted him on the shoulder. "See you tomorrow in class."

Graham had to wait until the following Saturday night to break it off with Carl… and it couldn't come too soon to suit Graham. Carl was getting so carried away that he sent flowers to Graham's apartment three times during the week.

Graham had prepared himself for this encounter and already made up his mind how to proceed. Just as with Trevor, he felt he owed more to Carl than just a few muttered magic words. After all, Carl had gone against his own sexual inclinations twice in one evening and had done things he would never have done if it hadn't been for Graham and the use of Robert's power.

Carl might have been a thoughtless jerk toward gays before the power had been used on him, but Graham was going to give him some respect now... more than Carl had ever given to gays before all of this happened. Carl was possibly a better person inside than even he realized.

When Carl pulled Graham over at the Annex parking lot again, Graham braced himself for the meeting he'd anticipated all week.

"Hi, there, honey," Carl said as he came up to the car window that Graham rolled down. "I've been looking forward to seeing you all week. It has seemed like forever since we were together last weekend. How about we go to that place I told you about for some coffee and a doughnut?"

"That sounds like a terrific idea, Carl."

"Then come get in my squad car, and I'll drive you over there."

"I'll tell you what," Graham said, "why don't I follow you in my car? That way... if we go to your place later, I'll have my car and you won't have to bring me back here to the Annex."

"Okay," Carl agreed. "Just back up and follow me. Don't get lost now." He grinned at Graham.

Graham waved, rolled up his window, backed up his car, and proceeded to follow Carl to the little all-night coffee shop. The big bay windows in the place were a little steamed over, which made it all appear to be warmer inside than it really turned out to be. Graham got out of his car and walked to where Carl, wearing that impressive uniform, stood holding the door open for him. They sat at a booth in the front window, and Carl ordered coffee and doughnuts for them both.

As soon as the waitress served them, Carl grinned at Graham and said, "Did you get the flowers I sent you this week?" He looked around to see if anyone had overheard him. Then he blushed a light shade of pink.

"I certainly did… you romantic devil, you," Graham replied. "That was very sweet of you. I would have called to thank you, but I figured I would see you tonight anyway so I could do it then. Thanks for thinking of me."

"I've been thinking about you every day. It's like a fever that I can't shake," he said. "Not that I want to shake it, of course. And you're not a sickness. I didn't mean it that way," he stumbled.

Graham chuckled. "That's okay… I understand." *And I'm going to give you the cure for that fever in just a minute.*

"Sometimes I guess I just say the wrong words," Carl admitted. "This 'being gay' stuff is all new to me."

"It's interesting you should say that," Graham said. "How did you feel about gays before you met me?"

Carl hesitated. "The truth?" When Graham nodded, he said, "I didn't think they were like real people. I thought they were just troublemakers who had decided to be different on purpose and then rub it into everybody's faces. Kind of like those hippies back in the sixties. Maybe not quite as bad as those jerks at the 1968 Democratic Convention in Lincoln Park when things got so rough… but at least pretty disrespectful. I was there, and I remember it."

"You really thought gays were dangerous troublemakers?"

"Well, maybe not as dangerous as those demonstrators were. But I thought gays were smartass agitators… who just wanted to be different for no good reason. But still real troublemakers, you know?"

Graham looked Carl straight in the eyes. "And now? Now that I've fucked you and we've had sex more than once."

Carl squirmed a little and looked around again to make sure that no one else had overheard Graham. "I'm still a cop, you know. But I see things a lot differently now. I never knew I was gay until I met you… but being with you has made me understand I was really wrong. We're just people like everyone else. I don't know why I didn't see that before."

"You still plan on harassing gays outside the bars?"

"Gosh, no! How could I do that when I'm one, too?"

"What if you weren't one, too? Would you feel the same way?"

"Well, it's hard to say, since I'm gay, too, after all," Carl said.

"But do you think you'd see gay people as just people… and not as dangerous troublemakers? I mean if you weren't gay."

"Well, sure. We're just people."

"Carl, look at me. How do you feel about me?"

"Why, you're the one that I want to be with from now on. You know that…."

Graham held up his index finger. "It ain't me, babe," Graham said softly.

Carl visibly shook for a second or two, and then he regained his composure. "What happened?" he asked. "What's going on?"

Graham smiled. "Why, you're just having coffee with a friend, Carl. That's all."

Carl suddenly turned red. "Oh, my God! What have I done to you?"

"Done to me? What do you mean? You haven't done anything to me. At least nothing that we both didn't enjoy, Carl…."

Carl blinked twice. "I took you home, didn't I?" he asked softly. "I tracked you down in Des Plaines, too! I sent flowers to you three times this week." He began to panic. "And I had sex with you twice last Saturday night! Oh, no! How could I do that?"

"Carlton," Graham said reassuringly, "You've done nothing to worry about. You wanted to experiment with something different… and you did. You had a good time, remember? We enjoyed our time together, but it just wasn't something for you to continue doing in the future. Isn't that right?"

Carl still looked a little confused. "Yeah, I guess that's about right." His eyes narrowed and he looked warily at Graham. "You're not mad at me, are you? I mean you weren't thinking of telling anyone about this, were you?"

"You mean telling anyone that a cop took me to his place where we had sex and that he followed me home and let me fuck him? With the lube that he bought himself?"

Carl gulped and almost visibly shook again. "Not so loud! You wouldn't turn me in, would you? It would be the end of my career!"

"I wasn't going to bring this up, Carl, but you just did. Do you remember the night we met... you threatened to ruin my teaching career at Maine Central? You were about to write a ticket when you saw my school sticker and said the kids should be protected from people like me. That would have been the end of *my* career!"

Carl blushed a deeper red and looked down at the table between them.

"Damn! I'd forgotten all about that. How stupid was it of me to say something like that? And here I am asking you to spare my job this time. I'm so sorry, Graham. I'm an idiot and a bully!"

"Do you think I should spare you?"

"I hope you will, but I guess I wouldn't deserve it."

"After all that's happened between us, do you think you would still threaten to ruin a gay person's career if you had the chance?"

Carl didn't hesitate. "No. Of course not. I know better than to do something like that now."

"Then I'll believe you, and I suppose we'll consider the subject closed. But I want you to think about some things. Carl, look me in the eyes. Do I look like I would do something like that to you? Don't you remember how you enjoyed holding me as we shared that new experience for you? Did I really give you the impression that I couldn't wait to tell everybody... and scream 'police brutality' the first chance I got? Come on, Carl. It may not have been something you'd ever want to repeat, but weren't we comfortable and tender and even caring together, just for a little while?"

Carl seemed to calm down. "Yeah, I guess we were." Then his eyes widened a little. "But you fucked me! Twice. Are you going to brag about that to your friends?"

"Carl, you don't have to worry about anything. What happened between us is completely private. I'm not going to run into the Annex and scream, 'I fucked a cop!' and you know it. I have too much respect for you. You should be able to figure that out, even though you haven't known me but a week."

"Respect. That's something I haven't shown to gay guys very much, certainly not to you when I threatened you that night. And you're going to respect *me*? Especially since I don't deserve it?"

"You *do* deserve it, Carl. Everybody does, in one way or another. Try to remember that, particularly when you're on duty around the gay bars. Okay?"

At last Carl was able to crack a little smile again. "Okay. I'll remember. You're something else, Graham Thomas. You really are. I'm pretty sure I'm not going to let you fuck me again," he laughed softly. "But I have to admit you've changed my way of looking at some things. I would never have told anyone this, but when I was a teenager I was curious about other boys and wondered what it would be like to fool around with another guy. I was too afraid people would call me a queer, so I never did anything about it. I guess without knowing it you fulfilled an old wish of mine. I don't think being gay is for me... but I'm glad to find that out for sure." He grinned. "Besides, it wasn't so bad at all. I think I owe you some thanks for what happened between us."

"Carl, would you let me hold your hands for a minute?"

Carl looked around the little coffee shop once more and saw that no one was looking at them. "I guess so." He put out both his hands, and Graham took them and held them both.

"I want you to remember that people can care for each other without being labeled gay or straight. We may not ever see each other again, Carlton Safranski... but I want you to know that I care for you in a personal way—not gay, not straight, just as one person to another person."

Carl looked at Graham without speaking for a moment. Finally with a few tears in his eyes he said, "If I were gay, I would fall in love with you in a heartbeat." He continued to hold Graham's hands. "And I hope we can be friends in the future. You've got my home phone number, and I've got your address, so I can find out yours. Call me up sometime. Or I'll call you. We'll have a beer and just talk. What do you say, Graham?"

Graham knew he was grinning like an idiot. "If you were gay, I think I could fall in love with you, too. And hell, yes. Let's be friends and grab a beer sometime. We might even go to a Bulls game! What the hell!"

Carl laughed. "I'll say it again. You're something else. I'm really glad we met." He looked down at his watch. "I hate to break up our love fest here, but I've got to get back on patrol. My break time is over. I'll see you later, Mr. Graham Thomas. You can count on it." He stood up, leaving money on the table for the tab, and waved to Graham as he headed out the door.

Graham sat there for a moment and finished his coffee. *I'm gonna miss that guy,* he thought. *Maybe we'll get together as friends, though. I meant what I told him. If he'd really been gay, I think I'd have wanted to develop an interest in more sports... just so we could be together....*

Even though he was a little waterlogged from all the coffee, Graham decided to go to the Annex for at least one drink. Maybe he'd find someone to share a drink with him... or maybe not. But Graham decided not to be frivolous with the power in the future. He didn't want to use it on just anyone who came along. It had to be someone with the potential to be a real lover. So he was determined not to use it on the first pretty face he saw. And that would be difficult because there were always so many tempting pretty faces there on a Saturday evening.

Graham knew he would have to overcome his natural shyness in bars and strike up conversations with different guys to find the right person.... He had always found this difficult to do. But after a little more than two hours in the Annex, Graham decided to give it up for the night. He had attempted to talk to several different guys, but he found that no one was particularly appealing to him... so his efforts were really only half-hearted. Even when Adrian showed up and tried to introduce him to a couple of his friends... it hadn't worked out.

Maybe I'm trying too hard. Besides, there will be lots of opportunities to use the power. It doesn't have to be tonight. So he went home alone... again.

CHAPTER TEN

GRAHAM decided to try a different bar the next Saturday night, so he drove to the Trip. He had only been to this bar a few times, but he liked its sophistication. The Trip had three levels: an expensive Italian restaurant in the basement, a cabaret stage surrounded by intimate tables beyond a large bar on the main floor, and a go-go boy dancing bar on the top floor, where five or six nearly nude college-age boys danced on raised platforms. They wore little more than G-strings, but these were constantly stuffed with bills from appreciative fans who splurged on their favorite gorgeous boys with generous tips.

Graham decided to try the cabaret floor. He ordered a scotch sour on the rocks and wandered around the bar area until he spotted an empty table near the stage, up the stairs. Just as he arrived and was about to sit down, someone else beat him to it and sat down first.

"Were you going to sit here?" the guy asked. "I'm sorry...."

"Oh, that's okay," Graham replied. "I'm sure I'll get another table in a few minutes."

"I wouldn't bet on that," the guy said. "The show is about to start, and the singer in this place is really popular. Want to join me? I'm here by myself."

"Are you sure you wouldn't mind? I wouldn't want to put you out or anything."

"Of course not. Do sit down and join me." He held out his hand. "My name is Aaron. Aaron Rutledge."

"Well, thanks, Aaron. I'm Graham Thomas." He sat down across the table from Aaron.

"Have you been here before?" Aaron asked.

"A few times this fall," Graham replied. "Not lately, though."

"Then you haven't heard the new singer. Her name is Andrea Casey, and she is absolutely wonderful. As a matter of fact, she's the reason I come here every week. She's sort of a combination of Streisand and Liza Minnelli. She does ballads... and funny songs and... oh, you'll see."

At that moment a strikingly beautiful, red-haired woman dressed in an emerald-green, low-cut formal gown came up the stairs and stopped at Aaron and Graham's table. She wore brilliant diamond earrings and a wide diamond necklace that matched the sparkle of her eyes. She smiled at the two men warmly.

"Aaron, you little doll," she said. "I'm so glad you're here again." She leaned down to kiss him on the cheek. "And where did you find this handsome one?" she asked, pointing to Graham with long fingernails painted a bright cherry red.

"Andrea, this is my new friend Graham. Graham, this is the famous Andrea Casey."

"You silly thing," Andrea said, flashing a smile with dazzling white teeth.

"Well, it's true, Andrea," Aaron protested. "This month's *After Dark* has a paragraph in it about you."

"It was just a little paragraph," she said. "Only a couple of sentences really. And I didn't especially like that comment about me trying to copy Streisand." She frowned.

"Ladies and Gentlemen," a loud voice announced over the sound system, "the Trip is proud to present the Five of Us, featuring the lovely Miss *Andrea Casey!*" The lights dimmed and a spotlight panned across the now-seated cute blond pianist and the three other tuxedo-clad musicians who had joined him on the stage. The audience cheered at the mention of Andrea's name.

"I've got to go," Andrea said, smiling broadly as the spotlight found her and followed her as she began to walk over to join the musicians. "I'll come visit you two for a drink after this set," she called from the spotlight at center stage before she turned to face the audience… and the cheers rose again.

"Isn't she wonderful?" Aaron gushed. "I just know you're going to love her, too…."

During the next twenty minutes of the set, Graham decided that he absolutely *loved* Andrea and the group. He also had a chance to study Aaron while Aaron enjoyed the show with such obvious delight.

Aaron appeared to be in his late twenties. He had a narrow face marked by an attractive boyish charm, and his wide smile was very appealing to Graham as well. Aaron was slender but athletic-looking, he had longish wavy blond hair, and his eyes were a deep sapphire blue. Although he was sitting, Graham guessed that Aaron might be an inch or two over six feet tall.

The more Graham watched Aaron during the show in the reflected glow of the stage lights, the more he realized just how handsome Aaron was. He became as excited about Aaron as he was about the musical numbers the group was performing.

"For our last number," Andrea said to the audience, "we're going to do a ballad… and yes, I know that it's kind of a downer… but I hope you'll like it anyway. For those of you who've heard it before, don't forget to sing along with the chorus at the end."

"'The Lady with the Braid'!" someone shouted.

"Hi, George," Andrea said. "I didn't see you. You belong in Faces," she said, referring to a drag bar. The audience laughed. "And one last thing," she said as the music began, "this Dory Previn song is for Aaron and his friend Graham."

Graham was surprised, but he smiled and gazed at Aaron who was blushing and grinning, too.

Aaron winked at Graham and took his hand across the table. "It's really a fairly sad song," he told Graham, "but it's so pretty."

It was indeed a sad and beautiful song that told the story of a woman so desperate to keep a man she'd picked up for the evening that she begged him to stay with her all night to keep her from killing herself. The song was sort of a downer, as Aaron had warned, but Graham enjoyed it almost as much as he enjoyed holding hands with Aaron while Andrea sang her heartrending version of it.

It was really catchy at the end when the audience joined in with the group to sing the chorus, "Going home is such a ride. Going home is such a long and lonely ride…." Graham thought about how the words were particularly poignant for him, having to drive all the way to Des Plaines alone late at night. Not just tonight, but every Saturday night.

When the song, the cheers, and the applause were over, the lights came back up and Andrea joined them at their table. A waiter immediately came to take their orders. Andrea ordered brandy, Graham ordered another scotch sour, and Aaron ordered a scotch on the rocks.

"Aaron's right," Graham gushed at Andrea. "You really are wonderful. And thank you for that last song. It was truly beautiful."

"Thanks, Graham," she replied with a dazzling smile. "I'm so glad you liked it. It was originally on an album by Dory Previn, but our version is so different that you almost wouldn't recognize it as the same song."

"I'm so glad you did 'I Wish I Could Shimmy like My Sister Kate' right at the last," Aaron said. "It's so cute—one of my favorites."

"Well, it's a change of pace. That's for sure," Andrea replied. "We just put little novelty songs like that into the set as a brief encore. So tell me, Aaron. How did you two meet?"

Aaron and Graham looked across the table at each other and giggled. "We just met when the show was about to start," Aaron admitted. "We both tried to get the same table."

"So you just met tonight?" Andrea asked. "And because of our show, too. Isn't that sweet?"

"Kind of a lucky break, I'd say," Graham replied. "It's pretty cool that you got us together, all right." He looked directly into Aaron's sparkling blue eyes.

"I agree," Aaron said. "We're just now getting to talk for the first time."

"Oh, I didn't mean to intrude," Andrea said, starting to rise from her chair. "And I need to make a trip to the little girls' room before the next set anyway. I'll just run along and see you two later. And save my drink for me... I'll finish it later. They run a bar tab for me here."

"You don't have to go," Aaron protested. "We're enjoying our visit with you."

"Now listen, Aaron," Andrea replied. "You just have a nice visit with Graham here. I really do need to take a break, and I'll talk to you both after the last set. There are a few other guys I promised to sit with tonight, too. You know how it is…. See you later." And she was gone.

"I didn't mean to make her go like that," Aaron said mournfully. "I don't get her to come to my table all that often. I hope you're not too disappointed, Graham."

"It's fine, Aaron. Besides, I really would like to get to know *you* better."

"Me, too. I'm glad you're at my table tonight. I was kind of lonely when I first got here this evening."

"So you're not with anyone right now?"

"My ex-lover Steve and I broke up about two months ago. It was my idea, so I'm not complaining or anything. It was really over a long time before that."

"How long were you together? If you don't mind my asking."

"I don't mind. A year. It wasn't all that big of a deal, I guess," Aaron said. "What about you? Are you with someone?"

"No," Graham replied. "My last lover and I broke up quite a while ago when I was still in college. He was a fellow college student in Texas. It just wasn't working out. And I haven't really had a boyfriend in the last few years." He looked down at the table with embarrassment as he added, "I'm kind of shy about meeting guys in the bars. Too shy, I guess."

"Are you from Texas, then?"

"Yeah. Amarillo, Texas."

"You won't believe this, but I'm originally from Amarillo, too."

Graham was shocked. "Really? That's such a huge coincidence."

"And it took Chicago to get us to meet," Aaron said, chuckling. "I used to go the Back Door in Amarillo all the time. Were you ever there?"

"Sure," Graham said. "I was there a lot of times back in the old college days. It's just our bad luck that we never met there some Saturday night."

"Tell me about it."

"So what do you do?" Graham asked.

"I work in a bank in downtown Chicago. What about you?

"I'm an English teacher at Maine Central High School."

"That's pretty neat… an English teacher. I'll have to watch what I say." Aaron chuckled. "Would you excuse me for just a minute? I have to go to the men's room. Be right back."

Graham was thinking only about Aaron while the guy was gone. *He seems like a great guy. And I might not even have to use the power on him. He seems to like me already, so this is really very promising.*

But the wait grew longer and longer. Graham began to worry when the band started to warm up and still Aaron had not returned.

Then he looked once more in the direction of the men's room and saw that Aaron was excitedly talking to another guy. They had their arms around each other's waists as they stood very close together, and Graham began to feel surprisingly jealous. He really got upset when he saw Aaron kiss the other guy on the lips. But before he could get up to do anything about it, Aaron started walking toward the table.

"Sorry to take so long," Aaron said, "and I really hate to do this to you when we were getting along so well, but I ran into my old boyfriend Steve over there. I haven't seen him but once since we broke up. Now it seems there may be some sparks left that we didn't know about, so we're going to a quiet bar for a drink. I really feel awful about this, Graham. You seem like such a nice guy, too."

Graham made a quick decision and pointed his finger at Aaron. He simply said, "You're the one." Once more the tiny bell rang.

Aaron looked at him and replied, "You know what? The more I think about it…. It's a really dumb idea for me to go back to Steve. We were washed up ages ago, even before we officially broke up. Just like I told you before. I can't imagine what I was thinking. Let me go tell him to forget the whole idea. I'll be right back this time—I promise."

Again Graham waited for Aaron at their table near the stage. *I wonder if I did the right thing. But it's not like I'm interfering with his life exactly. He broke up with that guy a long time ago…. And maybe the power will turn out all right this time.*

Aaron returned as quickly as he said he would. "Would you like to go somewhere so we can be alone together—you know, get to know each other better?"

"Sure," Graham replied. "I think that's a great idea. I live in an apartment in Des Plaines. It's about an hour's drive from here, you know…. Would you like to follow me in your car and go there?"

Aaron smiled. "I don't think I could wait that long. How 'bout we go to my place? It's a lot closer."

"Okay. That's fine with me," Graham agreed. "Where do you live?"

"In Evanston. Come on… let's go. We can talk to Andrea another time…."

Graham followed Aaron to the front door of the bar. As they walked out onto the street, Graham asked, "Where's your car? I'll just follow you. But maybe you'd better give me directions, too, just in case I get lost in traffic. I've only driven to Evanston once before."

Aaron simply laughed and pointed to a limousine idling in front of them by the curb.

Graham suddenly felt like he was in a movie. He had never ridden in a limousine before, except in his grandmother's funeral procession. He was speechless as Aaron's chauffeur opened the door for him and Aaron.

As they got into the car, Aaron asked Graham, "Where is your car parked? I'll have Charles drive by it so he can recognize it later when he comes back with one of the other servants to pick it up. Go ahead and give your keys to Charles, Graham. And don't worry about it. We'll have it safely at my place within the hour."

"You're serious, aren't you?" Graham asked incredulously.

"Of course. We'll take care of it for you. Won't we, Charles?"

"As you say, Mr. Rutledge."

Graham reached up to the front seat to hand the keys to the chauffeur. He told Charles where the car was parked so he could find it for later. Then they were on their way to Evanston. Within thirty minutes, they were in the exclusive Chicago suburb near the southern tip of Lake Michigan. The homes along this particular street, Graham observed as they drove by, were actually mansions like Graham had seen in the movies.

"I feel like this isn't real," Graham said to Aaron as the limo entered a circular drive that fronted a Tudor-style home with strategically placed outdoor lights among the gardens and trees.

"Don't be too impressed," Aaron warned. "When you're all alone like I am at the present, the place can seem more like just an empty shell."

"Your family doesn't live here?"

"Not at this time of the year. My father is working at our bank in Seattle, and my older brother is at the one in Baltimore. My assignment is to watch out for the family interests in our Chicago bank."

"When you said you worked in a bank, I thought you meant you were a teller or something," Graham admitted.

Aaron laughed. "That might be easier than serving as an officer, especially when everyone knows I'm the owner's son! But I'm not really complaining, you understand...."

"What about your mother? Isn't she here?"

"She's at our home in Amarillo at the moment. I believe that she said she might be back here for a few days at Thanksgiving, but I rather doubt that. Well, here we are."

The chauffeur opened the door for them, and they walked up majestic marble steps and entered the house through an elaborate oversized front door. The foyer was decorated with what looked like expensive antiques, and a rather grand mahogany staircase loomed before them. Large, exquisitely furnished rooms flanked both sides of the staircase.

A uniformed older woman met them as soon as they entered. "Good evening, Mr. Rutledge," she said. "Is there anything I can get for you and your guest?"

"Nothing right now, Marie. Thanks," he replied. "We'll just help ourselves at the bar. You can go on to bed. We'll manage until morning. But do have the cook have brunch ready at about eleven, please. Good night."

"Good night, sir. And I'll leave the message for brunch...." As she left, her footsteps on the marble floor softly clicked as she made her way toward some other part of the cavernous house.

"That's the housekeeper. I told her before I left that she needn't stay up for me, but that's just her way, I guess. She's kind of old school in her thinking."

"This place is really something," Graham cried, looking up the staircase that stretched forever... and wound up eventually at the third floor.

"I'd give you a tour, but we have better things to do." He winked at Graham and leaned over to plant a quick kiss on his cheek. "Want a drink before we go up to my room?"

"I guess so," Graham said, following Aaron into a large room to the right of the staircase. Aaron passed through a huge mahogany doorway and entered a drawing room with an elaborate mahogany-mirrored bar in the back of the room.

"That looks like something out of a movie set."

Aaron smiled. "Scotch sour, right?" he asked, and began mixing it before Graham could answer.

"Sure… that'll be fine. On the rocks, if you don't mind."

Aaron quickly mixed their drinks, handed one to Graham, and ushered him back out of the room and up the extensive stairs. The deep burgundy carpet completely silenced their footsteps as they made their way to the second floor. Aaron led him to the second room on the left of the hallway.

"Come on in and make yourself at home," Aaron said.

A small chandelier lit the corner of the massive bedroom. Graham was stunned at the beautiful appointments around him, accented by wall coverings done in rich shades of royal blue and cream throughout. Again, period antiques were scattered here and there, dominated by an impressive Tudor-style canopied bed with blue velvet draperies drawn back and tied from around it. Aaron turned on a small lamp on the desk at the far side of the bed and extinguished the corner chandelier. He smiled at Graham.

"Don't look so in awe of the place," he said. "It's just a bedroom, after all."

"But what a bedroom!" Graham exclaimed. "It's just beautiful."

"It's for sleeping, and *other things*," Aaron replied with a sly grin, "just like any other bedroom. Relax and enjoy it. I'll be right back." He opened the door to a deep walk-in closet and disappeared inside.

Graham didn't know exactly what to do. He was clearly out of his element, and he knew it. At home he just would have taken off his clothes, tossed them onto a chair, and climbed into bed with Aaron. But now he stood by the bed, nervously waiting for Aaron and sipping his drink. He almost wished he were back in Chicago in Carl's comfy apartment bedroom. *Almost.*

Aaron emerged from the closet completely naked. Graham stared at his beautiful body… sandy-colored hair lightly dusted his upper chest, and an enticing faint line of hair traced its way down to the navel. Slightly darker blond pubic hair topped a perfectly shaped hardened cock that swayed gently as Aaron walked. His nearly hairless balls hung low in a sac that extended about three inches below the base of his cock. His arms and legs were also lightly covered with the same pale blond hair as on his chest. His body was in excellent shape, but he didn't have particularly pronounced muscles like a wrestler or weight lifter... it was a neat and trim torso with no bulges or sagging skin. It was just the kind that Graham loved to touch and couldn't wait to embrace as soon as possible.

"Why are you still dressed?" Aaron asked. "I thought I gave you enough time to get rid of those clothes."

"Well, uh," Graham stammered, "I didn't know exactly where I was supposed to put them...."

Aaron smiled. "Tell you what... let me undress you myself, and I'll put them in the closet with mine."

Oddly enough, Graham didn't feel the least bit self-conscious as Aaron gently undressed him. He rather enjoyed the thrill of it.

When Aaron returned a second time from the closet, he took a sip of the drink he had left on the desk. Then he walked up and kissed Graham softly until it deepened into a french kiss. His strong arms enveloped Graham, and Graham felt like he was drowning in pleasure as those arms captured him.

Graham could feel Aaron's hot, teasing cock up against him, and he shuddered slightly.

"Let's climb into bed," Aaron suggested. "But first, let me switch on this night-light." Once that was done, he turned out the desk lamp and led Graham through the semi-darkness to the bed where they eased onto a luxurious mattress.

"Oh, this is a really good idea," Graham agreed. "I think I'll enjoy this even more since I can see you... thanks to that night light."

Once they were stretched out, and before Graham knew what had happened, Aaron was kissing him again, deeply like before. Their tongues met and explored each other's crisp, scotch-flavored taste. Aaron sucked so hard that Graham found it hard to keep up. Graham's cock ballooned to full size at the touch of Aaron's slightly larger cock rubbing against him.

Aaron then escaped from Graham's grasp, and down to Graham's cock. He licked it playfully before putting the head into his mouth and beginning to suck. Graham lay back, enjoying the moment.

Then Graham said to Aaron, "Let me have a taste of yours, too."

Aaron agreeably switched his position and moved around so Graham could take the larger cock fully into his mouth while Aaron continued to lingeringly stimulate Graham's cock. Graham knew he could come immediately, but he held back until he heard Aaron's groans of pleasure, indicating that Aaron was about to come.

"Stop!" Graham cried. "Let's not come so fast. Do you have any lube?"

"Sure. Right here in a drawer of the nightstand. I'll get it." Aaron reached over and got it for Graham.

Graham took the tube and applied some of the gel to two of his fingers. Then he put Aaron's dick back into his mouth, but this time he reached beyond Aaron's balls and found the tight circular muscle where he gently pressed his two wet fingers until they entered Aaron's pleasure ring. Aaron tightened up slightly until Graham found and fingered the sweet spot, causing Aaron to groan and relax.

Graham massaged inside Aaron's ass until he could tell there was no stopping the orgasm this time. Sure enough, Aaron spurted come into Graham's mouth in spasm after spasm. It made Graham so excited that his own climax came a few seconds later, shooting salty sperm into Aaron's waiting mouth. Graham shifted Aaron's body around to bring his lips back to where Graham could kiss Aaron and taste himself as well as Aaron when their mouths merged. Then they finally lay back exhausted, clinging to each other.

"I really wanted you to fuck me," Aaron said, "but I also wanted you to come in my mouth. So I went ahead and sucked you. Maybe a little later, we'll try again."

After a few moments of rest, they did. This time Graham gently eased his well-lubricated cock into Aaron's tight and enveloping ass... and he began to slowly pump as he filled Aaron and pulled back... in and nearly out, time after time. The warmth and perfect fit of Aaron's ass made Graham shudder again, but this time he came inside Aaron.

CHAPTER ELEVEN

"This time you fuck me," Graham said. Aaron took the tube and spread the gel all over his dick and gently, carefully fitted his cock into Graham's uplifted, waiting ass.

Graham knew that if he hadn't come twice already, he would have come again at the expert fucking Aaron performed on him. He grinned just because it made him so very happy when Aaron shot a hot load into him. It all felt so right this time. Then they went to sleep together, holding on to one another throughout the rest of the night in that luxurious and extravagantly comfortable bed.

FOR the next few weeks Graham felt as though he had left reality each time he was with Aaron Rutledge. His waking hours were spent at school as usual, but he spent every weekend with Aaron in Evanston. Only once had Graham managed to get Aaron to come to Des Plaines. And that was during their first week, a few days after they met at the Trip. Although Aaron said nothing negative about Graham's apartment, Graham could tell Aaron didn't particularly care for it. Aaron was more accustomed to a world of wealth and privilege rather than Graham's modest place in the western suburbs.

This became obvious because after that one weekend, Aaron always insisted that Graham come to his house. Every single Friday evening after they began their usual routine at the Evanston mansion, Aaron's limousine came to pick up Graham at the Des Plaines apartment… and it returned him on Sunday evening. Aaron was always inside the limo happily waiting for him.

Not that they spent all of their time in bed, of course. Aaron thoughtfully planned dinners at expensive restaurants and evenings at the Shubert or Studebaker or Blackstone theaters, and often found time for them to visit Andrea at the Trip. They became familiar visitors at the bar with Andrea, and she dedicated at least one song to them almost every weekend they were there.

But like all things in a dream world, it wasn't exactly perfect. A few things were beginning to bother Graham. For one thing, Aaron would never let him pay for anything. Dinners, drinks, theater tickets— whatever they did—were always Aaron's treat. Aaron would listen to no arguments on that point. One Sunday morning in the breakfast nook of Aaron's mansion, they were once again discussing it.

"Your teacher's salary would be strained to the breaking point if I let you pay for all the things we do," Aaron insisted. He reached to pour Graham and himself another cup of coffee from the crystal carafe on the table. "Besides, it's not a big deal to me. Money's for spending, and I want to spend it on *you*. My dad practically mints the stuff anyway…."

Graham was not convinced. "But it makes me feel bad when you pay for everything," he complained. "It's making me lose my self-respect. I feel like a paid escort—without the payment, of course. But all these perks that you provide are almost like being paid."

"Sweetheart," Aaron soothed him, "you're being silly. I wouldn't hurt you for the world... but you simply have to be practical about these things."

"Then why don't we just do some things once in a while that I can afford," Graham said. "That way I would feel a lot better about things...."

"We'll compromise, then. Part of the time you can take me out, but I'll cover the more expensive places like the theater and opera tickets. How would that be?" Aaron smiled his boyishly winning smile.

"I guess that would be okay," Graham grumbled. "But we don't always have to go to expensive restaurants, do we?"

"You're exactly right. We can go to McDonald's or Burger King or even White Castle from now on if that's what you want... anything to make you happy."

They both laughed.

But there was something even more important that kept Graham from being completely happy, too. And he couldn't really discuss this with Aaron. As time passed, he was beginning to feel very guilty about using the power to make Aaron fall in love with him. Not only had he taken Aaron away from a potential reconciliation with an ex-lover, but Graham also found that he wasn't really falling in love with Aaron after all. And he had really wanted to.

Oh, he was having a good time, all right. Aaron was terrific in bed and wonderful to look at... and they had fun going places and doing things together. But there was something missing... and it was a lack of emotional involvement on Graham's part. He felt that this relationship had been achieved much too easily because he'd used the power, and his own conscience was keeping him from really loving Aaron. The relationship was pleasant, but it wasn't honest. And Graham felt that more keenly every day that passed.

This isn't the way I thought it would be, because he doesn't love me from his own free will. He loves me because I made him fall in love. And I can't seem to make myself return the favor, either.

Although he was tempted to simply remove the spell from Aaron, he didn't do it for a very selfish reason. He enjoyed finally having a permanent boyfriend. He had been very lonely before he met Aaron.

Aaron might simply dump me if I broke the spell. So he was afraid to do it, and he kept their relationship going.

In the midst of his angst over how he'd captured Aaron's heart, Thanksgiving rolled around. Aaron was less than pleased that Graham had already agreed to spend it with one of his students and the boy's family.

"Why can't you just call the kid's family and cancel your plans with them? We could fly to New York and see the Macy's Thanksgiving Day parade, or we could go anywhere else you please," Aaron pleaded. "I just don't get why you have to spend the day with those people instead of with me. If you hadn't met me, and you just wanted company for the holiday, I could understand that. But this doesn't make any sense to me."

"Aaron, you know I'd love to spend the holiday with you, but I already made plans before I met you," Graham explained. "There's such a thing as keeping your word. Besides, this particular boy is really like a little brother to me. His mother even came to school for the sole purpose of meeting me and inviting me to their house. She thinks I've been a positive influence on her son, and she's counting on me to be there. I'm sorry, Aaron, but it just can't be helped… not this year anyway. We'll have other times together."

"All right. As long as you put it that way, I guess I'll just have to be a good sport and quit pouting. I give in." He smiled as though he were bestowing an expensive gift.

Graham chuckled. "How very generous of you." He came over to Aaron's chair, leaned over, and gave him a kiss. "But seriously, it's just one afternoon… and I'll spend the evening with you. You can pick wherever you want to go that night, and we'll have a good time."

Aaron sighed and nodded. "Okay. At least we'll have the evening…."

On Thanksgiving morning, Graham called Aaron at his mansion in Evanston. "Hi, honey," Graham said. "I just wanted to call you before I left for Trevor's house. Did you hear anything from your family today?"

"As a matter of fact, I did. Mom's still in Amarillo, just as I thought she would be… and Dad's still in Seattle. You'd think they weren't even married from all the time that they spend apart. I didn't hear from my brother though… but I think we'll all get together at Christmas. And that's another thing I wanted to discuss with you…."

"Not now, Aaron. We've already had the Christmas discussion about my trip to Texas. There's no way I can miss Christmas with my family. Anyway, I just wanted to wish you 'Happy Thanksgiving' before I leave. And I'll see you tonight."

"You have a good time with the kid and his family, and I'll be waiting for you to arrive up here later. Call me about an hour before you're going to leave the kid's house, and I'll send Charles to pick you up at your apartment, as usual. And later we'll talk about Christmas some more. Bye, sweetheart."

"Bye, Aaron." Graham sighed and hung up. "It's so hard to convince him about this…."

As he drove to the part of town where Trevor and his parents lived, Graham checked the little slip of paper on which he'd written the address. He'd never been to the house, but he was vaguely familiar with the neighborhood. The Randich family lived on an older but well-manicured street. Graham found the house, parked in front, and walked up to the front door. Trevor answered and cheerfully greeted him.

"Hey, Mr. T! I'm so glad you could come for the holiday. I really wanted you to be here… especially today," Trevor said, a little mysteriously.

"Thanks, Trevor. It was very nice of your family to invite me over. It's a long way to Texas. You know, Thanksgiving wasn't as important a family holiday for us as Christmas… but it's still an empty feeling when you live about thirteen hundred miles away from home and you certainly can't make it there by car very quickly."

"Wow. I bet that's quite a drive all right." Trevor opened the door wide and ushered Graham inside out of the cold. "Come on in and meet my dad. Mom's in the kitchen fussing around with some last-minute preparations." He led Graham into a comfortably furnished living room where Mr. Randich was watching a football game on television. "Dad, this is my English teacher, Mr. Graham Thomas. Mr. Thomas, this is my father, Darrell Randich."

Mr. Randich stood and offered his hand to Graham. "So this is the famous English teacher I've been hearing so much about," he said, smiling at Graham. "Just call me Darrell." He walked over to the TV and turned down the volume.

"Happy Thanksgiving, uh, Darrell. It was good of you to have me over today. I was just telling Trevor that it's a really long way to my home, and it just wasn't practical for me to travel that far for just a four-day holiday."

"Sit, Mr. Thomas." Darrell directed Graham to a wingback chair next to the sofa and close to the fireplace, which was cheerfully crackling in the background. "We're more than happy to have you with us. I believe we have you to thank for Trevor's renewed interest, or perhaps first time interest, in the academics... and perhaps for a career choice we really hadn't anticipated."

Graham sat down and said, "Just call me Graham. Well, I can't take credit for Trevor's fine schoolwork, but I'm pleased if he wants to enter into the teaching profession. He won't get rich, but the personal rewards can be great, I can assure you. Of course, we're all looking forward to his playing college football next year since he's got quite a talent for it. Any feelers from the colleges yet, Trevor?"

At that moment Olivia Randich entered the living room and sat next to her husband on the sofa. "I've done all I can in the kitchen until everyone is here," she announced.

"Someone else is coming?" Graham asked.

"Didn't I tell you?" Trevor spoke up. "I invited Eric Cernak, too." He gave Graham a secretive wink that no one else saw. "His parents went out of town, but Eric talked them into letting him stay here." He turned to his mother. "Eric is one of Mr. Thomas's students, too, but he's in a different class period from me."

"That's right," Graham agreed. "He's in my second period class. I really don't know him very well, but he seems to be a bright student and a pleasant young man."

Trevor beamed, and Graham was beginning to guess why. He also suspected that something important was in the air, and he wondered if Trevor had absolutely insisted on his presence for a reason bigger than just Trevor being kind to his poor old English teacher.

"I never noticed before," Darrell said, "that Trevor and Eric have gotten to be such good friends... again. I remember when the boys were in junior high he used to hang around here a lot, but then he sort of disappeared… until the last several weeks." He looked at Trevor curiously. "They've been practically inseparable lately."

Olivia just smiled and said nothing. Trevor continued to stare at Graham with a sort of idiotic grin.

Graham narrowed his eyes at Trevor. *Uh, oh. I have a feeling this is gonna be a Thanksgiving to remember. And I'm caught right in the middle of it….*

"Do you like oyster stuffing, Graham?" Olivia asked.

"Huh? What was that? Oyster stuffing?" Graham stammered. He was taken off guard by the completely different direction of the conversation. "I don't think I've ever had dressing with oysters. We call it 'dressing' down in the South, and my mother always makes it with corn bread and lots of ground sage."

"Well, you're in for a treat, Graham," Darrell said. "Olivia makes stuffing that's just out of this world."

The doorbell rang. "I bet that's Eric," Trevor said. "I'll get it."

"He's certainly excited," Darrell remarked. "It's only his old childhood friend. You'd think he was having his fiancée over to meet the folks." He laughed heartily.

Olivia smiled thinly.

Graham gulped and couldn't quite manage a smile.

Trevor brought Eric into the living room.

Darrell, Olivia, and Graham looked at the boys with surprise. They were holding hands and grinning at each other. Graham was almost afraid to look at the reaction of Mr. Randich, so he turned to Olivia first because she still seemed rather unruffled as she sat there smiling a little more warmly this time. Then Graham glanced back at the boys in the doorway, knowing that his suspicions had been confirmed. This was coming out day at the Randich house.

To his credit, Darrell kept calm. "Is there a meaning to this?" he asked quietly.

"Yes, Dad," Trevor answered. He let go of Eric's hand and put his arm around Eric's waist instead, pulling him close. "Eric and I are a couple."

"A couple of what?" Darrell asked without thinking.

Both Trevor and Eric chuckled, although it was a little nervously. "We're boyfriends, Dad. You know... a real couple. We hope to go to the same college next fall and stay together." Trevor's face was a few shades whiter than Graham had ever seen it.

Now Darrell was obviously thinking hard. The furrows in his forehead deepened. He kept his composure, but everyone could see that wheels were spinning furiously inside his head. He was quickly adding it all up. The recent closeness, the time the boys were spending together, the insistence that Eric come over for Thanksgiving... it all suddenly began to make sense... in a queer way, so to speak. Finally he relaxed a little and the perplexed look left his face.

"That's quite a pass you've just thrown, son. I think I'd call it a bomb."

Trevor looked at Eric a little more nervously this time.

Darrell turned to his wife. "Did you know anything about this, Olivia? Come to think of it, did you know anything about this, Graham?" he asked, keeping his voice very calm and even.

Olivia answered first. She had a look on her face like a determined mother lion protecting her cub. "I wasn't sure, but I suspected that something like this might be going on. They both were so intense and serious about being together so often. I thought they had become closer than ever before, but I didn't know anything definite."

Graham hesitated a few seconds, trying to decide just how much to say and whether he might make the situation even worse. "No, sir," he answered. "I have to admit that I am more than a little caught off guard by this turn of events. They didn't tell me anything about it." He looked as though he might be about to add something more, but Darrell interrupted him.

"I was just wondering if maybe that was why Trevor absolutely demanded that Olivia invite you to dinner today. Like to run interference for the boys...."

Graham took a deep breath and attempted a neutral smile. "I have a feeling that besides the obvious kindness about sharing the holiday... I'm here to be moral support. Is that right, boys?" Graham asked and widened his smile for encouragement.

Trevor smiled back at Graham, looking a little relieved. "You're partly right, Mr. T. I didn't want you to be alone on the holiday, of course... but you had already been invited before Eric and I even got together. We talked it over a few days ago and decided that this would be a good time to spring the news. Since you would be here anyway, the presence of our favorite teacher might keep us from being killed!"

"Now see here," Darrell began, "that's a little extreme to be saying something like that." He frowned.

Eric gulped and looked a little sheepish, but he stood steadily beside Trevor.

"That was just kind of a joke, Dad," Trevor said. "But we really didn't know how you would react to our news. We both decided that we wanted to be honest with you and not hide until we go away to college next year. We didn't want to drop a bomb on you, as you said, someday in the future."

"No... you decided to surprise your mother and me in front of company," Darrell said. Despite the severity of his words, he offered something close to a smile once more.

"Dad, this isn't just some decision Eric and I decided to make... to be gay, I mean. It doesn't work that way. It's just the way we are. We're gay, and we can't do anything about it. We've always been gay. When we were kids in junior high we suspected... but now that we're older... we know."

"*How* do you know?" Darrell queried and then attempted a chuckle. "Have you both tried girls and decided against them?"

"It's not like that. It's something that's just inside a person from the very beginning. Weren't you always attracted to girls, Dad? You didn't just weigh your options one day and say, 'I think I'd be better off with a girl because people would accept me better.' Did you do something like that, Dad?"

"Of course not. And don't you go thinking that I'm some radical who hates homosexuals. That's not true. I just didn't see it coming with *you*. That's all. You know what I mean... quarterback for the football team and all that... I'm just surprised." He paused and gave his son a look of concern. "You're sure about this, Trevor?"

"Yes, I'm sure, Dad. I hope you can understand—"

"Olivia, you haven't said very much. What do you think about all this?"

She gave her son a loving look. "I think Trevor is eighteen years old… he's a smart young man who's going to have a brilliant future someday in whatever he wants to do… and if he says he's gay and there's no question about it, then I believe him and support him. Do you have any thoughts about this, Graham? You seem to have walked in on a pivotal time in all our lives…."

"Of course, it's none of my business," Graham replied, "but I can certainly say that it takes a tremendous amount of courage to grab hold of a boyfriend the way Trevor did… and make an important announcement like this to the family. And I applaud you for that, Trevor. You, too, Eric. You're both very brave young men."

Darrell got up from the sofa and walked over to Trevor. He hesitated just a moment, and then he hugged him. "I love you, son. And I'll support you in whatever you do. You know that already." Then he grabbed Eric, too, and hugged them both. "When are we going to eat, Olivia?"

"My goodness," she said. "I've got a house full of men. I hope I have enough turkey, and more importantly… *pies*! Do you like rhubarb pie, Graham?"

As they made their way into the formal dining room, Trevor whispered to Graham, "Thank you, Mr. T, for being my friend… and just for being here on this important day!"

Graham gave him a quick hug. "You're a lot braver than I've ever been with my own family…."

CHAPTER TWELVE

CHRISTMAS was fast approaching, and Aaron was still trying to convince Graham not to go home to Texas for the holidays.

"You'd be gone for two whole weeks," Aaron complained. "I can't stand the idea of us being apart for that long."

"Why don't you go visit your mom and dad in Amarillo, then? Didn't you tell me that your father and brother were going to join your mother there for Christmas? We could go on the same plane and meet up during the holidays."

"No, my parents are coming here for Christmas," Aaron announced. "Along with my brother, who's coming in from Baltimore."

"Well, then that's another reason for me to be gone," Graham said. "How would it look if I spent the holidays here with your family in the house? I think they might just catch on."

"Maybe I'll just go ahead and tell them I'm gay," Aaron replied. "It's time I did that anyway."

"I thought you once told me your parents hated gays," Graham said. "You can't spoil your whole future with your family, not to mention your job, by spilling the beans because of me. You haven't thought this through very carefully...."

"I don't care," Aaron said petulantly. "I want to be with you."

"That's very sweet, but I remember not too long ago you told me to be practical," Graham replied. "Now it's time for you to do the same. Just keep quiet about being gay, if you think that they'd take it so badly. I'll only be gone for two weeks anyway."

"That's a lifetime."

"It's not. It's only fourteen days, and they'll fly by. Christmas vacation always does that. You'll see. Be reasonable and please just calm down about my trip."

"Oh, all right. But I don't like it."

Soon the Christmas holidays arrived, and Graham flew home to Texas to be with his family. When he got there at last, he found he had missed them more than he realized. An added plus to the vacation time away from school was the fact that Graham's best friend from college days, Rick Laine, was going to be in Amarillo, too, visiting with his family. Graham couldn't wait to see Rick and tell him about his adventures from this very unique fall. They had a lot of ground to cover when they got together.

The day after Christmas, Graham finally called Rick at his friend's parents' home. They agreed to meet for coffee and have a long talk at one of their old favorite watering holes—the coffee shop at the old Holiday Inn on Interstate 40. Rick now lived in Houston with a lover and didn't come home to Amarillo all that often. Graham knew he was lucky to catch Rick on one of the rare occasions they were both in town.

Graham got there first and found a corner table in the coffee shop. Just like in the old days, Rick was late. Graham smiled to think that his friend probably hadn't changed all that much over the years.

The waitress was an old friend, too—Alice Talbot. She had worked here since the old days when Graham used to meet Rick for coffee on late nights during the summer. That had been when Graham and Rick were both home from the different colleges they attended. But Graham knew Alice from even before that.... She had been a waitress at the Big Texan Steak Ranch, a restaurant that seemed like it had been around forever. When Graham was in high school, his family used to eat there fairly often, so he and Alice went back a number of years.

"How's it going, Alice?" Graham asked. "It's so good to see you're still here!"

"Things are okay, I guess. My back bothers me more as I get older, but I guess that's just nature," she replied. "My kids are all grown. Want to see what they look like now?"

"Sure. Let's see them."

Alice went to the counter, found her purse, and located the photos in her wallet. She was just showing them to Graham when Rick arrived.

"I can't believe they're so grown up," Graham said. "And these two are your grandchildren? They're so cute...."

"Thanks. I'm real proud of them. Hi there, stranger," she said to Rick as he walked over to the table. "How are ya?"

"Alice!" Rick exclaimed. "I can't believe it's you. I haven't seen you in years. " He gave her a huge bear hug.

"Let's not talk about how many," Alice said, and laughed. "I know you two—a few dozen cups of coffee. I'll just get the first two for you."

"Well, hello, you old Yankee!" Rick said with a big grin. "Get up here and give me a big old hug."

Graham stood up and embraced Rick. "I'm so glad to see you, too. I can't even remember when we had the chance to sit down together and have coffee."

"I think I overheard a similar conversation just a minute ago," Rick said.

"That's right," Graham agreed. "Let's not go into all that. Well, sit down and tell me all about Houston… and all about you and that lover of yours."

Rick told Graham about the happenings in his life since they last met, and Graham proceeded to tell Rick about the power and all that had happened because of it the past few weeks. They were now on their third cup of coffee.

"Oh, Graham," Rick said, gently laughing. "You're so silly. Have you been teaching creative writing again?"

"You mean you don't believe me?"

"Did you really think I would?" Rick asked. He drew an imaginary line across his forehead with his finger. "Do I have the word 'stupid' written across my face?" He laughed again.

"But everything I told you is true. The Robert Redford look-alike, the power, Margaret Hamilton—everything!"

"Either you've got a more active imagination than I remembered, or you've gotten into some powerful liquor since you got here," Rick said, smirking at Graham.

"I guess I'm going to have to prove it to you, Rick," Graham said. "All right, we'll use Alice and I'll show you. Alice," Graham called to her.

"Oh, come on, Graham," Rick sputtered. "Your little joke just didn't work…."

"Yes, Graham?" Alice said, returning to their table. "Ready for more coffee?"

Graham pointed his finger at her and said, *"You're the one."*

The bell sounded again, but, as always, only Graham could hear it.

"Graham, honey," Alice said, her face softening into a dreamy smile. She picked up the coffee shop check that she had left on the table earlier for the coffee. "I'll pay this. It's the least I can do." She put her arm around Graham's shoulders. "I've got a break coming in a few minutes so I'll join you. I'll sit right here beside you," she indicated the chair next to Graham. "By the way, I'm free tonight. Would you like to come over to my place? I can fix dinner for us—you know... candlelight and everything."

Rick was intrigued at what he was hearing. "Do you mean you actually want to date Graham?"

"That's too fancy a word for what I have in mind," she replied with a leer. "You know what they say, 'You can't rape the willing!'" She chuckled as she ran her fingers through Graham's hair.

"See what I mean?" Graham asked triumphantly. "It works. Just like I told you it would. Have you seen enough?" He turned to Alice, pointed at her, and said, "It ain't me, babe!"

Alice immediately returned to her normal demeanor. She looked a little puzzled and said, "Gee, Graham, I don't know what came over me... just forget all that foolishness I said. I'm real sorry. Oh, here you go," she added, putting the check back on the table as she started to walk away.

"Wait a minute, Alice," Rick interrupted. "I want to ask you something."

"Sure, Rick. What is it?"

"How long have you known Graham?"

"Since he was just a teenager. You were still a sophomore at Tascosa High School at the time your family used to come to the Big Texan when I worked there, weren't you, Graham? I remember it very well."

"Yes, that's right," Graham agreed. He turned to Rick. "What does that have to do with anything?"

"Oh, nothing," Rick replied. "I was just asking. Thanks, Alice. That's all I wanted to know...."

Alice walked away, and Graham looked at Rick. "What was that all about?"

"It just goes to show how far you'll go for a good joke. And I'll admit that it was pretty convincing the way she carried on about you," Rick added.

"What do you mean by that?"

"I just mean that you got here before I did this afternoon and obviously asked Alice to do that little act for me. And it was pretty good, too."

"But that wasn't an act. It was real," Graham protested.

"Oh, Graham, you're too much," Rick said, laughing again. "You're both really very good performers."

"So you still don't believe me, huh? Well, I guess there's just one thing left to do...."

"What's that?" Rick asked.

Graham pointed his finger at Rick and said, "You're the one." The tiny bell rang softly once more.

Rick blinked and stared directly into Graham's eyes. "I'm sorry I argued with you. We're such good friends... so close...." He reached across the table and took both of Graham's hands in his. "Graham, I've wanted to tell you for a long time... years really... that I still care for you the way I used to. Remember the affair we had when we were seniors in high school? I was crazy about you then... and I still am now! I just know we could works things out somehow. I could quit my job in Houston and move to Des Plaines. And then we could be together for always." He gripped Graham's hands so hard it hurt.

Graham pulled his hands free. "I think you've proved my point, Rick. It ain't me, babe!"

Rick looked blankly at Graham for a moment. Then he blushed, a deep red color that made his blond hair look even lighter. "I can't believe it. It's true. Everything you said is true."

"I tried to tell you, but you wouldn't believe me. That was the last thing I could think of to prove it to you. Convinced?"

"Am I ever," Rick said. "That power is really something. I'm amazed at the things I said to you."

"Don't let it bother you. As I told you, it's made people do very strange things and say a lot of things that they really don't mean and would never say otherwise. Imagine how I felt with that cop in my bed...."

"I see what you mean now."

Without any warning, the strains of "Dream a Little Dream of Me" sounded in Graham's ear... right there in the coffee shop. Robert, the Robert Redford look-alike from the Annex, came around the corner of the coffee shop from the motel entrance.

"Uh, oh." Graham exclaimed. "You won't be able to see him, but he's here."

Rick turned and blinked when he saw the movie star approaching their table. "I can't believe this. It's Robert Redford himself. Well, maybe I *can* believe it now. I wonder what in the world he's doing here?"

"Hiya, gents!" he greeted them cheerfully. "Surprised to see me?"

"You can say that again!" Graham agreed. "What are you doing in Texas?"

"I'm here because you're here," Robert said. "So this is your friend, Rick? Hi, Sport."

"Hi," Rick said. "But I'm kind of shocked that you'd appear in front of me."

"So am I," Graham said. "What's the deal?"

"Well, I knew you'd tell old Rick here everything so I decided not to wait until you were alone."

"But I don't understand why you're here at all," Graham replied.

"You're due for your final charge, Sport."

"What do you mean, final charge?" Graham asked.

"Well, you used the power on poor old rich Aaron, then on lucky Alice, and finally on Rick here. That's three from the second charge I gave you," Robert reminded him.

"But what did you mean by 'final' charge?" Graham asked.

"Didn't I tell ya? It must have slipped my mind. You get two full charges of three each. You've had those and already used them up. Then you get one final little charge that will work on only one person.

You're down to your last one, so hold out your finger." Graham did, and Robert touched it for the last time.

"You mean I just get this one more?"

"That's right, Sport. Too bad you wasted so many of your seven charges—Trevor, Dean Weinert, Carlton, Aaron, Alice, and—"

"Well, you don't have to do roll call. Anyway, the one on the cop wasn't really wasted.... I avoided a ticket... and saved my job!" Graham said. "And I had to use the ones on Alice and Rick to prove I was telling Rick the truth."

"Whatever you say, Sport," Robert said. "But you've only got one left... so you'd better use it wisely."

"Does this mean I'll never see you again?" Graham asked, a little sadly. "I'm beginning to get used to you...."

"Oh, you have such a way with words, Sport," Robert said, smirking slightly. "I like you, too."

"Well, I didn't mean it the way it sounded," Graham sputtered.

"No offense taken, Sport. And to answer your question... no, you'll see me again one more time. You could call it an exit interview. We'll talk then. Nice to meet you, Rick." And he instantly vanished before their eyes.

"If I hadn't seen it with my own eyes... and heard it with my own ears... I wouldn't have believed it!" Rick exclaimed. "And I'm still having trouble believing it."

"I know what you mean... and I've seen him three times... sort of... one way or another."

"Well, let's get over it because we've still got an important item left on the agenda for today's meeting," Rick said.

"What's that?"

"What are you going to do about Aaron?"

"Oh, yeah... I almost forgot all about him with Robert's appearance and all. What do you think I should do?"

"It's not important what I think. What you think is what counts. Do you love him?"

"I told you I don't," Graham said. "But I like having him around...."

"Is that enough to build a real relationship? Is it fair to Aaron? It sounds kind of selfish to me."

"No, it's not enough for a real relationship," Graham agreed. "And you're right… I'm just being selfish all right."

"Then you have to decide…." Rick stared deep into Graham's eyes. "What's the best thing to do… for both of you?" Rick asked. "You did admit that you're having trouble falling in love with him."

"That's true. My guilt at tricking him into falling in love with me certainly does get in the way."

"Graham, I've known you for years. I know you wouldn't do anything to hurt someone on purpose. You've really got only one option."

"Break the spell. I know that's what I'll have to do. Besides, it's not like I've never been without a boyfriend before. I can get used to it again."

"Exactly. But you've still got one charge left, as Robert put it," Rick said. "What are you going to do with that?"

"You pose a very good question. If I use it on someone else… I'll just be back where I am now… in the same boat as with Aaron. I'll have to give this some serious thought when I get back to Illinois. I'm not sure I will ever use that last charge."

Rick grinned. "In that case, you're going to have to be extremely careful where you point that finger and what you say… and I mean for the rest of your life."

Graham groaned. "You're right. I wish he hadn't given me that last charge…."

CHAPTER THIRTEEN

GRAHAM flew to Chicago and returned to Des Plaines the day after New Year's Day. He didn't want to waste any time in contacting Aaron, because he had decided to let the chips fall where they would. He called Aaron and got him to drive down to Des Plaines that same night. At around seven o'clock, Aaron knocked on the door of Graham's apartment, and Graham ushered him inside from the frigid hallway.

"Oh, Graham," Aaron exclaimed, "it's so good to see you again. I missed you so much all the time that you were gone." He threw his arms around Graham and began to kiss him.

Graham stood stiffly, allowing himself to be kissed. *This is just making what I have to do… that much harder.*

Aaron broke free from the kiss and exclaimed, "I have so much to tell you—it's just wonderful news."

"News? What do you mean?" Graham asked.

"Let's sit down, and I'll tell you all about it," Aaron replied. He led Graham to the sofa in the living room. "You're going to be so excited… maybe even more than I am."

Graham sat down next to Aaron. "What is this news that I'm going to be so excited about?"

"I've got you a new job. At the bank. With me." Aaron pulled Graham into his arms. "Isn't that just terrific?"

"You got me a job at your bank?" Graham was puzzled. "But I don't know anything about the banking business. How could that be?"

"Well, it has nothing to do with actual banking itself. It's more like in customer relations… and it suits you perfectly. You would do the writing and editing of the bank's brochures, publicity and advertising releases—that sort of thing. Since you're an English teacher, you know all about writing, and this fits right in with your talents. What do you think?"

"But I wasn't an advertising major in college," Graham objected. "I'm not sure I could do this sort of thing. Anyway… why did you get me a job? I've already got a perfectly good one teaching in high school."

"I know," Aaron replied, "but this pays more than twice your salary as a teacher… I know because my dad checked with the district administration office in Des Plaines to find out their salary schedules. And we could work together. Isn't that great? And even better yet… you can leave Des Plaines and move to Chicago where we can live together in my house."

"Quit my job? Move in with you in Evanston? Those are some pretty big steps, Aaron. I'm not sure I'm ready for all this…."

"We can finally be together like a real couple," Aaron exclaimed.

"I'm very curious about something, Aaron," Graham said. "How did you get me such a high-paying job at your bank? I have no qualifications whatsoever."

"You know that I'm an officer at the bank… and it's our family's bank. I can hire whomever I want. You know all that."

"You mentioned something about your dad. Did you discuss this with him? It sounds like you did."

"Yes, I did. Normally I wouldn't, because I can make personnel decisions without consulting him… but since you'll be living with me, I wanted him to know what I was doing."

"Didn't your dad want to know why you're hiring someone just out of the blue like that… and then moving the guy into his house?" Graham asked.

"That's the best part… and I saved it for last. I told him I'm gay! And you know what? He knew it already. He was so much more understanding than I ever could have guessed. He knows you're my lover and that we want to live together. Just think, this is the beginning of a new life for you… for me… and for us." He grabbed Graham and hugged him.

Graham pulled back from Aaron, held him by the shoulders, and said, "I just have one thing to say about all this."

"What?" Aaron asked.

"It ain't me, babe!"

Aaron's smile melted away like butter in the summer sun. He just sat on the sofa for a moment… and then he slowly looked around Graham's apartment, as though he were taking it in for the first time. Then he looked at Graham as if to say, *Who are you? And what am I doing here anyway?*

"Are you okay?" Graham asked.

"Sure. I'm fine," Aaron said, still with a rather blank look on his face. Then he seemed to remember all he had offered to Graham. "You know, Graham, this would be a very big career change as well as a lifestyle change I've proposed. You probably should think it over very carefully before you decide. As a matter of fact... uh, you're a dedicated teacher, aren't you?"

"Yes, I am."

"Then this may not interest you at all," he said. Aaron seemed to be weighing his words very carefully now. He continued, "You'd probably not even enjoy living in our house... it's so big and all. You're not used to it... you really might not be happy there."

Graham nodded. *And you might not be happy with me living there, either.* But instead he said, "I think you're absolutely right, Aaron. None of this is really right for me... or in my league, in a manner of speaking."

Aaron looked obviously relieved. "Well... do you want some time to think all of it over?"

"No, I don't think so. It's just not the thing I want to do," Graham replied. "But I want to thank you for the offer anyway... the job and the house. It was very kind and thoughtful of you."

"You know," Aaron said, looking at his watch, "it's getting late, and I have to get back to the city. Tomorrow's a work day... for us both. I think I'll just be running along."

He got up from the sofa and turned to look reflectively at Graham. "I'll call you sometime... maybe we can get together and have a drink or something." He looked as though he just couldn't wait to get out of Graham's apartment. "See you," he called as he opened the door and fled.

"So much for that," Graham said to the empty room. And it now seemed emptier than ever before. "I'm going to miss you, Aaron."

SINCE it was the last weekend of the Christmas break from school and Graham was feeling sorry for himself... now that it appeared that Aaron was gone from his life... he decided to call Carlton Safranski, his old policeman ex-lover. Graham found the phone number in his wallet and placed the call.

Carl answered on the second ring. "Hello?"

"Hi, Carl. This is Graham Thomas. From Des Plaines. Remember me?" Graham hoped Carl hadn't reconsidered staying friends with Graham.

There was a pause that lingered for just a moment. "Uh, sure. Hi, Graham. How're ya doing?"

"Oh, I'm a little down in the dumps. Remember how we said we'd have coffee or a beer sometime? You know… friend to friend?"

"Yeah. I remember." Carl's voice lost the hesitancy. "When did you want to get together?"

"Are you on duty tonight?" Graham asked.

"I'm on the late shift tonight, so I start in about an hour. But I can take a break later. You want to meet at that coffee shop again? Their coffee is pretty good. Remember?"

"You're right. Okay, can you meet me there about midnight?"

"Sure. That's before the heavy drinkers get on the streets when most of the bars close at two. I'll meet you there. You remember how to get to the coffee shop?"

"I'll find it. And Carl… thanks. I appreciate it."

"You bet, buddy," Carl said as he hung up the phone.

For a moment Graham considered how odd it was for him to be calling a Chicago policeman… and just for the purpose of lifting his spirits, too. There was something about that idea he wouldn't have believed just a few months ago. But things had changed greatly this past fall.

At a few minutes to midnight, he pulled into the coffee shop parking lot. He stared through the window at the place where he once sat with Carl and set the cop free from Robert's spell. He didn't see a police car in the parking lot, but he went inside and got a booth by the front window again… so he could see when Carl got there. He was just doctoring his coffee when Carl pulled up and parked.

Carl grinned at Graham as he came to the table. "You're still looking good, Graham," he said, reaching out to shake Graham's hand.

"You, too, Carl, if I may comment on the good looks of one of Chicago's finest."

Carl flashed a little grin. "You can say whatever you like to me, Graham. We have a special bond, you know."

"Sealed with a little more than just a kiss," Graham said so softly that no one else could hear him.

Carl blushed at that. "I wasn't going to bring that stuff up," he said. Then he chuckled. "But if it hadn't happened between us, I might not be the better person that I think I am now."

"You were always a good person, Carl."

"If we keep this up, anyone overhearing us might think we were lovers." Carl laughed softly. "So what's up, my old bed partner?"

Graham looked down at his coffee cup and sighed. "I'm feeling blue tonight, and I just wanted a friend to sit with me and hold my hand. Figuratively," he added when he saw the wary look on Carl's face. "You know I wouldn't want to embarrass you, Carl."

"You're not going to embarrass me. I'm a cop, and people don't usually mess with cops… except for maybe you."

"Well, here's the way it is…." Graham told Carl a brief version of how he'd won and then lost Aaron, leaving out the part about Robert and the power.

"Want my opinion, Graham?"

Graham nodded. "Sure. Let me have it."

"I think maybe you try too hard sometimes. I know you really want a lover, but it sounds like you need to give it a rest, buddy. Just let somebody come to you without you putting out so much effort. Maybe you should quit coming to the bars so often… and stop looking for someone so hard… at least for a while. What do you think?"

"Hmmm. I knew I called you for a good reason. You're probably right. I guess that I've been thinking so much about myself that I've overdone it. I think I'll take your advice and relax a little. I don't need to come over here to Chicago every single weekend."

"That's right. Give yourself something else to think about. You're a terrific guy, Graham. I told you that the last time we were in here. I said it then, and I'll say it again. If I were gay, I'd fall for you in a

CHAPTER FOURTEEN

heartbeat. So let someone else grow to feel that way about you, too. Things will work out for you. Just wait and see."

"I hope you're right," Graham said. "I'm glad I called you. You've already cheered me up a lot."

"Anytime, Graham." Carl looked at his watch. "Say, buddy, I hate to tell you, but this break has to be short tonight. I really need to get back on duty. Now remember though… call me anytime… and don't forget the Bulls game that we talked about. I'll take care of this tab. They never charge me for anything in here anyway. See you, Graham."

Just before Carl stood to go, Graham took both of Carl's hands and squeezed them lightly. "Thanks, Carl. You're a real friend."

As Graham drove home to Des Plaines, he felt better than he had for a long time. *Robert's dumb power spell at least got me a friend.*

GRAHAM returned to school from the holidays more depressed than he had expected. His visit with Carl hadn't cheered him for long. Even his students in class seemed more subdued than usual. But that was normal after a long holiday vacation from school. A notable exception to that was Trevor Randich, who happily greeted Graham in the hall before eighth period class.

"Hi, Mr. Thomas," he said. "How was your holiday in Texas?"

"Just fine, Trevor," Graham replied. "It was good to be with my family again. How was yours?"

Trevor smiled and said, "Couldn't have been better. You know what I got? A firm offer of a scholarship at the U of I! Isn't that great? All I have to do now is wait until signing day next month."

"Trevor, I'm so proud of you. I know you'll have a great career there." Graham reached out and shook Trevor's hand. "Congratulations."

"Thanks, Mr. T," he said. Then he lowered his voice so that no one else could hear him, and he added, "There's good news about my boyfriend, Eric, too."

"Well, spill it." Graham replied, smiling. "How's he doing? He doesn't say much in my morning class. He just sits there and grins at me an awful lot."

"That's the other part of the good news. He's going to school with me next year, too. His grades are high enough so he'll be accepted for sure… and his dad can afford the tuition. He was just waiting to talk to his dad about it until we heard something about my scholarship. He would have gone wherever I got a scholarship… so now we know for sure where we'll be together for college." Trevor grinned happily.

"That's great news, too," Graham agreed. "You know I wish the very best for you, Trevor."

"Thanks, Mr. T." The bell rang for class to begin, so they both hurried into Graham's classroom.

When the period was over, Graham went to the teachers' mailboxes to see if he had any mail or messages before he went to the teachers' lounge. There was a brief mimeographed note from Jack Richards, the English department chair. The message informed all

English teachers that there would be a short departmental meeting after school in Mr. Richards's classroom.

"Great." Graham sighed. "That's all I needed… a department meeting on the first day back from the holidays. I just can't wait." He went down the hall and walked into the faculty lounge. Once again he saw Mark Matthews sitting alone at a table. Graham poured himself a cup of coffee and went over to Mark's table.

"Want some company?" he asked.

"Sure. Have a seat," Mark replied. He saw the printed notice from Mr. Richards in Graham's hand. "I see you know about the meeting after school."

"Yeah, I just went to my mailbox. I'm so excited."

"I can tell," Mark said. "Your sarcasm is showing. But cheer up… maybe it really will be a brief meeting like the note said."

Graham looked skeptically at Mark as he sat down. "You haven't been to very many of Jack Richards's meetings, have you?"

"Well, no. I guess not." He chuckled. "Remember that this is just my first year here, and he didn't call but one or two meetings last semester…."

"He always says his meetings will be short," Graham said. "Oh, well. We'll just have to sit through it, I guess. How was your holiday?" And they proceeded to idly chat about the holidays, the newest movies, and the recent college football bowl games… for the remainder of the period.

As the time neared for the meeting, Graham got up and said, "I guess I'll go to my classroom and get my briefcase before the meeting. See you there."

"Hold on," Mark insisted. "I'll walk along with you. I don't need to go back to my classroom. Let's go to the meeting together."

"Fine," Graham agreed.

As he and Mark were entering Graham's classroom, Trevor and Eric walked past them. Both boys smiled at Graham and waved. Then, as they went down the hall, the two boys seemed to be in conference about something.

"They must be planning a hot date," Graham said softly under his breath.

"What was that?" Mark asked.

"I said they must be cramming a lot lately," Graham replied. "Trevor's grades are so high these days... I guess Eric helps him study."

It surprised Graham when Mr. Richards really did keep the meeting fairly short. He actually only had one item of business to discuss with the twenty-three teachers in the department.

"The only reason I called this meeting," Mr. Richards said, "besides taking the opportunity to welcome all of you back from the holidays... was to remind you that our literature textbooks are up for adoption for next year. Most of you know about the procedures that we follow for a textbook adoption... but I wanted to announce the names of those teachers whom I am asking to serve on the textbook committee."

Mr. Richards paused and smiled. "If your arms aren't strong already... they will be from lugging these heavy sample books around.

"Now I'll read the list of committee members... "

Graham was not really surprised to hear his name read as a committee member, but he was pleased that Mark would also serve as a member. *Maybe we can get to know each other better this way.*

There would be many meetings over the next two months, but Graham didn't really mind. It kept him too busy to worry about Aaron's departure or to reflect on his recent adventures using the power.

It didn't take long before Mark and Graham actually became friends, rather than just colleagues in the same department. This pleased Graham very much because he was really beginning to like Mark... quite a bit. Before their assignment to the committee, Graham had just been attracted to Mark's good looks. Now he began to see the person inside, too... and he liked what he saw. When the thought of using the power on Mark occurred to him, he quickly dismissed the idea. He didn't want any repeat of what had happened with Aaron. It wasn't a good idea, as he knew from his previous experiences.

One Thursday afternoon in February, the Maine Central High textbook committee was scheduled for a series of brief presentations from each of the competing textbook companies. By four thirty the presentations were over and Graham sat in a classroom student desk next to Mark after everyone else had gone.

"Thank goodness that's over," Graham declared with a sigh. "I'm exhausted after listening to all those promises from the book company reps."

"I guess it could have been worse. What if there had been ten companies competing for the book adoption?" Mark suggested.

Graham groaned. "Right. I guess we're lucky at that. Let's get out of here. I can't believe we're still sitting in these awfully cramped student desks."

"Maybe we're a little too big for them, but now I see how the students must feel. And we only had to sit in them for the afternoon...."

"It's a little early, but would you like to go out to eat?" Graham asked. "We could just sit and chat for a while before we order."

"Sounds good to me as long as we don't eat too soon. That luncheon spread those companies served us was pretty substantial," Mark said. "I'm not really too sure I want anything to eat the rest of the day."

"I agree. Maybe we could just have coffee. Or we could go out for a drink if you'd rather."

"Not me. It's a school night after all, and I need a clear head to finish up some grading when I get home. How about we meet over at the Rooftop Restaurant?"

Graham laughed. "I still think it's funny they call it that! It's a one-story little restaurant in a strip mall. I drove by there the other day and noticed that they've just about finished a new Kentucky Fried Chicken next door. I guess that's going to give the Rooftop a little competition."

"So would you want to go there?" Mark asked.

Graham rose and stretched. "Sure. I have to stop by my classroom to pick up some things, so I'll meet you over there in about fifteen minutes."

When Graham pulled into the parking area of the Rooftop, he was surprised at all the activity going on next door at the new restaurant. There were big trucks parked in the lot along with several other vehicles… but the oddest thing was how brightly lit the interior was. He got out of his car just as Mark pulled up and parked next to him.

"I wonder what's going on over there?" Mark asked as he got out of his car and joined Graham. "That looks more than just a little strange with all those lights."

"Yeah. The place is not even open yet, either. See that sign over there? It says the place opens next week."

"Oh, well," Mark said. "Shall we go into the Rooftop and be dazzled by the sights of the city… from way up there?" He smirked.

They strolled into the restaurant and selected a booth by the windows where they could look out and see the activity at the Kentucky Fried Chicken place next door. They were still a little puzzled by all the vehicles and people coming and going on the parking lot. A waitress came quickly to their table since there were very few other customers yet.

"What would you guys like to drink?" she asked as she handed them menus.

"I think we're both going to just have coffee for now," Graham said as Mark nodded in agreement. "We'll take a look at the menu, and maybe we'll order something else a little later."

"Coming right up," she said.

"If you'll excuse me, Mark," Graham said, "I've got to visit the little boy's room."

"I'm not going anywhere," Mark replied, still looking out the window.

As Graham headed for the restroom sign, he passed a jukebox on the way. The song playing was an old Tammy Wynette record, "Stand by Your Man." *I would if I had one. Must be a country-themed jukebox,* he thought.

When Graham returned from the men's room and passed the jukebox again, the song was just ending. The machinery whirred softly, and the next record began to play on the machine. It only surprised Graham a little bit that the song was "Dream a Little Dream of Me" by Mama Cass.

Oh, not again. And not in here with Mark sitting over there. Graham said to himself. He looked all around for Robert… with no luck… then he returned to sit down again at the booth opposite Mark. Two coffee cups were now on the table, and Mark was slowly sipping from one.

As Graham reached for the little bottle of clear liquid saccharine by the napkin dispenser on the table, the door to the restaurant opened and Graham, who was sitting so that he faced the door, did sort of a double take when he saw who walked in and passed him on the way to the counter of the restaurant. It was none other than Colonel Sanders himself, the Kentucky Fried Chicken icon.

The man was rather big, although somewhat short, and he was dressed all in white, including a white suit and a white dress shirt… just like he was in the TV commercials. The older man also had the famous white hair. It was almost like looking at a TV commercial that suddenly came to life.

"What's the matter?" Mark asked. "Why were you staring at that guy who just came in?" He looked beyond Graham's back and saw who Graham had been looking at. "Is that who I think it is?"

Robert certainly has a vivid imagination. I'll give him that. But I think that I'd better get over there to talk to him privately before he gets a chance to embarrass me in front of Mark.

Aloud he said, "I'll just pop over there and find out. I'll call you over if it's who we think it is." Before Mark could reply, Graham scooted out of the booth and approached the man in white, who now sat at the counter.

"Okay," Graham said to the man, "I get it…. and I can guess why you're here…."

"Pardon me?" the man replied, looking puzzled as he studied Graham. "Can I help you?"

"Hey, that's really good," Graham said. "You sound very authentic. I could almost believe that you're who you look like you are."

"Do I know you?" the man asked, giving Graham a puzzled look.

Graham laughed. "You're really a great actor. You just never quit, do you?"

"If that's a compliment, I guess I should thank you, but I'm not really an actor. I'm just a spokesperson. Since I sold the restaurants, the company has just hired me as part of the image."

"As usual, Robert, you're just perfect," Graham replied.

"I think you must have me mixed up with someone else," the man said. "I'm not Robert. My name is Harlan Sanders... and I'm here in Des Plaines to make a television commercial for Kentucky Fried Chicken. That's one of the newest outlets next door—"

"Sure you are. And I'm the Wicked Witch of the West escaped from Oz," Graham said.

Harlan Sanders stared at Graham for a moment. "I don't mean to insult you, sir, but are you feeling quite all right?" He called to the waitress. "Doris, would you come over here and tell this man who I am? He doesn't seem to recognize me."

The waitress arrived with the coffee that the man had evidently ordered. "Here you go, Harlan," she said. "Just let me know if you decide to order anything else. As I've told you before, we have some really good homemade pies out there in the kitchen. You might want to try a slice of the apple."

"Do you know this guy sitting here at the counter?" Graham asked, indicating the colonel. "I know he looks very familiar, but... "

The waitress laughed. "Of course he does. He's very friendly, and he has been happily visiting with our customers for the last day or two. Don't you know the famous Colonel Harlan Sanders who started the Kentucky Fried Chicken chain?"

"You think this is the real Colonel Sanders?" Graham asked.

"Of course it is," the waitress answered. "I told you he's been in here several times, and he's been nice enough to give autographs to any customers who asked. Some people have even taken his picture.... "

Suddenly Graham realized that he must have sounded like a complete idiot to the real Colonel Sanders as well as to this waitress. *This is all Robert's fault for confusing me! But that song on the jukebox....*

To the man in white, Graham said, "Colonel Sanders, I deeply apologize. I thought you were a friend of mine in disguise trying to play a prank on me. I can't tell you how sorry I am about this...."

Colonel Sanders smiled and nodded. "That's quite all right, young man. But you were beginning to make me question who I was."

"Do you mind if I call that guy over here to meet you?" Graham asked, pointing to Mark in the booth by the window. "He's another friend of mine…."

"Of course not," the Colonel replied. "By all means."

"Mark," Graham called. "It's really the Colonel. Come over and meet him."

Mark made his way to the counter to join Graham. "That certainly took a long time. What was the problem?"

"Just a little case of mistaken identity," the Colonel said.

Trying to change the subject, Graham said, "This is my friend Mark Matthews, Colonel Sanders. And I don't believe I told you my name. I'm Graham Thomas. We're both teachers at one of the local high schools."

Colonel Sanders smiled. "Nice to meet you boys," he said.

"Uh, I heard that you were giving autographs, Colonel Sanders. Would you favor us with yours?" Graham asked.

"It would be my pleasure," he said, reaching for a couple of napkins from the dispenser on the counter and taking a pen from his inside coat pocket.

"Do you mind if I ask you something?" Graham asked.

"Not at all. What is it?"

"If you're shooting a TV commercial next door, there's probably plenty of fried chicken over there. Why would you come in here?"

Colonel Sanders laughed. "Boys, I've had enough fried chicken to last me a lifetime. I never eat that stuff at Kentucky Fried Chicken!"

Graham, Mark, and the waitress all laughed.

CHAPTER FIFTEEN

IT WAS Saturday night again. After a moratorium of a few weeks from the bars, Graham had decided he was tired of sitting at home watching TV on Saturday night. *Besides,* he thought, *I only said I wasn't going to go to the bars every weekend anymore. I deserve a night out once in a while.*

He was almost finished getting ready for his night in the city when the phone rang. He answered, curious about who might be calling at ten o'clock on a weekend.

"Graham? Hi…. This is Aaron."

"Uh… hi. This is kind of a surprise. I'd more or less given up on hearing from you ever again. I thought about calling you, but I guess I just never got around to it."

"That's okay…. I really should have called you sooner. It was rude of me to practically run out of your apartment back in January when I was there that last time. I'm sorry I was so abrupt."

Graham hesitated. "It's really all right. I was pretty ungrateful after you went to all that trouble to find me a new job. And it was really generous of you to offer me a great place to live…. That mansion of yours is really special."

"Well, here's the thing. When I said all that and actually heard myself saying those things… it just suddenly didn't seem like something either one of us really wanted. I could tell from your reaction that it took you by surprise, and I felt like I had gone too far. I didn't even give you any warning. I should have discussed it with you when I first got the idea…. Then it all seemed wrong when I told you. I'm just sorry things worked out the way they have."

"Hey, it's just fine. I know exactly what you mean. All of a sudden it didn't seem like we belonged together after all…."

"That's how I felt, too," Aaron agreed. "But there's another reason I called. After we sort of mutually broke up, I ran into Steve again at the Trip. Remember him?"

"I remember seeing him from a distance that night we met. An old boyfriend, you said."

"Well, I didn't want you to find out by accident in case you and I ran into each other… like at the Trip, but Steve and I are back together. I think it's going to work out for us this time."

"That's great, Aaron," Graham said. "I'm happy for you."

"As I said, I wanted to be the one to tell you about it myself. I'd feel awful if you found out any other way except from me…."

"Aaron, I'll always wish you the best. You're a really terrific guy. I'm sorry it didn't work out for us, but that's just the way things happen, I guess."

"I need to go, Graham, but I really appreciate the chance to talk to you like this. I truly did enjoy all the time we spent together. I suppose it just wasn't meant to be... for us I mean. Maybe you could come to the Trip sometime and meet Steve. I've told him really nice things about you...."

"We'll see. It was nice of you to call, Aaron."

"Bye, Graham. You take care."

Graham felt a tinge of sadness. He had truly liked Aaron, but his guilt over the way their relationship was built hadn't quite gone away. He knew he'd done the right thing by letting Aaron go, but it didn't make him feel any better about his part in using magic on a really great guy. And he didn't think he was quite ready for drinks with Aaron and Steve at the Trip, either.

I haven't been to the Annex for a long time. I think I'll go back there. Maybe Carl and I could have a little reunion. He chuckled at the thought. *After all, I once had the "inside track" to his affections. Wait a minute, what am I saying? That's not funny. Carl really is a nice guy.*

So once again Graham drove across the expressway to the near north side of Chicago. This time there was no squad car waiting for him as he drove into the Annex parking lot. He bought a beer and looked around for a spot along the wall to park himself. It flashed through his mind that even though he'd stayed home for a while, his trips to the bars had become pretty routine and boring.

As he stood along a wall a little later, the song "Dream a Little Dream of Me" sounded once again, and Graham wondered what Hollywood personality would appear to surprise him this time. He looked around and saw Rock Hudson leaning against the wall next to him, nursing a beer.

"Oh, come on," Graham exclaimed as he walked up to Rock. "You can't be serious! Rock Hudson? Aren't you afraid you'll be recognized in here?"

"I think I look pretty good," Rock said. "And you can call me 'Roy'. You know... as in Roy Scherer... Rock's real name."

"I can call you a *psychiatrist*, too. At least I can call one *for you*."

"Careful," Roy said, "you'll hurt my feelings. By the way, did you know old Rock is from right here in Illinois? He was born in Winnetka."

"That's nice to hear. You sound like an encyclopedia. But you'll cause a riot if everyone sees you in here like that," Graham replied. "Do you really want to call attention to yourself this way?"

"Haven't you caught on to how this works yet? Nobody sees me this way except you. That's why no one else saw Robert Redford that first night that I met you."

"What does everyone else see?" Graham asked.

"They see an ordinary guy… one they wouldn't give a second glance."

"What about that time in Texas at the coffee shop?" Graham asked. "Didn't Rick see you the same way I did?"

"Sure, but that was because I wanted him to. That's the difference."

"Oh. Well, what are you up to this time? I haven't used the last charge, so this can't be my exit interview," Graham said.

"That's right," Roy agreed. "But that's exactly why I'm here. I want to know why you haven't used it. It's been a long time since I gave you that last charge. I need to finish up with your case and go on to someone else. You don't think I've got years to handle just one person, do you?"

"Frankly, I never thought about it," Graham replied. "I didn't realize you were waiting for me to use the power one last time."

"Haven't you found someone to use it on? You could just look around this bar tonight and find at least twenty interesting guys to use it on, couldn't you?"

"Sure I could… if I didn't care who loved me," Graham said. "But that would be sort of a gamble, wouldn't it?"

"Isn't life a gamble anyway? So is love, for that matter."

"Maybe so," Graham agreed, "but I'd like to be a little picky about whom I choose. You're certainly getting philosophical tonight, aren't you? But now that you're here and we're discussing this... I have a question for you."

"Let's hear it. Maybe I'll answer it, and then again maybe I won't," Roy replied.

"What was your real purpose in visiting me and giving me this so-called gift anyway? It really isn't very useful since it's not honest. Making someone fall in love with you in an artificial way doesn't compare with the real thing."

"How would you know? Have you ever found real love?"

"I guess not," Graham admitted. "But that still doesn't answer my question about why you appeared to me in these goofy disguises. Not to mention that I don't know who you really are... behind the celebrities you resemble each time we meet."

"I'll give you an answer. Sort of, anyway. You'll find out exactly why I appeared to you when this is all over... after your last use of the power. As to who I really am, it doesn't matter right now... but you'll be more than a little shocked... once we're all done!"

"Hmmm. That sounds like a cryptic riddle that doesn't really say anything... but I guess for now I'll have to just let it go. But back to real love for a minute. There is already someone I've met that I wish would fall in love with me."

"Who is that?" Roy asked.

"A teacher that I like at my school. But I doubt if you know him," Graham said.

"You mean Mark Matthews?"

"How did you know about him?"

"How do I know *anything* about you and your life?" Roy asked. "It's just one of my little secrets. But you're avoiding the issue. If you love Mark, why not use the power on him?"

"But I didn't say that I love him," Graham replied. "I just said I like him. But I think I *could* fall in love with him very easily. If I'm around him much more... maybe it'll happen."

"But why don't you just use the power on him?" Roy asked.

"I can't do it," Graham said. "You saw what happened when I did that to Aaron. I felt so guilty about it that I couldn't fall in love with him. No, if Mark falls in love with me, I want it to be because he wants to. Not because I used some trick on him. Besides, I don't even know if he's gay. Anyway, all my life I've been looking for honest love. I've learned my lesson about using magic… or *not using magic* is the way to put it, I guess."

"You mean you're never going to use that last charge of the power?"

"I don't know," Graham said. "I haven't given it a whole lot of thought."

"Listen, Toots," Roy said. "You've got to use it up so I can move on."

"And if I don't?"

"Then I'll have to keep coming around to see you. Forever, if I have to."

"Good," Graham said. "Then we can grow old together, and I won't be lonesome."

"Very funny," Roy said without humor. "You realize that I could appear in some really embarrassing disguises when I visit you. Would you like Tiny Tim or Mae West or Phyllis Diller… maybe even Liberace hanging around you at the bars?"

"That sounds like fun," Graham replied. "But nobody else would see them anyway… "

"I could fix that," Roy said. "As a matter of fact, I could appear in your classroom… in the middle of a parent conference… or in front of your folks when you're back in Texas visiting. There are endless possibilities."

"You wouldn't!"

"I would if you keep putting it off."

Graham thought this over for a moment. "Okay, I'll use the last charge, if you insist."

"I do," Roy said with a triumphant grin.

"Then *you're the one* I choose to use it on!" Graham said, pointing at Roy with his right index finger. The tiny bell sounded for a final time, and Graham set down his beer bottle and left the bar before Roy could say a word.

CHAPTER SIXTEEN

As Graham drove home that night, he hummed "Dream a Little Dream of Me." He had no idea what the result of his last use of the power would be, but at least it was done… and he wouldn't be tempted to use it on Mark. He even chuckled as he remembered the startled look on Roy's face as he had said the words of the power spell. *Serves him right!*

He halfway expected Roy or Margaret or Robert or whoever else to be waiting for him at his apartment when he got home. But there was no one there when he unlocked the door and went inside. He searched the apartment anyway—especially the bedroom—but it was empty. *Good! Maybe I've gotten rid of him at last!*

When Graham didn't have a visitor all day Sunday, he suspected Robert was planning to appear to him at school the next day… so he was somewhat apprehensive when he arrived at Maine Central High the next morning. However, there were no unhappy surprises waiting for him. He was a little puzzled but also very relieved. Every day for a week he waited for the ax to fall, but it didn't. That was as much a surprise as anything else that had happened to him.

ONE evening when Graham was at home watching TV, the telephone rang.

"Hello?"

"Hello, Graham? It's me," a voice said.

"Rick? Is that you?" Graham asked. "How nice to hear from you."

"Well, I just couldn't wait any longer to find out what was happening with you and the power and everything," Rick said.

"Hey, I'm sorry. I meant to call you to fill you in…."

Graham told Rick how he broke the spell on Aaron, how he'd begun to be interested in Mark Matthews, and how he used up the power on Robert himself… or at least on Robert disguised as Rock Hudson.

"Wow," Rick said. "You've really been busy. I'm glad you're not too disappointed about losing Aaron."

"That was for the best," Graham replied. "Just as we discussed at Christmas, it wasn't meant to be, I guess."

"At least you've got Mark," Rick said.

"Well, in a way. But we're only friends. I wish it were more than that, but I don't even know yet if he's gay. Remember how you used to tell me when we were in college that there were guys who came across as being super nice and friendly, but they weren't gay at all? You know… the type that's just naturally warm and charming and almost too friendly… but straight."

"I remember," Rick said. "And it's really true. They have what you might call a soft side to them that's kind of deceiving. You think they're gay, but they're not."

"I think that's the way Mark is," Graham said. "He'd probably be shocked if he knew I wondered what he looks like naked. He might even hit me if he knew that sometimes I picture myself in bed with him."

"What are you going to do to find out if he's gay?"

"I haven't got that figured out yet. It took all my willpower not to use the power on him. I'm just letting things run their course. If nothing ever happens, then it just doesn't happen…."

"Speaking of the power, I can't believe you actually used it on Robert himself."

"Neither can I. The idea just came to me when he practically threatened me if I didn't use it right away. I'm afraid I'm going to have to pay for my little joke one of these days, though, if it backfires on me."

"Well, keep me posted on what happens. I have to go now," Rick said. "Talk to you later."

"Bye, Rick," Graham said and hung up the phone.

He had barely had time to turn up the volume on the TV and sit down again when the phone rang once more. *Maybe it's Robert*, he thought, *and he's so angry with me that he doesn't want to face me in person*. But it wasn't Robert.

"Hello, Graham? This is Mark. I know it's a little late, but I was over at Kmart, and I just thought I'd give you a call since I'm not too far from your apartment...."

"What a nice surprise, Mark," Graham said. "Want to drop by for a drink?"

"Sure. That would be great. Give me the apartment number again. You're at Rockridge Apartments, aren't you?"

"That's right. It's building 1810, apartment 209... third building past the entrance to the complex, and the first section of the building... then the second floor."

"Okay. I'll be there in a few minutes, I hope—if I can find it in that big complex. Bye."

Graham was excited because Mark had never visited his apartment before. He glanced down at his clothes and wondered if he ought to change out of his well-worn college T-shirt and the same gym shorts he'd worn when Kent showed up that day.

Is this maybe a little too casual for entertaining company from school? Wait a minute. Hell, we're not going to the prom together, and this is just a short drop-in visit. It would be silly for me to dress up for Mark.

He started to head for his bedroom to at least put on some sneakers, but he stopped just inside the room in front of his dresser and looked at his image in the mirror. He saw the familiar red letters that spelled out Texas Tech on a black background with a big red "double T" insignia on his chest.

Hmmm. Maybe he'll think I look cute or maybe not. Who cares? What does it matter if I look like I'm settled in for a cozy night at home by myself? That's exactly what I was doing, and I'd be pretentious to act otherwise. Besides, he doesn't care if I'm barefoot and wearing my old shirt I've had for years. I'm being silly about this whole thing.

He walked back out into his living room and sat down to wait on the sofa without making any further preparations for the visit. He even left the TV on with the volume still turned down.

A few minutes later Mark knocked on the door, and Graham went to answer it. His heart began to beat a little faster as Mark walked through the door. *He even smells good,* Graham thought as he caught a whiff of Mark's cologne. *Cologne? It smells fresh.*

"You have a nice place," Mark said. "Lots better than mine."

"Thanks," Graham said. "Of course, I've lived here for nearly four years. It's taken me a while to collect enough stuff to make it look like a home… and livable. Have a seat, and I'll get you that drink. Is a beer okay?"

"Sure. That's fine."

Graham brought a beer to Mark and sat down beside him on the sofa, a discreet distance away.

"Do you mind if I use this ashtray?" Mark asked. "It looks almost too pretty to use."

"Go ahead," Graham replied, looking slightly puzzled. "But I didn't even know you smoked."

"I don't at school," Mark said. "I don't like the smell of smoke on my clothes when I'm teaching."

"Oh. Good thinking. The students would notice it right away."

"I don't really smoke much anyway… just when I'm a little nervous…. I bought these on the way over here."

Graham gave him a questioning look, but before he could ask Mark why he would be nervous, Mark changed the subject.

"I had forgotten that you told me when we first met that you were from Texas," Mark said, pointing to Graham's T-shirt.

"Didn't I tell you I went there for Christmas break? I guess I thought everybody knew," Graham replied.

"Where did you say you were from in Texas? Dallas? Houston? Austin?"

"No, it's in West Texas. Amarillo. Way up in the Panhandle on I-40 going west."

"Oh, sure. I remember now… and I should have remembered anyway because I have some cousins from Texas. And they're from Amarillo, too. It's quite a coincidence. Maybe you might know them… or you might have heard of them."

Graham smiled. "Of course it's possible, but there are over one hundred twenty thousand people in Amarillo. It would have to be really quite a coincidence…."

"They're the rich branch of our family. I almost never see them. My mother's sister married into their family. They own banks all over the place, including one in Chicago." He laughed. "That's as close to rich as I'll ever be."

Graham was truly startled to hear all this. *Surely he isn't from the same family as Aaron,* he thought. *That would be far too much of a coincidence.*

But he had to ask. "What are their names? Maybe I've heard of them after all."

"The last name is Rutledge. I have a cousin in Chicago, Aaron Rutledge."

Graham was so stunned he almost dropped his beer bottle. He didn't know what to say… and he saw that Mark was studying him quite closely because he hadn't responded. "I've heard of the family," he finally said.

"My cousin's five or six years older than I am," Mark said, "so we've never been very close. I've only seen him a few times in the last year or so."

"Really? That's interesting," Graham said, not knowing what else to say to Mark. He was afraid to admit he knew Aaron.

"But I did meet him a couple of weeks ago in Chicago for a drink at a place called the Trip. Have you ever heard of it? It's a bar with a sort of cabaret. They have a really great singer there named Andrea Casey."

Graham was now so shocked at what Mark was telling him that his mouth nearly dropped open. He put his beer on the coffee table to avoid spilling it, and he simply stammered, "Uh... I think I may have heard of it somehow...."

"You look upset about something," Mark said. "What's the matter?"

"Nothing. Nothing at all." Graham tried to smile, but he had a feeling he hadn't quite managed it convincingly.

"I can tell by your reaction that you *have* heard of the place... and I have a feeling you probably know it's a gay bar," Mark announced. "I guess this is as good a time as any. I've been wanting to talk to you about something...."

Graham examined Mark's face, which had become rather pale, as he feared his own had done. "Is this why you were nervous enough to smoke?"

Mark's hand shook slightly as he put out his cigarette and looked back at Graham. "Yes, that's exactly right. I'm afraid it gives me away. Look, I have a feeling I can trust you. We've become friends this year, and I wanted to have at least one person here in Des Plaines that I could be honest with about my... being gay!"

Graham picked up the beer bottle, took a swig, swallowed, and looked back up at Mark. "That's quite a confession. Why are you telling me about this? Not that I would tell anyone else, of course. You don't ever have to worry about that...."

Mark looked closely at Graham. "There's something I sense about you that makes me think you can keep a confidence... about anything."

"Do you mean you think I'm gay, too?"

This time Mark frowned slightly. "Not exactly. I didn't mean to imply that. I just meant that somehow I feel a closeness, a sort of camaraderie with you and no one else on the faculty."

"I see. Well, I'm honored that you feel that way and chose to talk to me about this."

"I have another confession to make," Mark said. "There was some wishful thinking going on, too."

"About me?"

"Don't be offended. Yes, about you. I've wondered all year long if you might be gay. I wasn't sure, of course. Tonight when I was shopping, I got to thinking about you. I knew you lived pretty close by, so I made up my mind to call you and come over to tell you about myself... no matter what the consequences. You helped me out by wearing that Texas Tech shirt, which gave me an opening to break the ice. I mean to talk about my gay cousin Aaron from Amarillo and all that."

"I don't know what to say," Graham admitted. "You've caught me completely by surprise."

Then he stopped, looked again at Mark, and gave him a warm smile. He hesitated for just a moment longer. "No. I'm being ridiculous. Of course I know what to say. I have a confession, too." He gulped slightly as though he were about to bite the bullet, which indeed he was. "As long as we're being so open with each other at last, I'll tell you that I've wondered the same thing about *you* all year, too. I'm gay, and I had no idea how I was going to find out about you, either."

Mark laughed gently as he leaned back against the sofa. "Wow. Now we both know, and it's such a relief! I can't begin to tell you." He took the cigarette pack out of his shirt pocket and tossed it onto the coffee table. "I don't need those anymore. I'm quitting these death sticks right now. I don't have a reason to be nervous now."

"I'll admit something else to you... finally," Graham said. "I've had my eye on you all this time... and that committee work we did together made me even more interested in you...."

"I could say the same thing about you," Mark replied. "So do you suppose that we might begin with... uh, maybe an introductory kiss right about now?"

Graham scooted closer and carefully put his arms around Mark. Then he kissed the man the way that he had wanted to for so long.

Mark put his hands up inside Graham's flimsy shirt and embraced him, too.

"Do you really have to wear this old shirt and these gym shorts?" Mark asked.

Graham giggled. "Do *you* really have to wear any clothes at all?" Without waiting to move to the bedroom, they stood and stripped off each other's clothes, right there by the sofa. Graham admired the naked body standing next to him for a moment... and it amazed him how much it had the same general appearance as Mark's cousin Aaron. Same blond chest hair, same blond pubic hair, same hair on his arms and legs. His hard cock was a little shorter than Aaron's, but that made it almost the exact same size as Graham's. Something they had in common.

"You're beautiful," Graham exclaimed. "I've wanted to see you like this for so long."

"I think you're the one who's beautiful," Mark replied. "And I'm so grateful you wore that shirt tonight, since it gave us a starting point."

"This mutual admiration society is nice," Graham said, "but I think we'd really be a lot more comfortable if we moved on into the bedroom. Want to join me?"

"Sure I do."

"Let's go."

"Okay. Let's not waste any more time, then," Mark said, leaning over to plant another little kiss on Graham's lips.

Graham took Mark by the hand and led him into his bedroom. He flipped the switch on the little lamp next to the bed, and then he pulled the covers back. "I'm so excited that you're actually here, naked, and about to climb into bed with me that... I almost don't know what to do! *Almost*, I said!" he repeated with a grin. "Come here, you delicious-looking, hot young English teacher! Let's talk about a thesis, the main idea, and some supporting details!"

"I learn better by kinetics," Mark smirked back at him. "You'll have to teach me with a hands-on approach. I learn much better by doing something... rather than just by hearing about it!"

"In that case," Graham replied, getting into bed and scooting over to make room for Mark, "let's begin with the first step. Lie down here next to me, and let's put our heads together. Both of them... upper- and lowercase!"

Mark laughed. "You're just almost too much. I can tell a relationship with you is going to be a real adventure." He lay down and melted into Graham's arms as they began with a deep, satisfying exploratory kiss while their cocks did indeed rub together, heightening their passion.

Their kiss became almost a duel. Each man explored the mouth of the other, sharing and learning all the little details of each other.

Mark reached between their hips and grasped both cocks and measured them with his fingers as he played and stroked slowly.

Graham looked down at both dicks clasped in Mark's hand. Since both cocks were almost exactly the same size in length as well as thickness, Graham thought it felt like his dick had simply doubled, and now there were two of himself instead of the usual familiar one!

As he watched, fascinated, Mark made a few more tentative strokes on both cocks. Then the hand searched even lower and explored Graham's balls, fingering the big jawbreaker-size orbs and playing with the abundant soft skin in the sac that held them. Graham's head was spinning in ecstasy as he uttered soft, deep-throated moans, which he hoped would encourage Mark to keep it up. Finally, though, as his load came ever closer, he gasped, "Do you want to fuck? Or would you rather suck? We could sixty-nine first—but I'm gonna come if you keep that up."

"Yeah," Mark replied. "Let's suck some dick before we do anything else."

"You've got it," Graham said, sliding down the bed to reach Mark's cock with his tongue while moving his lower body up to where Mark's waiting mouth could taste his dick. They lay on their sides tasting and exploring each other. A thrill raced once again through Graham's body as he took Mark's cock into his mouth, slowly at first, just sucking lightly on the head and then licking in a circular motion around it. Gradually he worked his way down the shaft until he had the full throbbing cock in his mouth. With one hand he played with Mark's balls and with the other he fingered the entrance to Mark's ass. He pulled his mouth away from Mark's cock long enough to murmur, "You taste so good. I want you to come so I can taste your sweet sperm and fill my mouth with it."

At the same time, Mark was sucking Graham's dick more rapidly, sliding along the shaft rhythmically, then stopping once in a while to lick the head and tease the slit of Graham's cock with his tongue...

tasting the pre-come that began to ooze. Graham began sucking again for a moment, but then he stopped and said, "It's not like we have to do *everything* tonight—"

"I know that," Mark agreed. "But don't talk so much… it's breaking my rhythm. I've got a hot dick here to suck." He returned to business.

Graham responded by sucking on two of his fingers, then carefully easing them into Mark's ass while continuing to suck Mark's cock. As soon as he found the sweet spot inside Mark and began to massage it, he knew that Mark's orgasm was coming very soon, for it was Mark who began moaning this time! He felt Mark's balls retract and Mark's cock harden like a rock as squirt after squirt of come flowed into Graham's mouth.

Graham's own dick soon released its load of come from the faster speed of Mark's sucking, so it was only split seconds after Mark's climax that Graham filled Mark's mouth with a load of salty come.

When their breathing slowed at last, and their heartbeats returned to normal, Graham released Mark's dick and moved himself on the bed back up to where he could kiss Mark's moist lips. This time they shared their salty maleness in a swirling kiss that lingered on and on.

At last they stopped, and Graham turned over onto his back, pulling Mark over close enough to him so Mark's head rested on Graham's chest. Graham ran his hand through Mark's soft hair and gently said, "I waited a long time to find someone to share love with me. I hope you're the one!"

The irony of his words didn't hit him until after he said them. *If Robert can hear me, I hope he knows that this time it really is the one!*

"It's a little early, perhaps," Mark said, "but I think maybe you just might be a keeper. Do you believe in fairy tales, Graham? Or in magic?"

"Oh, yes! I believe in them with all my heart. More than you can know." He thought he might share all those Robert Redford-inspired fairy tale magic adventures with Mark, somewhere down the line. But not tonight. It was already approaching the new morning, and he wanted to actually sleep with Mark… but already he was thinking he might actually have to invest in a much bigger bed as a playground for the two of them in the future. He truly hoped there really would be a

CHAPTER SEVENTEEN

future for them. He couldn't wait to discuss the possibility with Mark… just in case this potential beginning of a relationship was to work out the way he hoped.

THE next morning, Graham and Mark had to rise early so Mark could go home to change his clothes for the school day. Getting out of bed first, Graham stumbled into his small kitchen and poured water into the tank of his Mr. Coffee machine. Then Graham looked into the living room and grinned when he saw their clothes still scattered everywhere. He wondered if Mark was looking for his clothes in the bedroom, but he decided to say nothing and let Mark stay as naked as Graham. He certainly didn't feel any self-consciousness at his own nakedness.

"I hope you want a mug of coffee before you dash home to change clothes," he called out to Mark. The stream of coffee was already tinkling into the glass carafe.

"Do you mind if I shower here first before I run home to get fresh clothes?" Mark asked, emerging still naked from the bedroom.

"On one condition." His make-believe frown turned into another grin as he added, "And that's if you come here and press that beautiful sensuous body next to mine while giving me a big, pre-mouthwash kiss. I don't care how we taste first thing in the morning as long as we taste it together."

Mark laughed. "Hold your nose, then, so you can't taste my stale breath." He strode into the kitchen to join Graham, whose eyes widened as he stared in appreciation of Mark's erect cock.

It looks like his dick wants to touch mine, Graham thought as he smiled at Mark's hardened cock and reached out to grab it. He looked down and saw his own swollen dick, so he put them together in his hand and said, "Look how much alike they look. They could be twins."

Mark laughed again. "You say the funniest things. But you're right… they really do… and I'm so glad that they're together."

"Me, too." Then he released Mark's cock and simply enfolded Mark into his arms as they prepared to share their first morning kiss. But just before their lips met, Graham popped a hard candy into his mouth. He had been hiding it in his other hand, waiting to surprise Mark and sweeten both their mouths. The candy passed from mouth to mouth before Graham pulled away, crushed it with his teeth, and then shared it again with Mark.

"I can't believe you did that," Mark gasped, laughing once more. "You're just full of surprises."

"Well, I wanted our first morning kiss to be memorable. Now you can go get your shower, and I'll pour the coffee. Want any breakfast?"

"No thanks. I think I got enough nourishment during the night, if you know what I mean. All protein, too." Mark headed into the little bathroom and turned on the water in the shower.

Graham poured coffee into two matching mugs that he left on the kitchen table, and then he went into the bathroom to join Mark in the shower.

"Another little surprise," he said, as he pulled open the shower curtains and climbed into the tub. "I hope you don't mind."

"Not at all," Mark replied. "Why do you think I left the bathroom door open?"

"Good. You know what? I think we really are going to get along very well. I can just feel it…."

"Can you feel this?" Mark asked, as he ran the bar of soap all over Graham's chest and slid it down to his cock and balls. "I'll be happy to wash you all over."

"If you'll let me return the favor," Graham replied. "But we can't get as serious about this as I'd like because we still have to get ready for school. It's getting later by the minute."

"I know. I hate it that we have to hurry so I can drive home to change clothes. It takes a lot of time…. Of course when I came over here last night, I had no idea I'd be staying overnight."

"It would have been so funny if you had shown up at the door with a little overnight bag and a change of clothes in a suit bag."

Mark laughed. "That would have been more than just a little presumptuous… don't you think? And prematurely optimistic, I'm afraid."

"I have a thought," Graham offered. "And possibly this has occurred to you, too. We could stash a few of your clothes and toiletries here… so that if we really do decide we want to pursue a relationship together, we'll be prepared for times like this morning. Please understand that I'm not trying to rush things along too quickly. I just mean it would be more convenient to do something like that… if we keep this up between us."

"That sounds very practical to me," Mark agreed. "And I agree with you. We should see how things go between us before picking out the china, crystal, and silver patterns to register at the department stores for our wedding."

Graham laughed. "Exactly. And we'll put off an appointment with the realtors for buying a house together... at least for a few days anyway...."

Mark laughed, too. "Probably a good idea."

"To be serious for just a moment before we absolutely have to get dressed and rush out of here," Graham said. "I really enjoyed the evening with you, and I hope we have more like it. But we'll make sure we move at a pace that makes us both feel comfortable."

"Agreed. Now give me a quick kiss, and let's get going before—"

Graham put his wet arms around Mark's slippery body and kissed him again as they shared the memory of the crushed candy piece. "Damn! I think I'm going to have a very hard time trying to keep my mind on Cavalier and Puritan poetry in my senior English literature classes today! Maybe I should skip ahead to those Elizabeth Barrett Browning love sonnets we'll be studying next month."

"You can read love sonnets to me anytime you want—except right this minute," Mark declared. "We've really got to get to school! It might be just a little too coincidental if we were both late on the same morning and came into school at the same time together."

"That's true. The English office secretary might have a chuckle over it, but I don't think Mr. Richards would appreciate having to find someone to cover both our first period classes until we got there. He might actually have to cover a class himself."

"Heaven forbid! Ready to rinse?" Mark asked, offering his place under the showerhead. Graham turned around a few times under the water spray.

"At least we have conference period together. We can meet then and see how we might want to proceed. Maybe it's a good thing we have different lunch periods... it will give us a little more time to absorb and think about what's happened between us." Graham reached for a towel. "Wait a minute, and I'll get you a fresh towel from the linen closet in the hall."

"Graham," Mark began, as he dried himself with the towel that he was handed, "this is happening really fast, but it's a little like a dream come true. I mean... I've been wanting a boyfriend for such a long time."

"Mark, you took the words right out of my mouth."

All that day at school, Graham felt like he was still walking around in a thrilling, happy dream. When his conference period came at the end of the day, he eagerly waited for Mark to meet him at his classroom so they could walk to the lounge together. Trevor, who was just leaving Graham's class, came up to Graham before he left. The classroom was now empty.

"Okay, Mr. T," Trevor said. "What's up with you? You seem like a different person today—I can tell you're really happy! What gives?"

"I guess I am, Trevor, perhaps the happiest I've been in... well... maybe forever. We'll see, I guess."

"I know it's none of my business," Trevor said, "but Eric and I have noticed you in the halls with that first-year teacher, Mr. Matthews. He's really kinda dreamy to look at... and we think you should check him out. Why don't you try to find out if he's gay? Then you could have a friend here at school who's... uh, one of us."

Graham smiled because Mark walked in the door at just that moment and overheard what Trevor said. Mark looked a little shocked.

"It's okay, Mark," Graham said. "Don't worry about Trevor, here. He and I are old friends and have shared some secrets together." He winked at Trevor, and after looking around to make sure no one was seeing in through the door from the hallway, Trevor gave Graham a little kiss on the cheek.

"And you were right about Mr. Matthews and me," Graham said. "We're on the road to becoming... uh, really good friends."

"I'm glad—really glad," Trevor said. "I gotta go, so I'll leave you two *buddies* together. That's all I wanted to say... but it seems that you've already beaten me to it." He shook Mark's hand and said, "You'd be getting a really good one if you... uh, pick this one." He nodded toward Graham, winked at each man, and then walked out the door.

CHAPTER EIGHTEEN

Mark looked puzzled, so Graham simply said, "I'll tell you about it sometime. Come to think of it, you wouldn't believe a lot of it anyway. Now let's go to the lounge and have a talk over a cup of coffee...."

"Can't we each have our own cup of coffee?" Mark asked, smiling at his new close friend.

THINGS were working out so well for Graham in the weeks that followed that he nearly forgot all about Robert and the mysterious power. He had stopped waiting for the other shoe to drop, too. Not long after their first night together, they developed an exciting routine in which Graham and Mark spent two or three nights a week together, usually at Graham's apartment. On one weekend occasion, Graham stayed at Mark's place, but they agreed that it was easier to just store some of Mark's things with Graham, since his place was larger, and carry on from there.

One afternoon after school, they were sitting at Graham's kitchen table with newspaper movie ads spread out on the table.

"Do you want a beer or anything, Mark?"

"I'll take a Coke if we have any left in the fridge. I need a clear head if I'm going to get some essays graded later on tonight."

Graham reached into the refrigerator and took out the last two soft drinks. "Time to stock up at the store," he said as he handed one to Mark.

"You know, there's something kind of important that we haven't discussed in a while."

"What would that be? The rising cost of lubricant? I noticed the last time I was at Osco Drugs—"

Mark's laughter interrupted Graham's facetious reply. "Yeah. Right. That's our main concern these days." He grinned at Graham. "I was referring to the possibility that we might move in together one of these days."

"Hmmm. That's certainly something to consider… if we're going to continue along the path we've been going. I'm certainly for it. What do you think about it?"

"Well, on the practical side… we could both save some money by splitting the cost of one maybe slightly larger apartment. But I don't think money should be the real determining factor."

"I agree. Let's get right to the point," Graham replied. "The real question is how do you feel about me? And how do you feel about us now?"

Mark's face took on a more serious look. "Then I'll be blunt. I'm becoming crazier about you every day, and I'm up for something that could be lasting. I won't say the daunting phrase, 'I love you' just yet—but I see us moving gradually in that direction. What about you? How do you feel?"

"You certainly have a knack for putting my own thoughts into words before I can say them." Graham smiled. "You've cheated me out of sounding original. I'll sound stupid when I say ditto to all you've said."

"I'd never call you stupid, whatever you said," Mark replied through a smile on his face.

"Then I guess that brings us back to your original question. Shall we start thinking about living together? I've already told you I'm for it."

"So am I." Mark started turning the pages in the newspaper over to the classified ads for apartments. "Shall we take a look? We can look at the movie ads and decide later on a movie for this weekend."

"Then let's do it," Graham agreed. "Besides, if our relationship doesn't work out, we can still live together as roommates and save money. And you can be the houseboy—and keep the place clean!"

Mark stuck out his tongue at Graham. "In your dreams, old man. In your dreams. Come over here and sit next to me so we can both see the ads."

"My pleasure." Graham scooted his chair next to Mark.

After scouring a couple of columns in the ads section, Mark announced, "Here's an ad for some apartments over on Glendale Avenue. The rent is a little high… but we'll be sharing that… so maybe we could take a look."

"Two bedrooms, right? I'd like to have one to double as an office for us… with maybe a sofa bed in case we have guests… like family, I mean." He chuckled. "But I don't think we have to worry about a visit from my family. My parents don't really like to travel very much. They're not likely to drive all the way up here from Texas."

Mark chuckled. "We'll just have to make a little trip down there to Texas this summer, then—so that I can meet the in-laws. But let's just make sure that you and I share the bigger bedroom.…"

"I think we should drive over and take a look at these apartments, but.…"

"But what? You don't like the looks of those apartments from the description in the paper?"

Graham hesitated a moment. "It's not that…. I was just thinking that we shouldn't be in a huge rush to get a larger place. It should be exactly right. I think we should agree to look at several different ones in the area, no matter how much we might like the Glendale apartments. Let's not be in too much of a hurry to move until we find exactly what we both like."

Mark closed and folded the newspaper. "I agree. You and I are perfect people so we should have a perfect place to live." He grinned.

"I don't know about being perfect people… I wouldn't go that far. But this apartment where we already are"—he looked around—"will be all right for the present… at least until we find just the right one."

"Then it's settled. We'll go look at Glendale… but keep our options open!" Mark reached across the table and grabbed his briefcase. "I think I'll just get started on grading those papers. The sooner I finish, the sooner…." He glanced at Graham and grinned just before Graham gave Mark a little kiss on the cheek.

Graham watched Mark begin his work, but he was thinking about something else entirely—and it wasn't their discussion about a place to live.

Since Aaron is Mark's cousin… I'm going to have to tell him about the time Aaron and I were together last fall. We might run into Aaron and Steve at a bar or restaurant, and I don't want any awkward scenes or ugly surprises to come up. Maybe I'd better just quit putting it off and tell him.

Graham cleared his throat and began. "Honey, could I interrupt you for just a few minutes? I wanted to talk to you about something."

"Sure," Mark mumbled as he wrote something in red on an essay paper.

"Well… uh, you remember that you told me about your rich cousin in Evanston?"

Mark looked up from the paper that he had been grading. "Aaron? Yes, but I don't remember telling you he lives in Evanston, though."

Graham gulped and ran his tongue over his dry lips. "Uh, well, that's the thing. That's what I wanted to talk to you about, I mean. I've met your cousin."

"Really? Where did you meet? Was it in a gay bar in Chicago?" Mark asked nonchalantly.

"As a matter of fact, it was. The Trip, in fact. We both tried to get the same cabaret table just before an Andrea Casey show one night last fall. We met just by chance."

"That's interesting. Why didn't you tell me about it when we were first getting together? You know, that night with the Texas Tech T-shirt and all that."

Graham blushed a little. "Well, you see... uh, it was a little more complicated than just sharing a table at the Trip one night...."

"You're sounding very mysterious, sweetheart. Are you trying to tell me something?" Mark asked. "If you went to bed with Aaron, I'm not going to be angry over it. You and I weren't a couple then. You didn't ask me about my past, and I'm certainly not going to be critical of anything in your past, either. Even if it was with my cousin."

"I have to admit I kind of let him sweep me off my feet," Graham said. "We went to his family's mansion that first night, and it pretty much overwhelmed me. There was the chauffeur, a housekeeper, all those servants, that fabulous house.... I had never experienced that kind of life before, so it took me quite a bit by surprise. But we had a good time, and we liked each other for a while. And then it became an affair that lasted a couple of months, actually. We broke up right after New Year's, just before we started back to school after Christmas vacation." Graham then told Mark about the night Aaron had visited his apartment and about their breakup.

"You mean he had a new bank job for you? He wanted you to move into the Evanston house? And then he just stopped, reconsidered, and left with no further word?" Mark asked. "That really *is* very strange. I mean about the way he just broke it off with you."

"That was about it," Graham replied.

"You mean he didn't ever call anymore? He just left your apartment, and you never heard from him again? You would think he would give a reason for breaking up instead of just telling you to think it over and never contacting you again. Of course, I don't really know my own cousin all that well, but it still seems to me like there must be more to it than that. Are you sure you've told me the whole story?"

"No, he did call me back several weeks later to apologize and to tell me he's back with an old boyfriend. So it's been smoothed over between us, I guess."

"Why do I get the feeling you still haven't told me everything?"

Graham looked deeply into Mark's eyes. "Do you love me?" he asked.

"I'm pretty sure you know by now that I do, sweetheart."

"Do you think I'm a sane, normal person?"

"Graham, you're sounding *weird*. What haven't you told me?"

"Well, you're right. There's a lot more to it that I haven't told you. You're not going to believe it, though," Graham warned. "Hell, I wouldn't believe it, either. But I don't want to keep secrets from you. Do you remember when you asked me if I believed in fairy tales? Well, I've got one big fucking fairy tale to tell you!" So Graham proceeded to tell Mark *all* of it!

Mark laughed when Graham had finished telling his story, much as Rick had done at Christmas. "That's very creative, sweetheart," Mark said. "It sounds like a good enough story to write for publication. Is that what you have in mind?"

Graham could tell it was hopeless to think Mark would take such an admittedly ridiculous story seriously… so he decided not to argue about it or try to convince him any further. "Yeah. Maybe I will. It's possible one of those literary publications might be interested."

"Good idea. Would you mind terribly running to the store for some more Cokes? I really need to get back to my grading, and my throat is kind of dry…."

"Of course. Is there anything else we need from the store?"

And that was the end of it for the moment.

A FEW days later, Mark informed Graham that he had called his cousin Aaron. "I'd like for the three of us to get together for a drink some Saturday night."

"I don't know about that," Graham replied. "It might seem a little too strange for both Aaron and me."

"Oh, I don't think it would. Not for Aaron anyway," Mark said. "He seemed to like the idea well enough, and he said very nice things about you. I think he has only good memories of you, and he's convinced that his phone call to you, the one that you told me about the other day... pretty much cleared the air. He just wants for us all to be friends and get along."

"What did he say about you and me being together?"

"He's happy that you and I are together as a couple. He didn't seem all that surprised to hear we had become lovers... once I told him that we teach at the same school. He didn't even remember I was in Des Plaines when you were going out with him. He thought I was still in college. When I ran into him that time at the Trip, I don't think he was paying much attention when I told him I was out of school and teaching. I told you we didn't keep up with each other very often. We're just not all that close."

"I'm still not entirely sold on the idea," Graham said. "But if you really want to... we'll meet him sometime."

"How about this Saturday?"

"Uh, I guess so. Where? At the Trip?"

"That would be fun," Mark said. "You liked Andrea Casey, didn't you?"

"Sure. I really enjoyed her music. I suppose that's as good a place as any."

"Then I'll set it up. Just leave everything to me."

Saturday night came more quickly than Graham would have liked. He was afraid he just wouldn't have anything to say to Aaron. But there was no getting out of it now. They drove to the city in Mark's car, and as Mark was parking the car on the street a couple of blocks from the Trip, Mark said, "Did I tell you that Aaron will be with his boyfriend?"

"No, you didn't say anything about that. I saw the guy once, the night that I met Aaron at the Trip, but I didn't really meet him."

"I don't know him either," Mark replied. "I think his name is Steve something-or-other. But I guess we'll find out when we meet him."

"Yeah. What time are we supposed to meet them?"

"At eleven. That gives us about an hour and a half for dinner. I'm glad you suggested we try the Italian restaurant on the first floor of the Trip. I hear it's really good."

"I actually don't know for sure how good it is.... Someone just told me that once," Graham said. "But I thought we might as well try it, since it's right there in the same building."

They had just enough time for dinner before it was time to meet Aaron and his lover upstairs. As they were leaving the table, Mark said, "I enjoyed that. The food was great, just as you said."

"I liked it, too. It was a little on the expensive side, but we don't eat out that often in Chicago, so I guess we deserve a treat once in a while. Of course, you're a treat all the time."

Mark grinned at him. "I saved room for dessert—and it's going to be you when we get home."

The Trip was already getting crowded on the second floor when Graham and Mark climbed the steps and entered the cabaret area. They saw Aaron waving to them from up near the stage, where he and his boyfriend had already secured a table.

"Hi, Aaron," Mark said as they arrived at the table. "How are you?"

"Hello, little cousin," Aaron replied as he stood to hug Mark. "But you don't look so little anymore now that you've grown up to be such a handsome hunk of a man."

Graham smiled tentatively at Aaron and then looked more closely at the boyfriend Steve he'd only seen from a distance last fall. "Nice to see you again," Graham said to Aaron, offering his hand to shake with him.

"You, too, Graham," Aaron said. "I'm so glad you and Mark were able to join us tonight. I'd like you to meet my boyfriend, Steve Hartwood. I believe you just got a glimpse of him once."

"Hi, Steve," Graham said. "Nice to meet you."

"I'm glad to meet you, too," Steve replied. "Aaron has told me really good things about you. I've been looking forward to meeting you."

"And, Steve, this is my cousin Mark Matthews. He teaches with Graham in Des Plaines," Aaron said.

"I'm happy to meet you, too," Mark said. "I understand you and Aaron have a history together."

"Hi, Mark," Steve said. "Yeah, Aaron and I were a hot item a while ago. But we've just gotten back together this winter."

"Well, now that the introductions are over," Aaron said, "let's all have a drink. There's a waiter over there." He signaled to the waiter that they wanted to order. "I saw Andrea a few minutes ago, and she said she'd try to join us after the first set—if we can all squeeze around this little table."

The waiter arrived, the drinks were ordered and delivered, and the lights went down. An announcer offstage said in a deep, booming voice, "And now the Trip is proud to present for your enjoyment The Five of Us, featuring the lyrical stylings of Miss Andrea Casey!"

Warm applause greeted the announcement as a spotlight played first across the group's leader at the piano, then across the other musicians, and finally landed and stayed on Andrea. This time she was wearing a brilliant red gown with ruby earrings and a diamond choker necklace. As usual, the set that followed included a mixture of romantic ballads and familiar show tunes as well as some obscure, interesting, and amusing variety numbers to liven up the pace of the program.

Andrea brushed aside the applause. "Gentlemen, and what few of you who really *are* ladies," she said as the audience laughed. "Trash, maybe... but not *ladies*!" More laughter. "Just *kidding*, George—stop looking at me like that! Well, don't try to *prove it*!" She laughed along with everyone else. "Anyway, we all have our dreams, and sometimes we get lucky and those dreams actually come true. This next number is an old Mama Cass song that I hope will bring back some good memories for everyone."

Graham was more than a little startled as the band played the introduction to "Dream a Little Dream of Me." However, he soon got over the coincidence of the song and enjoyed her haunting rendition of it. *I guess I'll always think of Robert and his multiple personalities when I hear that song, though.*

After the applause died down, Andrea said, "Dreams and magic are kind of related, I think. This next tune is an old Doris Day hit from the 1940s." She glanced over at Graham and the others at his table. Then she smiled just before she began to sing "It's Magic."

In a way, this applies to Mark and me, Graham thought. *What a beautiful song.*

The applause was almost deafening as Andrea reached the end of the set. There were shouts of "More! More!" So the music started up again, and Andrea said, "You know what you're gonna hear!" She began to sing "What's a Nice Girl Like Me Doing, Working in a Joint Like This." The audience clapped and cheered... and then the set was over.

"I just love to hear her sing," Aaron said. "I wish the group could get a recording contract. I'd certainly buy their albums."

"I would, too," Graham agreed.

Andrea came to their table then. "I'm sorry, but I can't sit down with you guys right now! Mike, the bass player, got a bad nosebleed just at the end of the set, and I've got to go backstage to try to help him get it stopped. I'll try to see you later."

"Well, this has been fun," Aaron said after she left, "but Steve and I are going to drop by a friend's party for a while, so we need to leave."

"Oh, do you have to go so soon?" Mark asked. "Couldn't you stay a little longer?"

"Sorry, but it's a birthday party, and we promised we'd come," Steve said. "Maybe the four of us can get together again real soon."

"I hope so," Graham said as Aaron and Steve stood and said their good-byes.

"I guess it's just you and me," Mark said. "Well, I like that better anyway...."

"Me, too. Want another drink?"

"Sure," he said. "Aren't you glad we got together with them? It sort of bridges things over between you and Aaron, don't you think?"

"You're right," Graham said. "I didn't think so earlier, but I'm glad now that we came."

Without warning, Graham heard the sounds of "Dream a Little Dream of Me" again, but this time it sounded like the introduction on the old record from the jukebox. Just to be sure, he looked around to see if the band might be back already, but they weren't. "Did you hear that?" he asked Mark.

"Hear what, sweetheart?"

"Nothing, I guess. For a minute there I thought it sounded like the band was starting up for the next set," Graham replied. "Or maybe it was the jukebox way over there in the corner."

Oh, no! he thought, trying to brace himself. *Robert's finally back, and I'm scared of what he'll do to me now!*

But Robert didn't appear. Neither did Margaret or Roy or Rock or anyone else. Graham breathed a sigh relief, but he was still a little puzzled.

"What's the matter, Graham?" Mark asked. "You look kind of upset. Anything wrong?"

"I know you didn't believe my story about the power, but I just heard that song again—the one that's a signal Robert is going to appear! I was just looking around for him…."

Mark smiled. "But I'm already here, Graham."

Graham glanced across the table at Mark. "I know that. I said I was looking for *Robert*."

"You *are* looking at Robert," Mark replied. "You still haven't caught on, have you?"

"What are you talking about?"

Mark chuckled at his confusion. "It's me—Robert, Margaret, Roy. It was *me* all the time!"

As Graham stared at Mark, Mark faded and became the image of Robert. Then he faded again and became Margaret. He faded once again and became Rock Hudson. Finally he faded one last time and became Mark once more. "See? It's me! I'm all of them."

"I don't get it. If you're all those other people, where is the real Mark?"

"*I'm* the real Mark," he said. "I met you last fall at school, and liked you at once… so I decided to become the others and give you the *power*."

"I'm completely confused," Graham said. "What are you talking about?"

"Okay, let me back up and explain it to you," Mark said. "I know about that little thing you do—seeing a cute guy and pretending you're lovers… then imagining waking up with the guy the next morning."

"What's wrong with that? Anyway, I've quit doing it now that I'm with you.…"

"There's nothing wrong with it, but whether you were conscious of it or not, you were wondering what it would be like to make that person fall in love with you. So I gave you the power to do just that."

"But why would you do that if you were interested in me for yourself?"

"To get it all out of your system," Mark replied. "Forgetting the accidents with Trevor, Dean Weinert, and Carlton the cop, as well as the demonstrations with Alice and Rick, how did you feel when you made my cousin Aaron actually fall in love with you?"

"It made me feel guilty because it wasn't his free will," Graham said.

"Exactly. And that's why I didn't just make you fall love with me… when I easily could have," Mark replied.

"Wait a minute! Why go to all this trouble with the power? Why didn't you just tell me you were interested, or show up in a gay bar some night where we could talk and get to know each other?"

"You weren't ready yet."

"What do you mean by that? I've had lovers before."

"And how did they work out?" Mark asked. "Did they love you back?"

Graham thought about this for a moment. "Well, I think one of them might have, and possibly another.…"

"Hmmm. And did *you* love those two that you say loved you in the past?"

"Well, no. I guess not," Graham admitted. "What's your point? I still don't understand."

"For love to really work, both persons have to love each other. That hasn't been the case with you," Mark said. "When you were in love, you weren't loved back. And vice versa. You've had a tendency to see a cute guy and fall in love too fast. You've been very impulsive a lot of times. You haven't waited long enough to see if you've really met the right guy. You just charged ahead, trying to make someone—anyone—fall in love with you. You didn't give yourself or your potential partner enough time to see if you were meant for each other. You kind of let your hormones get the best of you. That's not love, you know."

"So you went through all of this rigmarole of the power to make me learn a lesson about making someone fall in love with me?" Graham asked. "Or rather… learning not to make someone fall in love with me."

"Yes," Mark replied, "but more than that, it made you take things very carefully and slowly with me. Remember how we just visited in the lounge first, and then we worked together on the textbook committee? For once, you slowed down and gave yourself a chance to get to know someone you were interested in. By the time we finally got together at your place, you were willing to take things very slowly. That's what you needed to learn before you found a lover."

"But why did you keep pushing me to use the power once you and I were getting along together?" Graham asked.

"You still had that last charge which you could have accidentally used on someone else. I needed you to get rid of it after it became clear that you weren't tempted to use it anymore… on *me*, for example." Mark said. "Do you understand now?"

Graham thought about all of this for a moment. "Most of it, I guess. This is all a little hard to follow. But I see that you really did go to a lot of trouble for us to get together."

"I thought from the very beginning that you were worth it, sweetheart," Mark said. "I wanted you to be sure you wanted me, and not just anyone who came along."

"Are you sure about it now? Sure about me?" Graham asked.

"Of course I am. Partly because you refused to use the power on me... as Mark. After all, you didn't want to force someone to love you this time. And you gave both of us enough time for nature to take its course."

"Oh, no!" Graham cried.

"What's the matter, sweetheart? What is it?" Mark asked, alarmed.

"If you're Mark *and* Rock, then you don't really love me!"

"Why would you say a thing like that?"

"I used my last charge on you when you were Rock Hudson at the Annex! You only love me because of the power!" Graham was almost in tears.

Mark smiled and then laughed softly. "Is that all? Sweetheart, it was *my* spell you used... so it couldn't work on *me*! It was like shooting me with a blank in a gun. I really love you just for yourself. Don't worry about a thing."

Graham sniffed and looked up into Mark's beautiful blue eyes. "Really?"

"Really." He reached out and took both Graham's hands and held them.

"But there's one really big thing that I still don't get," Graham said. "How do you have the ability to change into different people... and grant that power spell? Just who *are* you?"

Mark leaned over and kissed Graham gently on the lips. "I love you, sweetheart."

"And I love you, too," Graham said, "but who are you?"

"Graham, haven't you ever seen shows on television about characters who could do magic?"

Graham's look of confusion vanished, and his face lit up. "I get it! You're a *genie*... like on that show *I Dream of Jeanie*!"

Mark burst into laughter. "Don't be silly! That's just fiction.... There aren't really any genies in the world! I'm talking about the show *Bewitched*."

"You're a witch?"

"No, silly. I'm a warlock! Witches are female... warlocks are—"

EPILOGUE

"You mean that stuff like witchcraft and magic really exist… like with those characters on the show—Samantha, Endora, and Uncle Arthur…?"

"Well… not *exactly* like on TV, but there's more truth to it than fiction." He smiled and kissed Graham softly again across the table. The song started up again, but the two of them were the only ones who could hear Mama Cass singing "Dream a Little Dream of Me."

Sunday Afternoon... the next day

GRAHAM lay on the sofa in the living room of the apartment they had now begun to share, his head resting on two throw pillows. His eyes were closed, but he wasn't sleeping. Mark sat on the floor with the classified section of the newspaper spread out before him. Mark was still looking through the listings for local apartments, scanning for anything in the Chicago area that looked promising but that wasn't too far from Des Plaines.

Mark looked up from the paper and saw that Graham almost appeared to be asleep. He got up on his knees and quietly placed his mouth on the outline of Graham's cock inside those white briefs, which were all Graham was wearing. He blew hot breath onto the cock and waited for a reaction. He got one as Graham's eyes flew wide open.

"Damn! Who needs a blow dryer for my hair with your hot mouth around?"

Mark chuckled. "Just giving you a blow job, so to speak."

"Well, don't make it a half-assed one. Do it right if you're going to do it at all," Graham reached down to pull off his briefs, leaving a half-hard cock exposed for Mark.

"Yum! Looks delicious," Mark exclaimed. "But do you think there's anything left inside? I think I emptied it out last night."

Graham laughed. "You gave it your best shot... and I mean that in *every possible way*! And so did I... 'come' to think of it."

"Do you suppose other gay English teachers use puns like this all the time?"

"I don't think being gay has anything to do with it. We English teachers just like puns anyway, even if it is the lowest form of humor."

"I'll take your lowest form anytime you want to expose it, sweetheart," Mark declared.

"Enough. So are you going to see if you emptied me out or not?"

"Only if you scoot over so that I can get up on the sofa with you. Turn over on your side so I can climb up."

"Okay, but I expect you to strip off *your* briefs, too. I want you to give *me* a mouthful while you're at it. I'd like to see if you've got anything left in your tasty dick, too. Come on up here, you sexy thing."

Mark dropped his underwear and eased himself onto the sofa with Graham. He played with Graham's dick gently, running his fingers up and down the shaft while licking the head. With his other hand he softly kneaded Graham's balls, fingering the soft sac that held them.

Graham began doing similar things to Mark's dick and balls at the same time.

As he seriously worked at the job at hand, Mark began to establish a rhythm, plunging Graham's cock into his mouth and finally working it deep into his throat. Graham's dark pubic hair all but disappeared as he fully took in Graham's dick. Stroke after stroke brought whimpers from Graham as his climax got closer and closer... and then salty come flooded Mark's mouth and flowed down his throat.

In the aftermath of coming in Mark's throat, Graham sensed Mark was nearing his own climax, so he braced himself by putting his hands on Mark's thighs as he held Mark's dick in his mouth. Sure enough, Mark's load suddenly exploded. After a moment, Graham took Mark's dick out and just hugged Mark, rubbing his cheek up against Mark's genitals gently.

"Looks like the wells haven't run dry after all!"

"I really don't think you can empty out completely. Unless you just keep doing it without stopping. I don't think I could do that, though."

"Me neither," Graham said as he sat up and pulled Mark to his side so he could kiss him. "I really love you, Mark. I'm so happy we found each other."

"And I love you back, Graham. Both of us waited a long time for this...."

Graham kissed Mark again. "Want something from the kitchen? I'm kind of thirsty now. The salt in my diet recently has made me crave sodas."

"As long as you're *up*—please forgive yet another pun—go ahead and get me a Coke, too." Mark crawled back down on the floor to look at the newspaper ads again. "Want to stay in Des Plaines, or do you want to live someplace just nearby?"

Graham returned with two cans. He handed one to Mark and took a sip from his own. "Maybe we could get a place in Elk Grove Village, or maybe Arlington Heights, or even Park Ridge would be okay. I think Schaumburg is a little too far away. Since we're going to be living together, we might as well avoid being seen together constantly at the local stores, at the closer malls, or just around Des Plaines. You know how people like to talk in a small town." He sat back down on the sofa.

"Sound good to me," Mark replied.

Graham sat back down on the sofa, silently drinking his soda for a moment. "Mark, do you mind if we talk about some things that have been on my mind since last night? I'm still kind of overwhelmed by everything."

"Sure, sweetheart," Mark replied, looking up from the newspaper. "What's troubling you?"

"Are you really what I think you are?"

"If you think I'm a man in love with his gorgeous English teacher lover, then I'm what you think I am," Mark replied, smiling.

"That's sweet… but that's not what I meant, and you know it. Are you really a warlock like you said last night?"

"Yes. I really am a warlock." Mark laughed. "Warlocks and witches are not exactly like the characters of Samantha and her family and friends. That's mostly fiction. But as I told you last night… that show is more true than not, in a lot of ways. It's a good thing people think it's just fiction, though…."

"Can we really have a life together, then? I mean, if you can do all kinds of things like that TV show character. Won't we have a lot of problems?"

"Sweetheart, all couples, gay or straight, warlock or mortal, always have problems of all kinds. You know that."

"You have to admit that we're a special case," Graham said.

"In a way, we're *very* special. But we're not in a television situation comedy, either. We don't have writers dreaming up all kinds of interesting storylines with obstacles for us to overcome in a thirty-minute program. And we're going to live as normal a life as possible. I wish you'd just put it out of your mind and give us a chance to just be ourselves... and be in love."

"I want to do that, but this really *is* a big deal, honey."

Mark frowned. "This is why I really wish I hadn't had to tell you the whole truth. If I could have found a way to avoid it, I would have said nothing... but only because I don't want you to worry and think about it all the time. However, I guess it's just as well that you know right now... I would have had to tell you all about it eventually, I'm sure."

"Then you really think we can live a fairly normal life?"

"Pretty close to it, I think," Mark said.

"How old are you, Mark?" Graham asked. "I mean *really*?"

Mark paused. "Well, you really don't want to know the answer to that. But I've been around a pretty long time...."

"What's going to happen when I age and you stay twenty-one? I'll look like I'm robbing the cradle."

Mark laughed. "No, you won't. I've thought of that. I'll just cause myself to look like I'm aging right along with you. It will always look like we're about the same age."

"What about when I die, honey? I'm mortal."

Mark had no funny answers for that one. After a moment he said, "Sweetheart, everyone dies. It's a part of life. I can't stop nature for you, and I don't think you'd want me to. When you're gone... after a really long life with me... I'll grieve. You're my first real love ever... so I don't think that I'll ever have another one in the far future when you're gone. I'll just learn to live alone."

"We're getting morbid, aren't we?" Graham asked.

"Way too much. Just try to enjoy the life we're going to have together. That's what other couples do. They both know that one will usually die before the other, but they don't think about it all the time. Let's be the same way and just love each other for as long as we can."

"Okay, I'll drop all this sad and serious stuff. But I do have another question or two...."

"All right. Fire away," Mark said. "I'll tell you what I can."

"Is Aaron really your cousin?" Graham asked.

"What brought that on?"

"I thought that he might be a warlock, too. And maybe Steve is, too."

Mark giggled. "Aaron is not a warlock. His mother *is* a witch, but just like in any family, some characteristics are passed from one generation to another. Aaron didn't inherit the abilities. And neither did his older brother."

"Does Aaron know about you and your abilities?"

"No, he's in the dark about the whole thing. He doesn't even know about his mother… and don't ask me how she kept all that hidden from my cousins, because I don't have any idea."

"What about Aaron's father? Does he know about your aunt and your family?"

"Yes, he knows. My aunt *is* his wife after all. She knew she had to tell him when they married. But since the children are mortal, there was no reason to make an issue of it. I will tell you, though, this is the real reason why our family is not very close to Aaron's family. Too many tricky situations and questions might come up. That's why Aaron knows so little about me. I've had to keep my distance." He laughed. "When he was growing up, I had to assume the form of a little boy so he would think I was his younger cousin. It was actually kind of fun.…"

"That *is* kind of funny… but I wondered… if I were a girl and we had children—"

"Then there would be a fifty-fifty chance our children would be mortal. Want me to change you into a woman?" He laughed.

"Absolutely not!" Graham retorted.

"That's a good thing. We couldn't be lovers if you were a female. I'm *not* into girls."

"Are there very many gay warlocks?" Graham asked.

"Yes, there are many… but they're mostly in show business."

"You're making that up!"

"Actually, I'm not." Mark laughed again. "How do you think all those stars stay looking so young for such a long time? Plastic surgery?" He laughed again. "Of course, eventually they allow themselves to look old, and they pretend to die. But they're still around in a different form."

"I don't suppose you'd care to share some names with me?"

"I'm not supposed to do that. Sorry."

"Incidentally, something else has dawned on me… about you, I mean…."

"Oh? Something else?"

"I've been thinking everything over since last night at the bar, and I remembered something about that night you first came over to my apartment. About the way you… uh, behaved."

"What are you getting at?"

"I'm talking about that little act you put on about acting nervous, and having to smoke a cigarette, and all that nonsense. Remember how your hand shook as you admitted that you were gay?"

Mark grinned. "Oh, that. Well, I had to be convincing, didn't I? It wasn't time yet for me to tell you everything. First I had to see if we had a chance to make it as a couple. Don't be mad about it."

"I'm not mad. It actually seems pretty funny when I look back on it. Especially the time I told you about Robert Redford, which of course was you, and that whole thing with the mysterious power. I don't know how you kept a straight face when you suggested I get the story published!" He paused and thought for a moment. "And there's another thing, Mark Robert Margaret Rock," Graham said.

"Oh yeah? What's that?"

"What do you really look like? Without all the disguises. Are you wearing a disguise right now?"

"That's easy. I look just like I do right now. I never hid that from you."

"Wow! Then you truly *are* a very handsome devil. I'm so glad this isn't just some created disguise you use."

"It's not. This is the real me. You and I are both pretty easy on the eyes, and it's all natural," Mark said. "At least as natural as a warlock like me can be, that is."

"Okay, sweetheart, let me ask just one last thing, and then I'll hush about all this. What if we really were to get into some very serious trouble? What would you do?"

Mark got up off the floor and moved up to sit next to Graham on the sofa. He took Graham's face into his hands and kissed him, deeply and totally. Then he pulled away slightly so he could look at Graham. "I'd get us out of it, and then I'd write a TV series or a book about our adventures."

Graham laughed out loud. "Okay. Change of subject. Do you know what I wish I had?"

"Yes. An old jukebox," Mark said after kissing him again. "Don't worry. I'll get you one."

GENE TAYLOR was born about fifty miles south of Dallas in Corsicana, Texas, and he actually got to see what the city looked like twenty-six years later when he visited it briefly for the first time. He grew up in a different part of the state and thus knew very little about his birthplace. He had heard that there was a bakery there that sold wonderful fruitcakes online for Christmas presents, however!

He graduated from a large university in Texas with a double major in English and history, a few years later earning a master's degree at the same school. Since then he has lived in California, Arizona, Illinois, and Texas while teaching in high schools and selling antiques and collectibles in various shops. Currently, he has a booth in an antiques mall called As Time Goes By, but he usually spends his time writing novels and short stories. In addition, he often allots some time to playing records on his restored 1947 Rock-Ola jukebox and on his 1961 Wurlitzer 2500 jukebox!

A few years ago he was greatly surprised to learn on a genealogy website that he is a direct descendant of Geoffrey Chaucer (his nineteenth great grandfather on his father's side). He wishes he had known that when he was teaching *The Canterbury Tales* in British literature classes.

At the moment he is single, but he never gives up hope of finding someone to share his interests in reading, writing, antiquing, and playing slot machines and roulette in Las Vegas! You can write to him at genetaylor957@yahoo.com.

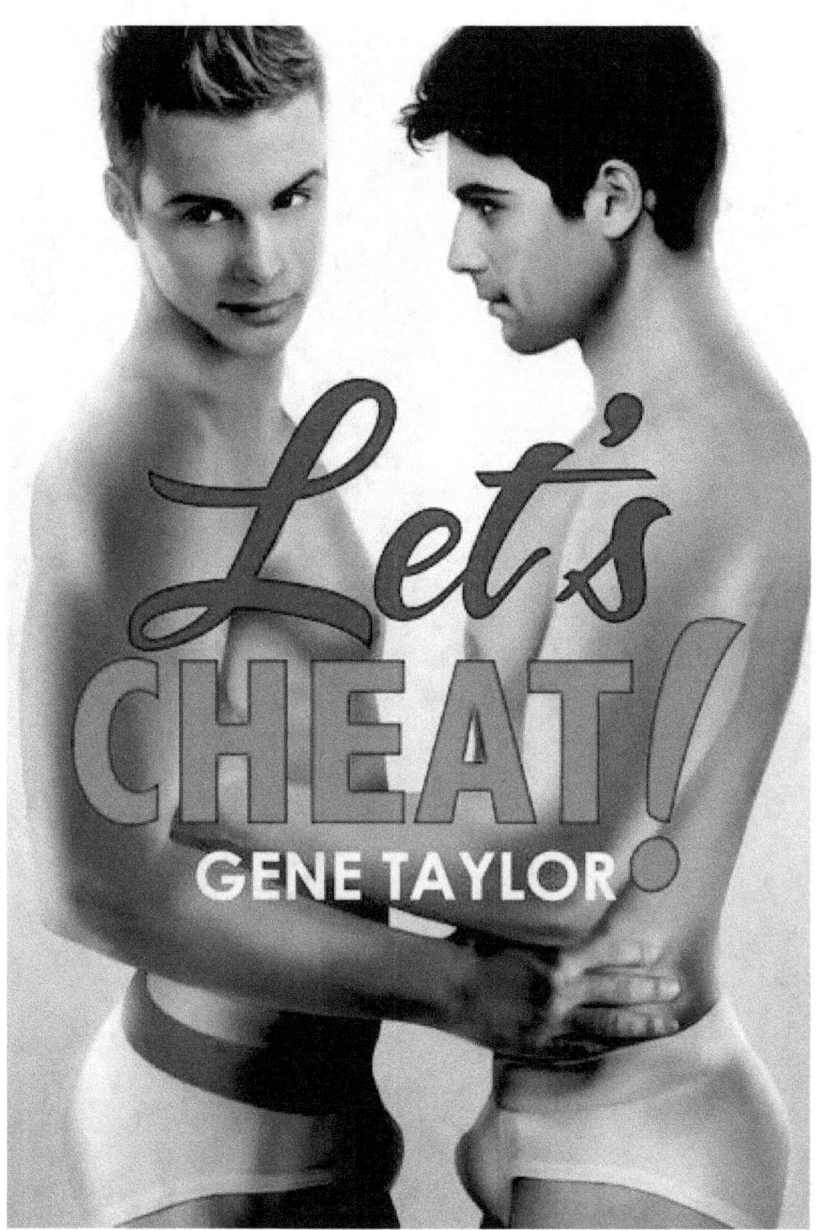

Also from DREAMSPINNER PRESS

ONE *True* THING

PIPER VAUGHN & M.J. O'SHEA

http://www.dreamspinnerpress.com

Also from DREAMSPINNER PRESS

Until It's
Time To Go

Connie Bailey

http://www.dreamspinnerpress.com